621 Pleasant St. • Boulder, CO 80302

May 4, 2021

Jenn Ashworth
36 Derwent Road
Freehold, Lancaster LA1 3ES
United Kingdom

Dear Ms. Ashworth,

Owl Canyon Press is pleased to announce the forthcoming publication of *The Ubnetter Blog* the new novel by Brett

The Upsetter Blog

The Upsetter Blog
A Novel

Brett Marie

Owl Canyon Press

© 2021 by Bret Marie

First Edition, 2021
All Rights Reserved
Library of Congress Cataloging-in-Publication Data

Marie, Brett
The Upsetter Blog —1st ed.
p. cm.

ISBN: 978-1-952085-09-3
Library of Congress Control Number: 2021936803

Owl Canyon Press
Boulder, Colorado

Disclaimer

For my Miss Marie

What could he want - and what could they want, those who shriek in ecstasy at his song? And what did I want, watching them, taking notes? Whatever we wanted, it wasn't what we would get.

Stanley Booth, *The True Adventures of the Rolling Stones*

Intro

November 5, 2003

"We want Jack! We want Jack! We want Jack!"

It starts with just one voice, some anonymous drunken loser without a girlfriend to embarrass, hidden deep within the chattering mass of denim and leather. Cliché to begin with, those three syllables sound particularly obnoxious coming from just one person. But a restless herd of kindred spirits surrounds him, each cut from the same Miller-soaked cloth, and his knuckleheaded call-to-arms is all they require. Within seconds, loner turns to leader as his chant catches the fancy of an eager crowd.

"We want Jack! We want Jack!"

Two hundred fists punch the air with each shouted word. Scattered rebel yells provide shrill counterpoint as the atonal anthem crescendos. The noise crests at an oppressive volume, when suddenly the refrain disperses, melting into a tide of self-satisfied cheers. The crowd has found release, but the focus of its anticipation remains unchanged: the stage remains empty.

Peering out the control-room window onto the club floor, I have to admit I'm impressed. I say as much as I turn to the object of their desire. "What do you have to say about that? They weren't doing that six months ago."

Jack Hackett answers with a shrug. This is the most elaborate and articulate he's been with me all day; the kid has been downright catatonic since I greeted him here at the Mint this evening. His sullen eyes bulge like gumballs from his pale, gaunt face. Leaning with one hand against the mixing board, he slouches limply forward, his head upright at an angle that calls to mind a marionette with all but one of its strings cut.

His mood, I understand, was better this afternoon. I'm told he spoke at full voice, instructing the Mint staff to place a 'Reserved' placard at a table directly in front of his microphone. He insisted she was coming—that she must be coming, that she wouldn't stay away from him on a night like this. As much as I would have cringed at such delusional talk, I would take it in a heartbeat over his crushed silence now, as it becomes apparent he was wrong.

"We want Jack! We want Jack!"

The soundproofed walls are no match for the pounding of the renewed chant. Louder this time, the words manage to breach the kid's eardrums, and he breaks his sightless stare.

There are seven of us cocooned with the kid in this compact control room: me, my son the Fan, the kid's three bandmates, the roadie, and the engineer. Fourteen eyes watch the kid reach into the knapsack at his feet.

"We want Jack! We want Jack!"

His hand emerges clutching a yellow CD case. I recognize the cover photo, the blue block letters across the top: it's his Chuck Berry greatest-hits collection. As he locates a CD deck in the rack full of recording gadgetry, I entertain the thought that he will counter the crowd's onslaught with a full-volume 'Johnny B. Goode'. Maybe, I think, the driving rhythm will jump-start his heart, and we'll have him back.

"We want Jack! We want Jack!"

But then the light jangle of Berry's guitar makes a meager peep between chants. I don't need to hear the first line to recognize 'Memphis, Tennessee', the closest thing the kid will find on that CD to a song that can evoke his pain. My silly illusion of a moment ago dissolves even before Chuck's soft plea to Long Distance Information comes in.

"We want Jack! We want Jack!"

My fellow control room inmates sit silent for some time. Over the outside din, Chuck begs for the listener to get in touch with his Marie. A full verse plays before the Fan gets fidgety. "Great song!" he says, and waits for the kid to agree.

"We want Jack! We want Jack!"

The kid stares hard at the nearest speaker. The Fan looks at me and frowns. Jack's bandmates stare at their leader, murmuring among themselves.

"We want Jack! We want Jack!"

Another minute passes before Berry's guitar chimes in to bring the curtain down on the song. At the same time, the faithful outside break up their chant and applaud themselves once more. With the clock ticking down to zero-hour, the seven of us watch Jack reach for a button on the CD player. And now the jangle is back, light and sad as before, and here is Chuck's voice, just as pleading. And Jack's eyes, now sunken a smidgen further behind his bangs, stare just as intently at the speaker playing his request.

⌘

We live and die by coincidence, don't we? Well-timed bolts from the blue send us reeling from one life-altering event to the next, finding their logic only as a series of blind ricochets stretching back to the Big Bang. Every instant a trillion atoms bounce off each other to spin off down new and unexpected avenues, while the doors to the old slam shut behind them.

Soul-mates meet by chance. Lightning strikes men dead. Ignore the millions of near-misses. Give credit to the divine. Do that, and you can enjoy the fantasy that we are more than merely so many billiard balls waiting to be sunk into our respective pockets simply by the laws of physics and luck.

Billiard balls, or marbles. A boy grows up in a small New England town, steeped in the music of his day, dreaming of worldwide stardom in the mold of his hero Elvis Presley. He spends his paper-route money on a rock 'n' roll guitar, learns a few chords. All seems to flow toward his destiny as surely as a river to the sea.

But more powerful than a healthy boy of fourteen, mightier than his planet-sized dream, is the force of a tiny cat's-eye marble, lying by chance on a patch of hard earth along the third base line of the sandlot where on a summer's day he joins a pick-up ballgame.

What explosive power that small marble exerts on a teenager racing for home plate, when it absorbs the boy's full weight at just the right angle, when it rolls a mere inch under the sole of his sneaker. For the chain reaction it sets off, starting with the fall that snaps his left middle finger, derails him from far more than a run scored. The splint it earns his hand, his finger's failure to heal enough to fret his guitar properly, they knock him sideways from his destiny, sending him careening down a wildly different track. What a mighty David's stone that cat's-eye is, fired from the sling of a blind, capricious fate.

This notion enjoys a firm place in the bedrock of my brain, a place into which years of experience have served only to further entrench it. As I stand in a small control room, in a Los Angeles nightclub one night in November, watching John Preston Hackett III sit in quiet desolation while beyond the door two hundred voices chant his name, this idea's place seems permanent, assured.

But the billiard balls and marbles of fate are still colliding, and they are indeed powerful things.

Verse

My first run-in with Marty was no happenstance. It wasn't until the next time he engineered a meeting, months later and without pretense, that I came to recognize his M.O. But I should have known from the start.

Staking out my building from across the street, he would have watched me come in from my morning run, then step out again a half hour later. I can picture him tailing me on foot, like a private investigator, all the way to the Wild Oats Market a few blocks away, before happening to be in the market that day in February.

But as it happened, one twist of fate worked in his favor. At the moment he chose to make contact, as I perused a shelf in search of a carton of soy milk, a particularly delightful sight entered my field of vision. Chestnut locks flowed just past her shoulders, turning up at the ends. From a placid, olive face, her brown eyes gazed past long lashes at items on the shelf.

Her figure was what got me. She might have intended her loose shirt to conceal her pregnant belly, the long skirt to mask a laden waddle she might have found less than beautiful. That would have been a shame; I am at a loss to name the swell of motherhood before my eyes if I cannot call it beauty. I stared unabashedly.

It was in this state of enthrallment, watching this sweet creature reach for a can on a shelf, that Marty caught me. Lucky devil—he got me at my softest. "Uncle H!"

I whirled around toward the sound of his voice, self-conscious like a voyeur. For the first heartbeat, I didn't recognize him. Few who had known the Marty of my memory would have expected to see his face under a short haircut and bottomed out with a collar and tie. But thus far I was 'Uncle H' (and not 'Henry' or 'Mister Barclay') to only one person. His name leaped out when I opened my mouth to speak. "Marty!" I gave him a good laugh with my next line: "What brings you over the hills? You have a girl in this neighborhood?"

"In West Hollywood? Uh, no." And that was all the ice he needed to break. "But seriously, what a coincidence! And right when I'm..." He had the act down: the widening eyes, the slowly spreading smile. "Listen, Uncle H," he said after a long moment. "We gotta catch up on things. Why don't you visit me at my office? Are you free for lunch tomorrow? I'm up to something, and I tell you, the man upstairs must want you in on it. Why else would he have led me to you, now of all times?"

My expectant olive beauty chose that moment to wheel her cart past us. Chestnut poured over my field of vision, and her perfume teased the air around us. The combination compromised my defenses. Turning back to Marty, I saw all the wrong things: how his cinnamon hair was now tousled by hair gel rather than last night's pillow; his smart, starched shirt; a collar of sublime geometry; a tie that shimmered but didn't blare. And, warmed by a perfumed olive glow, my heart would not stay hard enough to allow me so easily to dismiss my own godson. "We'll see what happens," I said.

With a lock on what he had come for, off he dashed with a quick word of farewell. And yes, perhaps I should have found our whole hit-and-run encounter suspicious. But I wasn't in that frame of mind. Not yet.

⌘

The front gate of Marty's office opened from the sidewalk into an open-air path lined with fica plants and ivy. Marty leaped out as I reached his front door, and wrapped me in a bear hug. "Uncle H! It's been way too long!"

"Hasn't it?" I groaned, and patted his back until he released me.

We each took a step back. "You look good!" he declared. "Still running?" I nodded. "What's chasing you?" He cackled. "And I take it you're still popping those vitamins like Tic-Tacs." His smile broadened. "Well, they've paid off. Just invest in some hair dye, and *I* could pass for *your* uncle!"

It was easy to return the compliment. "If your father could see you today..." I mused aloud.

"Thirty-three is as good an age as any to grow up, I figure. I hit my lifetime quota of mornings waking up on the floor."

I followed him through the entrance into a modest reception area. A red Ikea couch beneath a framed late-sixties movie poster faced a low coffee table on which sat a small statue of the Buddha, cheerily entreating visitors to choose from a selection of magazines. At a desk to the right, a pretty Persian-looking girl murmured into a phone while staring at a computer screen.

"I'll spare you the grand tour for now," Marty said. "First, I want to let you in on what we're about. Besides, our lunch is getting cold." He motioned toward a sliding door that led to a tiny patio. A minute later he was pulling naan breads and curries in Styrofoam tubs out of a paper bag ("Indian—got it right across the street."), placing them with the care of a gourmet chef on a wooden picnic table.

He shifted to catch-up talk as we filled our plates. We spoke some more about his father ("I think he'd finally be proud of me."). He asked about my boy Patrick, born the same year and in the same city as Marty, now living in another universe across town from this place ("He's well, got placed at a health food store, bagging goods."). We talked about impending war as if it were the weather ("Yeah, I wish it would all just blow over.").

Then Marty took a breath as he poured a steamy curry over a helping of rice. "Okay. So. When was the last time you bought a copy of *Rolling Stone?*"

"You're asking the wrong person." I kept one eye on him as I piled rice onto my fork. "Probably when they last mentioned me. Seventy-five, maybe."

"Well, you haven't missed much. I let my subscription expire after they put Al Gore on the cover, but I should've let it happen way sooner." He shoveled a forkful of food into his mouth and continued speaking behind it. "Anyway, they're all the same. *Spin,* all of 'em."

"I suppose you intend to do something about it."

He winked as he swallowed. "You know it." He turned his fork toward me and began poking at the air to punctuate his speech. "I'm here to redeem them. This here is the beginning of *Upsetter*" poke "*Magazine.*"

I let my eyebrows jump but could muster no more. "Listen," he went on, "I don't expect to run a juggernaut like *Rolling Stone* out of business. But I plan to at least fire a few shots across her bow. Let them keep putting out fluff. Their readers can come to *us* for insightful commentary on pop culture."

"And you have the resources to start with nationwide distribution?"

"Well, as I see it, we can start with just a website. The internet's the New Frontier, right? And it's been making it a lot easier for the little guy to make a dent these days. And as for the print edition, that's what this office is for. I've got a whole staff of people working full-time calling on potential investors who may want in on the Next Big Thing in Rock 'n' Roll." A grain of rice flew from his lips and across the patio as he spoke. He gave it no notice. "I want you to be in on it, too."

"Uh-oh," I quipped. "Here's where he asks me for money."

"No. No, Uncle H. This is where he offers you a job."

"Do telemarketers make more than minimum wage?"

"Ha," he said. "Anyway, here's the deal: we have this pitch that we go over with investors, and I've got a similar package to line up advertisers, where we outline the first few issues in a nutshell. The centerpiece idea is a chronicle of an up-and-coming rock band as they go on their first tour and cut their first album."

"What instrument will I play?"

Without as much as a smirk he carried on. "I've got this friend with an indie label, and he just signed this amazing group. They're going on the road in March, and when they come back, all tight from months of playing, we're gonna do a live recording at a club on Pico."

He paused, as if to allow me to finish his proposal for him. I let the silence grow.

"See," he finally continued, "we figure that the three of us—his label, the band and my operation—can all gain exposure by printing the saga of this debut recording. And to get a jump on it, we thought we'd start by posting it online, while the tour's happening, as a blog."

"A 'blog'."

"Yeah, that's internet-talk for an online journal."

Another pause, this one shorter.

"Anyway, we've been pitching this whole scheme with the idea that a classy author will do the piece."

"Oh, yes, of course," I offered in place of the groan I felt building, "lend it some *gravitas*."

"Something like that. And they always ask who we can possibly get who would fit the bill. " He broke into a grin. "And you know whose name always comes up first."

He didn't wait for my reaction. "I tell you, Uncle H, this is the part that feels so good—so right." He cast a wistful eye somewhere beyond the whitewashed brick of the patio wall. "You know, when I was at UCLA, they had this class, 'Mid-Century American Road Fiction' or some other stupid-long name," he rolled his eyes, "and I used to meet girls, and they'd be carrying *Till It Hurts* to class. And I'd be like, 'Hey, would you believe, I know the guy who wrote that? My dad was his editor!'"

"I don't know which I find more galling," I interrupted, "that they were still subjecting young people to that book in the late eighties, or that you spent your college days using your father and me as a pick-up line."

"Make fun if you want, Uncle H, but it's true. And that's the thing. Working this pitch, I've come full circle. I'm back to telling people, 'Hey! You know that guy who did that great thing way back when? *I'm his godson!* And he's gonna do something great *again!*' And this time, can you believe it? I'm gonna be the one who gets him to do it!"

He went silent, holding onto my gaze. I broke eye contact with him after a few long seconds, looking down at the stone patio between the slats of the table as the farcical parry and thrust of my refusal commenced.

"Now, you'll probably want to see what the band is like before you decide..."

"I won't."

"... whether you want to be a part of this thing—"

"I don't."

"—and it just so happens they've got a gig lined up tomorrow..."

"Good for them."

"... at a photo gallery downtown." His tone sharpened. "Come on, Uncle H, don't just dismiss this. Look around! Have I ever done anything nearly as committed as this? This is something I've put a lot into, something close to my heart. I deserve a fairer hearing than you're giving me."

I pushed my plate, still half full, away from me, smiling as I sought words to soften the blow. "Marty, if your father were at this table, he'd be blubbering with pride." I leaned forward onto my elbows. "But I'm not the kind of writer who could do your act justice."

"And why not?" he snapped. "You and I both know what a closet rocker you are." He returned to smiling. "Do you know what my dad told me, out of the blue, a month before he died? He said that when you were fourteen you bought a guitar. You told him you were gonna be the next Buddy Holly. He said you learned all the chords to a bunch of songs, you wrote some tunes of your own, and you were really gonna do it. *You* know what happened next."

"Is a picnic table appropriate for this?" I asked him. "Perhaps I should be on your couch."

"Which hand was it?" His eyes narrowed as I tucked my hands beneath the table. "I'm guessing it was your left. If it was your right hand, you could've still practiced chords with your left, or found a way to strum in a cast. Even with your finger not healing right, you wouldn't have had to give it up." Now it was his turn to lean forward at me. "Uncle H. This is your chance to chase that dream."

I sighed, long and heavy. "Marty. You're talking about a dream from 1957. It's been forty-five years. And think about all those years, while you're at it. If you put my name on a project like this, it will make it seem dated right out of the box."

"Well, here's what you do," he said. "Come downtown tomorrow and see this group for yourself. I think you'll be pleasantly surprised. We'll talk about specifics then, when you change your mind." With that he rose from the table.

We parted as we had met, as godfather and godson. After another hug, Marty mustered up one final cheer with his goodbye wave: "See this band! America needs it!" I raised my palms as if to say, 'You never know,' got in my car and pulled away.

⌘

My phone was ringing when I opened my front door. Dashing into my living room, I picked up the receiver just in time to rescue the call from my answering machine. "Hello?"

"Dad." Patrick's voice was heavy.

"How's my boy?" I felt my voice rise in pitch.

"Bad. Mister Rogers died."

"Oh, no. When did you hear that?"

"This morning. On TV." I could hear the congestion of his grief while he waited, breathing through his mouth into the phone.

"Did they say how he died?" My free hand grabbed the TV remote off the coffee table.

"Cancer." He sniffled. "Stomach cancer." Another sniffle. "Does that hurt a lot?"

My thumb hit the mute button and twitched over and over on the channel changer. No buttoned sweaters, no clanging trolleys; across nine channels I caught glimpses only of a talk-show stage, a trio of scantily clad brunettes in reality-show semi-focus, and scattered shots of desert-camouflaged soldiers heaving duffel bags across Kuwaiti sandscapes.

"Dad?"

"Yes, kiddo," I finally told him, "I'll bet it hurts."

"But not anymore."

"Not anymore."

"Dad? Do you think Mom will see him?"

"I wouldn't be surprised." I winced at the lie.

"'Member what she told you, Dad?" It was a delight to hear the laugh that escaped him, but his falsetto imitation of his mother was piercing in my eardrum: "'I'm raising our boy with Mister Rogers!' Remember that?" My rueful chuckle took some effort.

My remote-control thumb had stalled on a local newscast. A neatly coiffed female correspondent held a microphone to a crew-cut, square-jawed fellow in a beige military jacket. "Dad?" Patrick said after a minute. "Do you think Stacy's okay? She liked Mister Rogers, too."

"She'll be all right, in time." The cameras switched to the studio desk, at which the two anchors engaged in banter with the sportscaster.

"I didn't mean to hurt her, ever." Patrick's voice was pleading now. "I only said what you told me."

I sighed. "You never told me her brother was a soldier," I reminded him. "And what I said was more about the president than the Army."

"It's not your fault, Dad."

"Thank you, Son."

"Why'd it hurt her feelings?"

I took a deep breath.

"Dad?"

On-screen, a field reporter bounced a microphone between himself and the Anaheim Angels' manager. "Spring training starts tomorrow, doesn't it?" I said.

"Dad."

"Sorry, kiddo." I took another breath. "Look at it this way: what's the most important thing I've taught you?" I almost added 'the *only* thing' in jest, but it felt a hair too close to the truth.

In a rote monotone, he recited, "'Always do what you think is right.'"

"Whatever you do?"

"Whatever you do."

"Good people live like that, right?"

"Right."

"And your Stacy's a good person."

"Yeah."

"How about her brother?"

"He's nice."

"So. Your girlfriend—"

"*Ex*-girlfriend."

"—and her brother, both do what's right to them."

"Yeah."

"Now how would *you* feel if someone said you were doing the wrong thing?"

"Bad."

Here came my point. "I guess it hurt her because she's good. And *he's* good, too." I bit my lip and waited for his appraisal.

"I miss Mom."

Deflated, I could only agree that I missed her too. I couldn't admit defeat though, and racking my brain for something I could offer to console him, I blurted, "Now, how about I take you out tomorrow night?"

⌘

We parked near the gallery's address in a neighborhood one might confuse with a run-down part of Brooklyn. Along the barren side street under the distant neon glow of Library Tower's crown, a few scattered Skid Row denizens patrolled, pushing metal shopping carts that chattered, 'tack-tack-tack,' down the sidewalk.

As incongruous as it was for a photo gallery to set up shop in such a derelict area, there it was: fifty yards down the pavement, the only building in eyeshot with light in its barred windows. A crowd of people spilled out of its doorway; within its walls throbbed the beat of live music. Patrick quickened his step. "We're missing it." He waded through the gaggle of people and disappeared inside. I traced his path at my own pace. Like an image coming into focus, the music's bass-heavy hum became a sharp guitar roar as I crossed the threshold into the gallery foyer.

Before me, a single guitar player chopped out a chugging blues-rock riff on a hollow-bodied Cadillac of a guitar, while the bassist and drummer countered with a swinging rhythm right out of Little Richard's 'Rip it Up'. All of it, down to the band's quasi-uniform of blue denim jackets and black jeans, seemed perfectly unoriginal. But the lively snap of the rhythm, set against chunky chords that stomped around the beat, stirred within me a giddy spirit, the new-found memory of which, despite me, made me giddier still.

There was no stage, only an implied square on the white linoleum, bounded in back by a few amplifiers, and on either side by two black speakers on tripods. In front of this arrangement, ten or twelve listeners littered the floor in patches of two and three. This vast gulf was accentuated all the more by the bright gallery lights which glared down on every corner of the room.

I had to turn and peer out into the street to confirm the sight of a crowd that should have been crammed, sweaty and ecstatic, all around me. There they were, no hallucination, thirty-odd college-aged kids, holding glasses to their chests and flapping their lips at each other.

Patrick was across the room, exchanging excited pats on the back with Marty. The two began gesturing at each other in a sort of kabuki dance, the barrage of the PA forcing them to turn a quarter decade worth of catching up into a game of charades. Far too easily I navigated the floor to greet them.

I nodded at Marty, then turned up a palm at the sparsely populated floor. Marty shrugged, then mouthed "L.A.," before brightening as new activity onstage caught his eye.

The kid slunk into view, sheepish like an eight-year-old in the school play who knows he's forgotten his lines. Despite his smart attire (maroon velvet jacket, tight black jeans), I thought that he might be some stagehand when he reached center stage and began adjusting the microphone stand. But as the music came to a sudden snare-drum halt, like a light switch had been thrown open he was seized with a spastic rage. He tore his mic stand from the floor with both arms and gripped it like a weapon. And in that heartbeat, with a shriek he began to sing.

Two words—"*Oh, you*"—thundered from his wide-open mouth before the band came crashing back in behind him and all intelligibility was lost. The words *'love,' 'soul,'* and *'heart'* floated above the murk of his vocal in the first verse, leaving the rest of the lyrics asphyxiated in the fog of sound.

It didn't matter. The tone of his voice carried his message, and his madman's dance embellished the tale. A lyric would come out as a sneer and he would check himself, his next line soft and rueful. Then all at once he would throttle the microphone and spit out his words like a curse. He did it all with perfect pitch—even the tortured wail he let out to herald the guitar solo was on-key.

The guitar player stepped forward. A shower of blue notes poured from his amp over the non-crowd. Their non-reaction to his six-string salvo seemed not to bother him; in fact, his eyes never left his fretboard. Turning back toward the drummer, the singer wrenched his mic stand from the floor and swung it wildly, its base flying at the guitarist's face. The guitarist stepped out of the stand's swing radius as though avoiding a mild draft. He continued his solo while the singer rested by the drum kit, tapping a foot and breathing deep with each bar.

The singer returned to center stage, eyes half closed. The final verse he delivered in a long sigh, and as the music softened, the first full line I could understand came out deadpan:

"And here you'd thought I'd die."

A swirl of guitar notes, a crashing chorus and finale, and this heartsick boy's song of wounded defiance met with defiantly tepid applause. The kid stared hard at the wall opposite him. His cheeks twitched for an instant; only when his scowl returned did I realize that this had been a smile of thanks.

Seconds passed like days as he stood at center stage biting his lip, still holding the boom with both hands. His knuckles turned white while the drummer twirled a wing-nut on a cymbal. The band exchanged glances and launched into a slower rocker. As the blast of music hit him from behind, the kid let go, shutting his eyes and tilting his head back. It was the first fleeting moment of the set when I detected release. But as the bars went by, his eyes narrowed, his jaw set, and his hands crept back onto the mic stand.

He stood stock-still as he sang the first verse, glaring at the entrance. Then, as the band crescendoed into the chorus, he slid past the microphone, half danced past the stage monitor, and vanished through the doorway.

From his place beside me, Patrick floated toward the door, as usual all curiosity and no inhibition. He stopped short of the opening and craned his neck to see outside.

Throughout all of this, the trio of musicians played on. The chorus retreated into the next verse, wordless, like the soundtrack to a movie. With a wall of framed photographs blocking our view of the kid, the effect was as though the projector light had gone out.

Midway through a spirited guitar solo, the singer shot back through the doorway and raced to the stage, looking wide-eyed over his shoulder. A second later, a blond Sasquatch of a man stomped in, his face beet-red and his eyes shooting fireballs at the kid.

Patrick was not trying to break up a fight in the making. As the singer brushed past him, my son had whirled to face the stage, and so had no warning before the burly berserker piled into him. My poor boy went sprawling, sliding a good foot as he hit the ground. As I rushed to peel my son from the floor, the man froze, his eyes suddenly soft. He turned back and stooped down, reaching Patrick at the same time as I did.

The dazed grin on Patrick's face made it obvious he was okay. His unwitting attacker studied Patrick's face for a long, horrified moment, registering fully my boy's almond-shaped eyes and tiny, folded-over ears, then over the ongoing wash of music hollered in my ear, "Is he okay?"

"Ask him yourself," I replied, as jovially as I could.

The man repeated the question, over-enunciating each syllable into Patrick's ear. My son nodded, all smiles, pulling himself up by the man's shoulder and giving him a forgiving handshake. Relieved, the man turned his attention to the stage once again as we headed back to our place with Marty.

But where before we had stridden across a vast linoleum prairie, we now had to pick our way between thickets of onlookers. Throughout the room, eyes darted back and forth between the singer and his new friend, who stood in front and shook his head, a look of manslaughter aimed between the kid's eyes. A pretty young girl tugged at the man's arm, trying to stay him with her uneasy gaze.

With the caged lion stewing in the front row, the bassist and guitarist stepped front and center, leaving a gap only the length of a guitar neck through which the singer could be seen. The kid moaned on, seemingly aware of the new situation only inasmuch as the phalanx around him restricted his movement.

A few feet tapped among the new crowd. Some heads nodded. But most of the audience merely gawked at the kid and his opponent, waiting for the fuse to run out. Gradually, however, the maligned brute's posture relaxed, and his lady's pull turned into an embrace. The song tempos slowed, the guitar strumming softened, and the eyes around the floor ceased darting, settling on the kid with the microphone, the only person in the room who couldn't seem to simmer down.

Through two slow blues numbers he smoldered behind his human shield. The lyric of a final ballad floated over the music in a confessional tone.

"And it pierces me with sorrow,

Between my ribs a bayonet,
That my night of all tomorrows,
Was for you another evening to forget."

The last ringing notes of this love song were buried in an avalanche brought on by the closing number, an epic rocker whose guitar crunch devoured the vocal. And for at least this finale a few audience members danced in place as if they were watching a rock 'n' roll show.

As he sang his last chorus, the kid stepped forward between his guitar-wielding comrades and took a bow at the feet of Blond Bigfoot. The man caught some gesture I missed from where I stood; he snarled and took a swipe at the kid. But the kid was spry, and danced back between his friends, who closed the gap between them once again.

With his closing line, the kid surveyed the crowd one last time. Then he slammed down the mic stand and bolted to the doorway at stage left from which he had come. In front of the stage the brute shook his girlfriend from his arm and stormed off in pursuit, leaving the young lady calling after him and all eyes on his back.

The band built a guitar castle on the song's furious beat, then came to a crashing halt. The room erupted into applause. Marty dashed to center stage, grabbed the mic, and thundered like a Baptist minister, "Give it up for Jack! Jack Hackett and the Flak Jackets!" The applause redoubled, then died down into a gossipy rumble as an old soul number chimed in from the PA.

The crowd dispersed after the kid's pursuer emerged from the back doorway wearing a puzzled scowl. The man found his girlfriend, threw up his hands, and began shaking his head and kicking the linoleum.

Patrick bounced across the floor to the big fellow. A protective urge pulled me along with him. The man and I exchanged nods. His blonde companion, still hooked to his elbow, lowered her gaze to the floor.

Patrick held out his hand to the man. "Hi again!"

"Hello." The man reached out his hand, clasped my boy's for a second, and withdrew it.

"Why'd you chase the singer?"

The brute looked stunned for a moment. When he spoke again, it was in that slow, enunciated cadence to which I have had to grow accustomed in my son's presence. "He stole my, uh, joint, right out of my mouth." He mimed the action. "Before I could light it."

"Is that what he gave you in the last song? Your joint back?"

Scowling, the man put out his palm. In it he held a pile of crushed green marijuana buds, interspersed with shreds of white rolling paper.

Patrick's laugh might not have been wise in the presence of a large, angry man. But his mirth was contagious. The man dropped his awkward stare and allowed a chuckle. Still staring down from his right arm, his girlfriend smiled and nuzzled in closer to him. And finally, as the two turned toward the exit, the man allowed words to leave his lips in tones that didn't grate with awkward condescension. "Take care, man. Sorry about runnin' into ya."

In an instant, Patrick pivoted, springing off into the stage area to greet the players before they finished taking down their gear. I refrained from joining him, preferring to ponder the music-themed photographs on the wall to my right.

It was here that Marty caught up with me. Beaming with pride, he clapped my arm. "What'd ya think?"

I shrugged. "They'll go far once the singer gets out of the hospital."

"Oh, Jack's fine—he's always got an escape route planned." He nudged me a few feet over to the makeshift bar in the corner. "Can I pour you a drink?"

I shook my head. Marty grabbed one of the half full wine bottles and filled his glass to the brim. His first sip took care of a third of the contents. Thus fortified, he leaned in close as though he were sharing a secret. "So have you come around?"

"They're very good," I conceded. "But Marty, did you really expect me to change my mind?" I locked my eyes on his. "I have things to do here."

His eyes flashed. "What are you doing that's so important? Apartment hunting?" His index finger went to his chin. "Patrick just told me something interesting. He said he's probably moving to a new home in Culver City. Culver City! How many years has he lived just around the corner from you? I figure if he's heading there, *you* must be, too. And why the hell would you be leaving *your* place—for Culver City!—unless..." His finger left his chin and shot straight up, as if pointing to a light bulb that had just switched on atop his head. "Unless you can't afford to stay?"

"Are you finished, Mr. Mason?"

"Look. Uncle H. I know how money goes. It's a miracle you made your movie rights payoff last as long as it did! Now listen to me. This magazine isn't some xeroxed school paper. I've got some big-time investors already, and I'm finding new ones every day." He lowered his voice. "This job could buy you time."

Over Marty's shoulder, Patrick waved his arms in an air-guitar windmill for the bass player.

"I'll cover your rent back here, plus your expenses on the road, on top of your pay." A whiff of alcohol on Marty's breath made me realize how close he had gotten to me.

"I still think you're asking the wrong person."

"Well, you keep right on thinking until you start thinking otherwise."

Patrick had finished making the rounds of the musicians and found us by the table. He beamed as if he'd just been a witness at Kitty Hawk. "They're great!" he gushed to Marty. "Thanks for telling Dad about them!"

"Aww, it's nothing!" Marty patted my back. "Now he's just gotta tell the rest of the world."

At Patrick's quizzical look I cringed, realizing what Marty was up to. But though I could have strong-armed the conversation into a hasty goodbye, something held my tongue.

"I'm giving your dad the chance of a lifetime." Marty gave me a sidelong grin, then gave Patrick a run-down of his proposal. Patrick's eyes grew wider with every word.

"Oh, man!" he cried when Marty was finished. "Dad! You gotta do it!"

I held up my hands. "But I have you to think of, too, Son." I felt guilty adding, "What about you and Stacy?"

"Stacy who?" he countered, then laughed loud and long at his joke.

"I'm serious," I said.

"No, Dad. I'm okay. I was sad. But look now. I'm happy! See?" He gave me a molar-baring smile. "Come on Dad, do it. It'll be cool. I'll be fine. I'm grown up."

"See?" Marty looked ready to uncork champagne.

"Not so fast. You might regret picking me. I'm a nobody—worse than that, I'm an *expensive* nobody." Under Marty's smug eye, my whole argument suddenly felt like a Hail Mary pass. "My rent is sixteen hundred a month."

"I'll give you the full amount of the lease up front."

"Have they got a tour bus?"

"A minivan. I'm renting a little Kia for you to drive. That gives you some freedom to get away from them on their downtime and find an internet café."

"I'm useless with websites."

"But not with email, I'm sure. You write your entry up and email it to me, I'll grab the juicy bits and post them."

"How often?"

"You give me regular posts, I have 'em up like clockwork every Monday."

"And column inches?"

"Follow your muse. I'll take a paragraph or a novel if it captures Jack."

"And when does this all kick off?"

"March nineteenth. They play the first show at the Mint in West Hollywood. Then you're off and running."

"And it wraps up..."

"We've got them all up and down the Coast through till end of June. Come back, break for a week and record their triumphant homecoming on the Fourth of July."

My eyes betrayed my next question; he cut me off before I could ask it, silencing me with a dollar amount that seemed a mistake, a misplaced decimal adding a zero to my pay.

"How is the print edition going to sell if you've got the content up on the internet for months beforehand?"

He had begun speaking before I finished my sentence. "... only posting some of what you write online. We hold some of the best parts for the print edition. We'll spatter the site with ads for the mag, so all the kids who read and reread your priceless prose will rush out to snap up copies of the first five issues of *Upsetter*. I'm sure each one'll be a collector's item."

Black-framed photographs hung on either side of him. A dozen figures of rock history preened, postured, scowled and sneered at me over his shoulder as he talked.

"I'm thinking you have to write the whole you-are-there, warts-and-all thing," he said. On the wall behind him, Chuck Berry duckwalked toward the camera. "You write everything you see, right? All the gory details, band fights, groupies, debauchery." He puckered his lips over that last word. "I'll cut out the dangerous stuff—you know, the break-up-the-band stuff or the cart-'em-off-to-jail shit—before I post it. But when we do the mag, we stuff some of it back in. And then the book! We cram the rest in for the book, once their record's scaling the charts. It'll be a smash! And from your hand? It'll be a literary event!"

To Berry's left, a sunglassed rocker lounged in an airport, leaning against a sign: 'Patience please. A drug-free America comes first.'

"I know we're starting small. You may feel a bit like you're slumming. But we're going to grow them as we go. Radio, posters, everywhere the boys travel. Think of this tour like a snowball!"

Over his other shoulder a group of young punk rockers made rude faces in what looked like a London alleyway. Their defiant bad-boy poses muddied their faces, but the mud didn't quite hide the smooth shine beneath. Hell, they probably didn't even need to shave more than once a week.

"What are you smiling at?" He turned to look behind him.

"Nothing."

Scanning the rows of photos for a moment, he zeroed in on one to the left. He let himself be distracted just long enough to tap the glass over Elvis Presley and say, "That's my favorite." His dream would not stay on hold any longer, though. "So," he said. "Uncle H. I've been patient. But we're getting close to the kickoff here. I need to know if you're in the lineup."

I nodded as if deep in thought, shifting my gaze at intervals between Elvis's black-and-white rendering and Marty's pulsing temples. I held out for a few long seconds before glancing at my boy. "Patrick would never forgive me if I turned you down."

"Yesssssss!" My boy did a clumsy kick in the air.

Marty clapped me hard on the back. The motor in his jaw sprang to life again. "...biggest thing since...we'll all be rich...bring back rock 'n' roll..." It spewed out so fast the words edged each other out before their meaning could take hold. I stood with a bemused grin, my mind leaving Marty to drone on to himself as I let my eyes follow the magnetic current toward Elvis on the wall.

He stands with his feet apart, a pigeon-toed Colossus of Rhodes, strumming an acoustic guitar which can only be a prop, competing as it is with bandmate Scotty Moore's hollow-bodied electric—itself surely no match for the high-pitched, pubescent wail of the crowd.

"...make music matter to people again..."

His eyes are almost completely shut, as they should be—it's what he's hearing that holds the secret. Everything else is a distraction.

"...can't hurt your career, either..."

And his mouth is wide open, you can see down his throat. In his ecstasy, he has a look of a baby crying out at first breath. These *are* first breaths he's taking, his first in a new world partly of his own making.

"...you know why records don't sell anymore?..."

Throughout his rise, critics of all stripes are accusing him of stealing the sounds of the race records of his day. But an honest listen to any of his early singles is enough to kill those assertions. He borrows sounds, pinches moves from across the tracks, but no more than his colored contemporary Chuck Berry, who sings countrified boogie with a twang ambiguous enough to garner airplay on a healthy number of white stations.

"...not downloading, it's because the music sucks..."

The stance, the pose, the face. In other shots I have seen, Elvis toys with the crowd, his face like Faust at the first inkling of his power, feeling his oats as he teases, astonished and emboldened.

"...it's a whole scene just waiting for this band..."

Here, though, he's just lost, giving himself up to the tidal wave of the music, dragging the crowd in to be baptized with him.

"...conquer the world..."

It will go on to kill him, slowly, inexorably. A pity. But a small price to pay, when all is said and done, for a gift that we who live on will treasure forever and ever.

"I tell you Uncle H," Marty said, "we're at the best part right now. It's all ahead of us."

I shrugged. "We'll see what happens."

Chorus

March 19, 2003

Look at Marty Drennan, editor-in-chief of our own *Upsetter Magazine*, holding court in a stage-side corner booth at the Mint on Pico Boulevard. You'd never know from his face that there was anything amiss. Pausing from his animated conversation with the fellow who sits across from him, he raises a hand and calls "Over here!" with an air of grandeur. He holds fast to a triumphant grin while my son and I weave between empty tables to reach him. And when my son asks, "Did they cancel it?" he's ready with a laugh.

"Jack Hackett and the Flak Jackets, cancel their tour opener? Hah!" He and his friend slide sideways to make room for us. My son sighs theatrically with relief as he takes a seat beside Marty. He's been waiting for this night ever since seeing the Flak Jackets for the first time last month, at which time he declared himself their Number One Fan. (Earlier today, when I asked him how he wanted me to refer to him in my writing, he told me, "Dad, just say The Fan!")

"Still, it's a shame." I have to raise my voice to overcome the PA music as I take a seat beside Marty's companion.

"What shame?" Marty clings to his grin. "So our Dear Leader picks tonight to start his damn war. You think he's upstaged us?"

I feel guilty sweeping my hand across tonight's audience: two unkempt young men in cowboy shirts at the bar, two bartenders standing with their arms crossed by the cash register, and two waitresses chatting idly among the empty tables.

But Marty has lost interest, with the low turnout, with our arrival, with everything except whatever he was talking about before we showed up. He and his friend sit tall, neither looking in the least embarrassed at the small white placard which, absurdly, declares their booth 'Reserved'. They drink red wine in small but frequent sips, and a minute later, when they notice us again, their conversation barely pauses for introductions.

"Fritz here runs the Flak Jackets' label." Marty stuffs these words into an unrelated, already overloaded sentence. The duo's continued stream-of-consciousness banter volleys back and forth at a rate faster than my speed of thought.

My son the Fan watches his childhood friend Marty with passive but unblinking eyes. After a long minute waiting patiently for his buddy's attention, he looks the other way, to the side of the stage a few feet away.

I try for a time to follow the conversation, give up, and settle for the plaintive howls of Otis Redding that drown out every other word. Our record mogul Fritz rests his pink-silk back against a purple velvet jacket draped over the seat. Hairless on top, he has his sides cropped, and two wide muttonchops reach out along his jawline, striving in vain to link up at his chin. As if to be ironic in the dim lighting of the room, he wears oversized round-rimmed shades that give him an extra-terrestrial air. Neither the reptilian pulsing of his bald temples nor the eerie way his lip draws back from his crooked bottom teeth in an inverted smile when he stops talking does anything to humanize him.

Eventually he finds me beside him, and yells in my ear, "Henry Barclay, right? I dug your Jesus book." I could correct him, explain the difference between a carnival performer and the King of the Jews. Instead I nod my thanks.

"You done anything since then?"

"About a dozen first chapters."

His finger darts out first at Marty and then the stage. "We'll change that."

He goes on, regaling me with his soliloquy on the sorry state of American music, intercutting with reasons the Flak Jackets are the remedy for these ills. He needn't bother—I catch only about a third of his convoluted, run-on sentence. The rest is lost beneath the swirling organ of 'Mustang Sally'.

Ten o'clock rolls around. Showtime. No one moves to begin the proceedings. Sitting half out of the booth, the Fan pumps his leg up and down as he scans the room. His eyes lob question marks at me. Marty and Fritz have returned to their verbal table tennis, leaving us to parse the words of some gravel-voiced hipster warbling over a gritty guitar-and-drum vamp permeating the room.

At five after ten, two young ladies enter and wend their way to a table in front of the stage. The first is short, slim and fetching in a sleek black dress. Stray light from the stage illuminates her face as she sits down, revealing a picture of Hispanic beauty framed by teased, shoulder-length hair. Fritz taps my elbow. "The bassist's chick." He flicks his tongue across his upper lip. "But look at the new piece she's brought."

The new piece follows her friend to the table, taking all eyes with her. Her figure rebels against the conservative cut of her navy-blue dress. Piled atop her head, her auburn hair cascades in waves and curls down her back. When she sits, stray ringlets swing and bounce around her doe eyes. Her friend speaks into her ear, and she breaks into a sheepish giggle-grin, covering her mouth as she laughs. That sweet gesture lifts the darkness of the room and stirs a flutter in my heart.

It is now ten-fifteen. Marty raises his eyebrows at Fritz. "Shall we?" Fritz throws up his hands, at which Marty scoots past the Fan and disappears through a curtained doorway behind our booth at the side of the stage.

"We've stalled long enough," Fritz tells me. "He's gone to round up the fellas."

Marty reappears after another minute, hopping onto the low stage and grabbing the microphone up front. "All right!" he barks. "Nice to see you all here." His laughter at his own statement reverberates awkwardly in the empty spaces of the room. "Uncle H—uh, Henry Barclay." I find myself straightening in my seat. "Blogging this tour for us, ladies and gentlemen, we're very honored—Uncle H, you mention this disgrace..." he gestures at the unoccupied tables, and his face turns mock sinister. "I edit you out." Well, kiddo, here it is in black and white. Do your worst.

"Anyway! We're here to witness history. Ladies and gentlemen, to inaugurate their first-ever nationwide tour, here are Jack Hackett and the Flak Jackets!" He offers his applause into the microphone. His amplified clapping all but drowns out the self-conscious smattering of applause that trickles out at his announcement.

Three urchins hustle onto the stage and take up their instruments. The process outlasts Marty's and the audience's show of appreciation; they plug in amid a stony silence, broken only by a startling cry of "Yeah!" from the Fan.

A staccato A chord coughs from the PA. The guitar player, a scrawny, acne-scarred Asian-looking boy with a greasy black mop covering his eyes, nods at his bandmates. The equally emaciated redhead on bass answers with a brief arpeggio and flashes a half smile. And with a snare-drum burst from the drummer their preparation is complete.

For an instant they stand motionless at the ready, like runners poised in their starting blocks. Look at them now, before the blur of motion obscures them: the Bass Player, standing with his hands on his hips like some hippie comic-book superhero, bass guitar hanging like a pendant from his shoulders; the Drummer, sitting with shoulders up as if he's ducking something, turning his messy-maned head to look to the Guitarist with eyes which, though bare, I will affix with thick-lensed glasses when I call his face to my memory; the Guitarist, probably Japanese, gripping his ax with both hands and gazing outward at the sound booth across the room, jet-black bangs hanging like a veil over his eyes.

The Drummer strikes the match, counting one-two-three-four on his hi-hat. With the crash of the cymbals and the opening punch of a finely-tuned bass and guitar riff, the fuse is lit.

The Fan is dancing in his seat. Over his shoulder something tugs at the curtain drawn across the doorway at stage right. For a split second, a face pokes out, eyes taking aim at the stage. He jerks his head back, his dirty-blond bangs falling over those eyes as he disappears again, curtain all aflutter like the ripples on the water when the otter ducks back under.

Four bars later, the curtain is thrust to the side, and the kid launches himself onto the stage. His momentum carries him to his mic stand, beyond it as he takes hold of it, planting his feet at the lip of the stage and tipping it forward so that they both lean precariously over the first row of tables. He hovers like this for an impossible moment, somehow pulling back in time to save himself from falling over.

As the intro gives way to the verse, the fuse on this powder keg runs out. I brace for the blast as the mic stand rises and slams back down on the stage.

But the expected boom is a muted pop—on his cue he mutters, "Shit!" and misses half the first line.

He recovers quickly though, and the band plays, cooking to a slow boil. The kid sings his song like a homeless man trying to ward off the deadly gloom of night. "*I'm still standing*," the kid sighs, "*though I can't tell you how.*" His eyes are shut, and after this line he winces.

Between verses he jerks the mic stand off the ground and swings it sideways. The heavy round base hits the headstock of the bass player's Fender. The bass player shakes his head, not missing a note as the impact knocks his instrument back. The kid stops in midswing and brings the boom back to the fore, setting it gingerly down at his feet. Now something else catches his attention.

The girl stares up at him, wide-eyed, a hint of a smile on her lips. She does not turn away. The seconds go by; his eyes remain fixed on her. He begins to sing again, his trance unwavering; her only response is to bow her head slightly, absently running her finger along her collarbone.

The song rolls on, the snare drum popping like bottle rockets going off in 4/4 time. The kid continues his anxious confessional, and throughout it, his eyes will not let go of her. He puffs himself up, struts a little during the guitar solo, pumps the mic stand in the air with both hands, all with a strange hopeful look pointed squarely at this new figure.

The girl seems no less transfixed, merely smiling up at this boy pouring his heart onto her table. As the first song ends to minimal applause, she does not clap, but only broadens her grin, letting her lips part.

The guitarist hacks at his strings after only a few seconds of silence. The kid turns his head, suddenly remembering that he is onstage. Turning back toward us, he lets one eye leave the girl. And from this moment on, he proceeds to remind us that he is great.

The remainder of the show is an unrelenting exorcism. Our hero claws at his eyes, tears at his collar, stomps, hollers, wails, and pleads—all on the beat, all in tune. It is a testament to his ability that when he has led his band back through the stage-side curtain, I find that the mere act of watching him has left this old man too exhausted to applaud.

The Fan offers the cheer of a dozen men; he and our two companions at the corner booth manage between them to drown out the other ten people in the room. Marty pats the Fan on the shoulder and winks at me. "I'm glad *someone* in this town gets it." Then, with Muddy Waters piping up overhead, Marty nudges the Fan out of the booth and motions for us all to follow him.

⌘

The Mint's backstage area is in fact its own outbuilding, located across the club's tiny alley parking lot. The smell of incense, weak but off-putting, is the first thing to greet us as we enter what looks like a cross between a recording studio and a bordello lounge. Dominating the room to my left is a large mixing board, crowned behind with a giant computer screen. A dozen guitars of various types and vintages hang from a velvet-covered wall, surrounding the door through which we've entered. In the far corner a door, plastered with a collage of magazine photos, sits ajar. A toilet is visible beyond it. To my right is a circle of plush chairs and sofas, mismatched and draped with multicolored scarves—draped, as well, with the spent bodies of the Flak Jackets.

"Great set, boys!" gushes Marty, to nary a raised eyelid from the sprawled figures. He wades between outstretched legs until he reaches the kid, sunken into the center of a large couch and stewing in his own sweat. He pats the kid's thigh. "Jack, that was awful selfish of you back there, putting your mark on the only free pussy in the room."

The kid opens one eye and makes a pouting face. Marty pats his leg again, then returns to my side. "So listen up!" He sounds like a little league coach trying to rally some reluctant troop of nine-year-olds. "I want you to meet my Uncle H! That's Henry to you boys. He's the one blogging the tour, so I want you all to make sure and show him your best side."

While his friends smile and nod, the kid pulls himself to his feet and takes a step toward me, arm outstretched. As I take his hand, he forces a smile.

"I'm Jack," he says. "And that's all you get."

"You're really great!" the Fan blurts at the kid. He turns and points at the other band members. "You're all great!" The drummer and bass player murmur their thanks, while the guitar player finally pushes his bangs from his eyes and cracks a meek smile.

"You liked that, huh?" A tablespoon of sugar coats the kid's voice; strangers tend to serve their words to my son that way. "Well, you got lots of friends? 'Cause otherwise we're gonna have a pretty dead-sounding live record come July."

The bass player sits up. "Hey, I did my part. Gabby even brought a friend this time. I wanna know what happened to the Japanese contingent."

The guitar player's left hand idly fingers chord shapes on the neck of his guitar, which sits upright against the arm of the couch. "I don't know," he says, revealing a heavy accent. "I told people."

The drummer chimes in earnestly, "I didn't manage to get anyone, but you know my situation."

The bass player shoots him a wry smile. "No worries, pal. We can't ask you to keep good time *and* have friends now, can we?"

Fritz adjusts his bug-eyed shades. "Don't worry, boys. Tonight was a fluke. Who knew we'd be competing with Saddam Hussein?" He guffaws, his face all yellow teeth. "But seriously, you'll be on fire when you get back in July—a line around the block. And even if there's not a single person here, we can add a crowd afterwards." His eyebrows bounce up and down. "*Frampton Comes Alive*, man. Done in theaters. They slapped an arena crowd on that puppy, six months later it's arena crowds he's playin' to."

We fall silent for a long minute. Finally the bass player breaks our spell of reflection. "So, uh, Uncle H," he says. "Are you gonna ask us any questions, or are you just here to capture the ambience?"

Perhaps it's arrogance which puts my finger to my lips and draws from me the chiding words: "Not another word, or you'll ruin your mystique." Over the bass player's laughter, I ask for the Flak Jackets' names.

"Let me, Dad!" the Fan blurts. He points to each band member, a well-studied schoolboy showing off for teacher. The Drummer: "That's Tim." The Bass Player: "That's Caleb." The Guitar Player: "That's Joe. He's from Tokyo." Once each player has nodded at his introduction, the Fan conducts his own short interview. "Where're you playing next?"

Caleb the Bass Player fields the question. "Joshua Tree, Saturday. Turnout oughta be better. Weekend—bombs dropping on TV won't be such a novelty anymore. Plus it's not L.A., so you don't have *that* problem."

"Yeah, *that* problem," echoes Tim the Drummer, shaking his head for good measure.

Caleb frowns. "What I don't get is this: what about Silver Lake? Can't these guys get us Spaceland? That's the gig we need."

I await a rebuttal from Marty or Fritz, but their spot on the carpet is suddenly empty. Caleb the Bass Player points to a low, closed door opposite the entrance. "They're off on something else, man. I guess we're just not exciting enough for 'em." He smiles. "Or maybe they want the stuff in your blog to be a surprise." This earns a cheerful laugh from Tim the Drummer.

Joe the Guitar Player (from Tokyo) picks his guitar off the floor and starts noodling. The Fan's leg starts pumping to the implied beat.

Tim the Drummer turns to me with the look of a gracious host. "So you're a big writer, I hear."

"I'm a writer," I reply.

"Well, I should come out and admit that I don't know your work." He contorts some guilt into his expression and asks meekly, "Would you mind telling me some titles of yours I might want to check out? I *am* a big reader."

I give him the only title he'll ever manage to unearth. Caleb the Bass Player remarks in his friendly way that forty years have passed since its publication. "What did you do after that?"

"Among other things," I reply, "I moved here."

"And what prompted that great career move?"

I give him a flavor of my circumstances at the time: the purchase of movie rights by the ambitious studio, the promises of creative control and artistic integrity, the waste pit that was New York City in the mid-seventies, my wife's insistence that things would be better for our son here.

He raises an eyebrow. "And...?"

I don't bother with my associates' excuses, about the rise of the blockbuster, and the death-blows dealt to the serious-picture market by the releases of *Jaws* and *Star Wars*. I have always found their cocaine habits a far more convincing explanation, but I spare the band my moralizing. "It didn't pan out."

Tim the Drummer turns to the Fan. "And did you mind coming here?" He looks a little too directly into my son's eyes, speaks a hair too slowly and a touch too loud.

The Fan looks flattered to be addressed. "I love L.A."

"Do you miss anything about New York?"

"Just the Yankees. Dad and Aunt Ruth and me went to a playoff game. Last year. Do you like baseball?"

The Flak Jackets all shake their heads. Caleb the Bass Player explains for himself, "I'm from Kansas City. Hasn't been much to like about baseball there for a while, I don't think."

Our small-talk grows sparser, more forced, until finally Caleb gives up on it. He turns on a small television by the couch; the others swivel around to gawk at it. A foreign city skyline takes up the screen; a solitary plume of smoke rises in the foreground.

The TV volume is off, but for a while no one speaks. Caleb the Bass Player is the first to break the façade of solemnity, sniggering, "Boy, I'm all for gettin' Saddam, but did they have to pick tonight to do it?"

Tim the Drummer's eyes bulge like something wants to burst from his head. "Hey, hey, we promised, no politics tonight." He wags a finger at his bandmate. "Agree to disagree, remember?"

"I'm just sayin'." The bass player looks to Jack and Joe the Guitar Player for support, but the kid holds his gaze fast to the screen, while Joe watches his fingers on the neck of his guitar.

For another minute the TV flickers while the musicians stare. The Fan's eyes dart between them, looking steadily more helpless as his new friends refuse to be bored and move on. This is our exit cue.

"Lemme pee first, Dad," interrupts the Fan when I start to say goodbye. He darts into the bathroom in the corner.

Just then the front door lurches open, and the lovely Latina labeled earlier as the Bass Player's Chick practically falls into the room. "Heavy door," she observes, caressing her shoulder.

Her sweet-faced companion dips a delicate toe in behind her. Some reflex at the sight of this beauty turns my eye to the couch. The kid is scrambling to his feet.

"We were waiting for you!" the Bass Player's Chick complains. Her accent is vaguely Mexican; her tenor flirts with a whine that is pure San Fernando Valley.

Caleb the Bass Player slides an inch to the side and extends a beckoning arm. "Sorry Gabs, we had to get through with the backstage orgy first."

"Oh, you pig!" she squeaks, and scurries over to slap at him before he tugs her into his lap. From the couch she says, "Boys, this is Wendy."

The girl, Wendy, gives the room something between a nod and a curtsy. Joe the Guitar Player looks up from his instrument long enough to twitch his lips into a smile. Caleb lifts a hand from his girlfriend's midriff to wave. Tim the Drummer, still standing, takes half a step toward her before Jack knocks him back into his seat on his way past him.

The girl stands just a foot away from me, but even as he brushes past me, I can tell the kid can't see me. He extends a hand to her; the tension which has limited his face to either a smirk or a scowl suddenly lifts when she clasps his fingers. He breathes his name, "Jack," like he's holding a little bird that he's afraid might fly away. She blinks her understanding, while her free index finger traces the line of her clavicle under the collar of her dress.

The moment must end. He drops his hand to his side. She looks away. He opens his mouth, lets his jaw dangle for a few awkward seconds before abruptly asking, "You want some chips?"

"Sure." She looks a little stunned, but not enough to erase the smile from her face. The kid turns toward the door to the back room; she follows a foot or two behind him.

"I never met that one," says Caleb after the two have disappeared through the back door. "She from work?"

His girlfriend nuzzles her forehead into his chin, as if trying work herself back into the forefront of his mind. "She's brand new, like, this week. She comes from, like, New England. I don't think she has no friends here." She shrugs with one shoulder. "She seemed nice, so I told her this was the place to be tonight."

"Well, if you've got any more friends..." Tim says.

"I have to take her home soon," Gabby goes on.

Caleb pouts. "You gonna drop her off and come back?"

"Oh, no," she says. "We both got work tomorrow."

Caleb looks at the back door. "Well then, I guess Jack better work fast."

The sound of the toilet flushing vibrates through the wall in the corner, followed by the rush of the tap. The door opens, and the Fan appears, looking pleased to hear conversation flowing again.

"Some tour kick-off," moans Caleb. "My legions of fans stay home, my groupie takes off before midnight...." He shakes his head until Gabby gives him a pitying kiss.

Making his way to my side, the Fan spies the new face, and points to the space Jack has left on the couch. "Where's Jack?" I point to the back room. He looks again at Gabby; when he turns back to me his eyes are wide. "He's with that girl! Isn't he?" This gets a big laugh around the room. "Well, say bye to him for me." I yank the door open. "You guys are great!" he calls as he walks through. "Number One!"

It is midnight when I get home after dropping the Fan off at his home a block away. The evening hasn't been without its highlights, but overall I'm disappointed. I surprise myself, therefore, in plugging in the laptop computer that has lain dormant on my desk since virtually the day I bought it three years ago. I do so only to see if the word processor is properly installed so that I may begin my blog tomorrow morning. When I next look up from it, I am surprised again: the time is now four-thirty in the morning, and I've racked up five thousand words.

⌘

March 21, 2003

And as quickly as the tour kicked into gear, the brakes are on. The band's next show isn't until Saturday night, leaving the tour still feeling imminent rather than ongoing. In a bid to keep the blog's momentum up, Marty arranges for me to sit in on the band's last home-base rehearsal. Sensing an opportunity, I make sure I'm allowed to bring a guest.

Throughout the trip from his home to the shack off Sunset Boulevard where the band has booked time, the Fan hurls questions at me. "What songs will they play?" "You think Joe'll let me play his guitar? I still know the chord you showed me. A major."

The rehearsal space is walled with blackened concrete and smells of years of takeout meals spilled on the sooty shag rug. Despite the unglamorous setting, for the first fifteen minutes the sheer awe of sharing his heroes' inner sanctum is enough to muzzle the Fan. When he finally gains the gumption to speak, he asks me the obvious question: "Where's Jack?"

Yes, the fact is inescapable: the three players before us in this dingy room rehearse familiar riffs with only the occasional "*Bap!*" or "*Ooh!*" overlaying them. Joe and Caleb move around the raised platform that simulates a stage, but each makes sure to leave empty the few square feet around the center microphone stand.

They get through another two songs, tinkering here and there with arrangements, before the Fan addresses his question to the band: "Where's Jack?"

Caleb chuckles. "Yeah, you know it."

"He oughta be here soon," says Tim.

"Don't bet on it." Caleb's eyes roll. "He was talkin' last night about seeing that chick this afternoon."

The Fan springs into the conversation. "The girl from the show?"

"He's all googley-eyed again." Caleb is nodding. "Probably tryin' the ol' 'How about one for the road?' routine."

"A ladies' man?" I gather.

"I wouldn't say so, really," says Tim. "In the year I've known him, I've only seen him with a couple of girls, and they just kind of came and went."

Caleb agrees. "'F you listen to his lyrics, he seems to always be getting fucked—in the wrong sense of the word."

Tim grimaces. "He'd kill us if he heard us talking about him." He looks at me. "He was, uh, reluctant, to have someone blogging the tour."

"Really." My suspicion is confirmed.

"Yeah, well," Caleb comes in, "he's been sayin' to Marty how this is about music, you know, not like 'Entertainment Tonight' or something."

"I see." I shrug. "I'll try not to stray into soap opera."

"Don't worry about my Dad," says the Fan. "He's great. He wrote *Till it Hurts*."

"Oh, we know," Tim bubbles. "We're very honored!" Joe, smiling blandly, turns his guitar up so that his playing is just audible through his amplifier. Tim takes the cue. "Anyway, we should get back to work."

They tinker with another two songs. The Fan inches toward Joe's side of the platform, eyes on the sunburst Fender Telecaster the guitar player has placed in reserve against the wall. He squats to sit on the edge of the stage, within arm's reach of the instrument. In a moment of quiet between songs, he raises a hand to get the fellow's attention, and with a combination of raised eyebrows and pointed fingers he begs permission to pick the guitar up.

With a friendly nod the guitar player grants it. I watch my boy carefully take the guitar from the wall and gingerly bring the strap over his head. He strikes a pose worthy of the greatest guitar hero before setting about putting his fingers in place for his A major chord.

The Flak Jackets start another song; the Fan cries out in delight. "I know that one!" I see his lips saying. And after having seen the band only twice, he is ready to chant the chorus when the guitar and bass start pounding on top of the drums' crescendo.

The bass player then makes the Fan's day. With a wry grin he steps to the center microphone and points it in my son's direction. My boy needs no more encouragement than that. Eyes and mouth wide open as if trying to take the surprising scene and swallow it whole, he reaches the microphone in two bounds. Swinging Joe's Telecaster in his best rock 'n' roll flourish, he howls the tail end of the chorus. Though for words he can only approximate with "… *and I'm a ba-ba-da-da-bam, riding ba-da-do rail*," he just about has the melody line, so that when Caleb and Joe come to their own microphones, their "*Ooh, third rail*" makes a decent harmony.

They're on the last chorus when Jack shuffles in. The Fan pulls out of the singer's space, giving a sheepish smile and a reverent bow. The Flak Jackets ride the outro while the kid wanders around the room, apparently taking in the sound from all angles.

The Fan is shrugging off his borrowed accessory before the last chord is struck. "I was just playing around."

"That's fine." The kid is smiling, but an uneasy look pulls up his brow.

"How's your sweetheart?" Caleb's smug delivery draws a stern look from Jack. "Ooh. A heartbreaker? All those moony eyes for nothing?"

"It's not like that, asshole."

"My, such language! Well, in that case, when's the date? And you'd better both thank Gabby when it comes to the toast!"

Jack steps onto the platform. Caleb backs up a step, impish glee radiating from his face. The kid mumbles, "Cool it," then leans in to the bass player's ear and whispers something.

Caleb nods, the grin still plastered to his face. "Okay, that's cool. Hey, I'm happy for you."

"How about we play a little?" Tim says. Joe nods in agreement. The Fan, cowering at the edge of the platform, claps his encouragement and scurries to my side.

Caleb and Jack drop their baggage as the music kicks off. Jack gives the band satisfied nods at intervals. As Joe fires off a volley of guitar notes to hit the climax of the solo, Caleb turns from watching Jack's back and makes a 'come-hither' motion to the Fan.

The Fan's finger, touching his chest asks, 'Who, me?'

A laughing nod from the bass player: 'Yeah, you!' He taps his microphone and cocks his head back: 'Get up here!' The Fan cries out "Yeah!" and bounces onto the stage as Jack moves in to sing the final chorus:

"I'm a fifth wheel spinning backward kicking up sparks,
About to run up against the third rail.
Gonna light up like a comet's tail,
When I run up against the third rail."

My son takes up Caleb's whole microphone for a bar before Caleb nudges his way beside him. His gruff voice breaks here and there, and for words he substitutes a bevy of '*da-da-da*s,' but the harmony he ekes out is not without its ragged charm. Tim smiles winningly and hits the crash cymbal in congratulations when the Fan looks back at him.

Caleb shoots a smile of his own back at Tim, as if to say, '*Look at us, giving this handicapped person a treat.*' I ignore this, just as I ignore the uneasy tightness of the kid's awkward smile. They might not be what I perceive them to be—and besides, the complex of intense feelings that radiates from my son's face easily blocks them out.

"Ooh, third rail."

I can watch the crease in his brow as he struggles to hit the first word of each line in tune and on time.

"Aah, fifth wheel."

I can watch his eyes dart around the room, imploring everyone to see him shining and to understand his gratitude for this chance to live a little dream.

"Ooh, third rail."

I can share his smile as the song's simple refrain stretches on for a minute, and the three-and-a-half-part harmony melds closer together. I can feel proud of my son and appreciate what his new friends have done for him.

The song comes to its conclusion. Over the ringing final chord the Fan gestures at Jack and the Flak Jackets, holding up his forefinger and mouthing "Number One!"

⌘

March 22, 2003

At the Avis on La Tijera, Marty treats the pre-rental inspection of a dull-silver Kia Sephia as if it's the unveiling of a Cadillac. From there I follow his Dodge to a bungalow off of La Cienega whose tiny pool-house Tim apparently calls home. The Flak Jackets are at the curb, Tim closing the hatch on their overfilled white rental van when we pull up.

Marty indulges in some backslapping, capping a short rah-rah speech to the boys with "Onward to victory!" His aftershave hangs in the air around us, as if he's marked us for the journey, long after the dust from his departing Dodge has settled.

Nothing remains now but to pile in and move out. I suggest that the boys might want to take turns riding shotgun with me, so that we might get better acquainted. Each band member agrees to this, although Jack has to cross, uncross and finally drop his arms at his sides before he can stammer, "But—okay, yeah." With that, they make designations: Caleb to drive the van for this leg, and Tim, as they put it, to be my "wingman."

Tim emerges from the group's huddle and shakes my hand like a man running for office. As we get into my Kia, he pulls something out of the inside pocket of his jean jacket. Bubbling "Look at this!" he slaps a decrepit copy of my novel onto the dashboard. "I just got it yesterday, after practice. A guy on eBay was selling it right here in town. I was the only bidder. I went to Glendale to pick it up—to save on shipping."

"Oh, well done. And what is my current market value?"

"Forty-nine cents." He says it apologetically. "Ended up costing me more in gas to get it."

"Sounds about right."

The boy laughs with earnest sincerity. "Well, pages one through six at least are fantastic. It's truly an honor to have such a virtuoso blogging *us*."

"Don't mention it." Please.

The white van ahead of us, which has been listing from side to side as its occupants make a final pre-flight rummage, suddenly leaps from the curb and careens into the street. I let it disappear; we have our directions in the car, and I'm too old to play races.

Tim's zest is unrelenting. When I ask if he minds my recording our conversation, he offers to hold the tape machine. I roll down my window three inches before pulling out, then watch him as, with studied precision, he sets his window to the exact same height.

We cover personal background while snaking down La Cienega. He entered this world in 1980 via Salinas ("Steinbeck Country," he asserts with evident pride). His upbringing, "right out of the fifties," included classical piano lessons from the age of five. These lasted right up until he was ten, "and I was quite good!" But his dad inadvertently corrupted him, "blew it for me," the day he brought home a copy of the Traveling Wilburys' debut record. "Jim Keltner," he intones to me meaningfully. "After hearing those drums on 'Rattled', Mozart and Brahms didn't stand a chance."

"How did you come to the Southland?"

"Well, I figured that it wouldn't do me much good to be the best drummer in Salinas. I guess you could say," and here his voice rises to an absurd grandiosity, "I was lured by the bright lights of Tinseltown."

That gets us to the on-ramp. We head eastward, gliding smoothly past Downtown on a 10 Freeway remarkably devoid of traffic. Tim makes throwaway comments as we approach the interchange alongside the downtown copse of skyscrapers. His eyes beg me to fill the gaps he leaves. I throw him a line, inviting him to try the car radio. He dives for the 'On' button.

The car speakers thud with a bass-heavy beat. "Hmm," Tim says as he starts poking the 'Seek' button. "Not a big lover of Outkast—though I respect them... And same goes for Nickelback... Wait. This has a CD player, right?" He opens the knapsack at his feet. "I've got the perfect thing for this trip."

He pulls a disc from his bag and slides it in the player. A flurry of fiddle and country guitar notes floats gaily from the speakers.

"What's this?" I ask. The nasal-sounding good ol' boy who picks up the verse doesn't seem to have much in common with the Flak Jackets' repertoire.

"It's Gram," he answers. The singer cuts in to wail a few lines in a wistful drawl. "Parsons," Tim continues. "That's where we're going."

"Is he from Joshua Tree?"

"Oh no," he laughs. "He died there. In the early seventies. This is the guy who created country-rock." A fiddle player silences him with a frantic solo.

He tries at frequent intervals to jump-start the conversation, but the music draws my ear away from him. I switch off my recorder, and let a ticky-tack drumbeat move us along through a concrete corridor walled with commercial, industrial, and residential complexes. The walls grow gradually shorter, gaps begin to appear between them, and there comes a point about an hour in when I look to my left and see a bare brown virgin hillside, and a barrier-free shoulder that stretches on into the far distance.

Leaning back in my seat, I restart my tape recorder. "How did you come to play with the Flak Jackets?"

"Not much of a story there. I answered an ad."

"What caught your eye about it?"

"Well for starters it was the only one that wanted a rock 'n' roll drummer. Seems funny, but you don't see that too often anymore." He rolls down his window to match the level of mine. "The band was just starting, but they were all together already. Jack, Caleb, Joe. I was the final piece."

"And what did you think of them from the outside?"

"Jack's the king," he blurts. He sits up, swivels a few degrees toward me. "I mean, Caleb and Joe are perfect backup, but it's *his* show, don't you think? You know, the songs are great, and that's him. And he delivers them just perfect, and he's exciting to watch, even from behind. It's an *honor* to play for him."

Surely there are more blanks to fill, but the landscape expanding before us tugs hard at my eyes, and I find myself too distracted to come up with more queries. I shut my recorder, and finally, Tim settles for silence. We climb over hills, through valleys and across fault lines into the bleakly beautiful high desert, watching the landscape unfold as the post-midday sun sails amid dwindling patches of cotton-candy clouds.

⌘

What are we doing in Joshua Tree? The only sign that denotes any human activity in this region is a massive banner in nearby Twenty-Nine Palms, replete with yellow ribbons, advising us to support our troops. Still, Tim at least is adamant: this is more than a tour date.

"The hotel here is Marty's treat! He's booked us each our own room!"

"That's extravagant."

"Yeah, but Marty knows. Gram came here with Keith Richards. They got stoned and spent the night in the desert looking for UFOs. He came here a lot to rest. And the last time, he OD'd." He falls silent as we pull up to our destination, a quaint motel perched on the highway side.

I switch off the ignition, sigh with the relief of a man beyond my years that the day's journey is over, and step out of the car. The desert air is warm and, with a gentle intermittent breeze, invites deep breaths. The scarcity of buildings, the absence of trees beyond the spindly Joshua trees that are the town's namesake, the dearth even of clouds in the sky, all of these things I take in with a strange exhilaration.

Tim is stretching, pulling one arm behind his head with the other. He drops both arms to his sides when we make eye contact and reaches back into the passenger seat to pull out his knapsack. "May as well bring our stuff in."

The drone of an approaching engine breaks the desert calm. "Here comes the cavalry," quips Tim, squinting down the highway. Indeed, it's the van which last we saw sling-shotting around the corner toward La Cienega a few hours ago, a little dusty but otherwise intact. Caleb, still at the wheel, attempts a thirty-five-mile-an-hour right-angle turn into the motel drive, applying the brake at the last possible second. The vehicle sways violently and jerks to a halt uncomfortably close to where I stand. The three Flak Jackets descend from inside laden with the remains of a take-out lunch.

"Howdy slowpokes," crows Caleb. "Where you been the last hour?"

Joe lifts a white plastic bag and holds it out to me. "We bought you lunch," he says. "Chicken wrap." He struggles just a little with the *r*.

What appears on the outside to be an unremarkable motor lodge is on the inside a fairly pleasant bed and breakfast. A great stone fireplace reigns over a lobby adorned with Mojave-themed photos and artwork. These generic Southwestern touches aside, the T-shirts, books and other themed memorabilia showcased at the front desk suggest that the keepers of this inn know full well the legacy they have inherited. Tim fills me in on that legacy as we await our keys: "Gram passed away *in this hotel*." His eyes gleam reverently. "Room 8."

And to see his face when his key is handed to him, you would think he won the lottery. "Room 8!" he repeats, looking with wide, glowing eyes at the number on the key-shaped holy grail in his hands.

Caleb performs an angry soliloquy: "Dammit!" Joe smiles graciously. But Tim's eyes are on Jack. The kid's brow falls a hair, his jaw slackens a touch, and a thin veneer of dejection is pulled across his eyes.

Tim's eyes move back to the key, and the light in them flickers. He turns it over, back again, shakes it hesitantly. But his smile never falters. He is smiling as he holds the little brass talisman out to Jack. He smiles as he looks over at the awaiting hotel clerk and says, "Do me a favor, will you? Switch my room with Jack Hackett?"

"You sure?" the kid asks. Tim nods. Jack takes the keys with surprised thanks.

A silence follows this exchange, one that grows uncomfortable, most palpably on Tim's face. Finally, he grabs his knapsack from the floor. "All right! Let's get settled in!"

We make plans as we move along the walkway to our rooms. The band has sound check. The old man—me—has time for a much-needed nap. We will reconvene for the show.

Our party stops, predictably, at Jack's room. The kid turns the key and enters. Over his shoulder, Tim exclaims, "And the stone was rolled away!"

"Let's not get carried away," says Caleb. Tim thus quieted, we file in. I bring up the rear, leaving the door open for a quick exit; I am growing weary of all this necrophilia.

Tim has been silenced, but his religious fervor emanates from his pores so that I can just about smell his awe. Caleb breaks the short silence with a deliberate wet blanket, "Ya know, it ain't even the same furniture — and that picture sure wasn't lookin' down at him when he croaked." He points to a framed photo on the wall, depicting a cheerful young hippie, presumably Mr. Parsons, sitting in an ornate armchair.

The visual thus betrayed, Tim shuts his eyes. I can almost see the million tiny feelers snake out from all over his body, searching, grabbing for any vestige of the supernatural force that might remain locked in here. Jack is watching him as well. "O-kay," the kid mock-yawns. "'Bout time we broke up this little séance. Before Tim starts singin' country songs in tongues."

To which Caleb adds, "Or just creams his jeans."

⌘

Tim greets me at the club's entrance, taping an 11"x17" poster to the door. Jack stands in black ink on yellow paper, eyes squeezed shut and mouth agape, with the band in heroic action at his flanks. A stylized band logo graces the top. The venue name (with the exclamation "Here!" in brackets beside it), and the date and time ("Tonight!"), are scrawled across the bottom in black ink that has yet to dry. Tim points to the poster and blurts, "Our advance publicity!"

The joint isn't empty, thank goodness, but neither is it abuzz. Patrons dressed in sloppy-fitting T-shirts and jean jackets look intently at their glasses or blankly around the room. Said room is western in décor, all woods and rawhides, but the horned skull that hangs on the wall is just another brushstroke. Underneath I can still make out a familiar canvas: low stage, bored staff, sparse, bored clientele.

To their credit, the Flak Jackets converge on the stage with far more bounce than the occasion merits. They re-enact their ritual, band warming up for Jack, Jack skulking onto the stage and indulging in his public primal-scream-therapy.

The locals clap lightly when the group offers them gutbucket blues. When the beat swings and the guitar clangs, they clap lightly. Jack, in fleeting seconds, opens his soul and bleeds on them, and as he sews himself back up they clap lightly. And at a table near the stage, to my shame, I clap lightly along.

Midway through the set, Jack peers out into the dark beyond the stage lights with a steel-eyed squint. For what or for whom he's looking, I can't tell.

"'Wild Horses'!" calls out a plump, wispy-haired oaf at a table near mine.

Like a cat's for a string, Jack's eyes pounce on the man. For a second, he braces for motion as his eyes betray a lightning calculation, a thousand chess moves and one upending of the board considered in the draw of a breath. Instinctively I edge my seat away. The man's glassy eyes harden and his pudgy jaw sets as he smells a confrontation.

In the time it takes for the clanking of a beer glass to reach four walls, the audience snaps to attention. The stare between the kid and the stranger forms its own spotlight, and edges up the temperature of the room. Jack is near critical mass when Joe, alone among us in his ignorance of the coming blast, cuts into the intro to the next song.

Jack exhales, and in one syllable—"Hah!"—pops like a soap bubble the apprehension of the audience. "'Wild Horses'? You got the wrong band!" he laughs. A chuckle ripples through the room while he gears up to sing. When I turn to the goof who initiated the standoff, the goof is laughing too.

There is a marked change from this point. Jack has stopped searching. For fifteen minutes he's on, and it is only because I have borne witness to this before that I am not floored by the performance.

With the show's last chord still whining in my eardrums, I take my thoughts out into the crisp night air. In time, the Flak Jackets begin appearing and disappearing, carting their gear back to the van. Aside from Tim, who has an insipid one-liner prepared for each time he passes me, they labor in silence, dragging their feet in the gravel under the weight of their amplifiers.

When they have trudged the last piece out, Caleb closes the back of the van and exhales in exclamation. He looks to Jack. "No sense hittin' up the barkeep for pay, huh?"

Jack nods in bewildered agreement. "Sound guy mentioned free drinks, though."

"Hey, we get 'em for something!" And as the four head back to the door, Caleb claps Tim on the back. "Hey! Drummer Boy! You're designated driver! You can order my second round!"

⌘

March 23, 2003

The next morning, I don my frumpy jogging pants and gray T-shirt, and go for a jog along the highway side. I return to my room aglow with sweat well-shed, take a refreshing shower, and enter the dining room looking for all my advanced years in better shape than the spring chickens who trickle in one by one over the next twenty minutes.

A red-eyed Jack Hackett appears first in the doorway. Light stubble muddies his face like bruises along his jaw. Tufts of greasy hair meander from his scalp in a dazed whimsy. He licks his lips absently, but stops when he registers me. He falters, like he's walked into the wrong room, but does not turn away. "Mornin'," he mumbles, and heads for the buffet table to pour out a bowl of cereal before taking a seat beside me.

"How was your night?" I ask.

"Not bad."

"Sleep well?"

"Yup." More silence as he takes a mouthful of cereal and holds it in his mouth, jaw motionless, as though the very crunch of his teeth may give away more than he can allow.

A protracted, staged yawn emits from the hall. Caleb swings through the doorway a second later. "Mornin', early birds!" he says, clearing his throat with the same breath so that the words come out in a growl. "How'd you beat me in here?" He pulls up a chair across from us without taking any food and slumps down with his chin resting on his fist. Jack and I return to our meals. The kid's jaw begins to work.

When Caleb fails to contribute in word or deed to the scene, the kid frowns. "Jeezum Crow, Caleb, why the hell d'ya get out of bed?"

Caleb dons a mask of effrontery, heaves himself up and out of his chair, and plucks an apple off the buffet table. "Jeezum Crow!" he chuckles to himself. "Who the hell says Jeezum Crow?" He holds the apple up on display to Jack, stares the kid down for a long second, then takes a bite as he sits back down. Fragments of the fruit stick out from between his teeth when he speaks: "Got a long drive ahead, right? Gotta get up and out."

My spoon has rested in my empty cereal bowl for a few minutes when Tim and Joe drop in, one after the other. Joe peruses the buffet and grabs a sticky bun. Tim, looking squeaky clean and bright-eyed like the teacher's pet, chirps away while he assembles an elaborate feast.

"Boy, it's just that right temperature outside to wake you up!"

Caleb spins his apple core on the table like a top. Jack looks upon the act with mild bemusement.

"Man, I thought *L.A.* was dry!"

Joe hovers over his sticky bun, picking off chunks and placing them on his tongue. The gratification evident in his consumption of each morsel is surprising.

"Great show last night!"

Joe reaches for a packet of sugar. He nudges his thumb and forefinger into the sachet, and sprinkles a pinch over the already sugar-glazed bun. White granules fill the folds and fissures along the surface. Caleb raises his eyebrows in amusement.

"I tell you, I won't soon forget coming here! I really feel like Gram is *here* somehow." Tim puts a tall glass of orange juice on the table and sits down.

"Sounds like someone in the van got contact high," cracks Caleb.

"No, I mean it. I think we all made a connection last night—"

"Not from the stage, that's for sure!"

"—and I'm glad we came here. This'll stay, with *me* at least, for a long time."

Glancing at me, Jack mutters, "I dunno, I'm kinda over it." Tim's face falls; the kid amends his words: "But yeah, I'm glad we did it, I guess." He tosses his spoon into his empty bowl.

"So, Vegas next!" Tim blurts.

His words kick-start the next leg of the tour. Beside the van an hour later, the boys huddle to choose my traveling companion. Caleb looks to Jack, looks at Joe, and raises his hand. "I might as well."

⌘

The desert road, after the splendor of its vastness has faded, is a non-entity. In the desolation from horizon to horizon on the route to Vegas, the landscape collapses in on itself until the highway becomes a narrow corridor with sepia-colored walls. Driving through it gives the feeling of those dreams of pushing forward with all one's strength and only inching ahead. You can floor it, watch the desert crawl by like a slug, and then glance at the speedometer to see you've cracked ninety.

A companion throughout this journey is a blessing, even if, like Caleb Porter, the Bass Player, he suffers from a loud mouth.

"I'm the All-American boy," Caleb declares early in our journey. "I can talk sex, drugs and rock 'n' roll—but I know guns and God, too." His first choice of music, decided upon and jammed into the CD player before I can gather the courtesy to offer its use, is an Elvis Presley compilation. I commend his taste and he waves it off: "It's in our blood, ain't it?"

It comes as a surprise to him that some on this planet can remember a world before 'Heartbreak Hotel', that some took in Elvis with uninitiated eyes and ears and had to decide what to make of him.

"But you went for him?"

"Almost as madly as my sister did."

"How about the Beatles?"

"Are you doing a piece as well?"

Caleb has his head halfway out the window, letting the wind brush the greasy mop from his face and erode from around his eyes some of the remaining hung-over puff. He falls back into his seat. "Just want to get to know ya, Uncle H," he says. "Answer me that, and I'm all yours."

"I liked them."

"Past tense." He's perceptive.

I stop my recorder and plot the arc of my tastes as they evolved from the sounds of the day to the standards that were still around for the squares who couldn't keep up.

"So you went easy listening."

"I went to Sinatra."

He wrinkles his nose. "Sinatra." He says it quietly again. The last strains of 'Love Me Tender' fill the silence that follows. Then, as though searching for something to redeem me, he asks, "You like Ray Charles?"

"I love Ray Charles." And then, seeing in his eye that we can now be friends, I engage him about Elvis.

"I got it from my dad—my love for the King. Dad was into the rockabilly thing. Like, obsessive." He pushes his hair back from his face. "He was, like, Daddy Cool, you know? Slick-back hair, sideburns. In his *fifties*."

Elvis is getting all shook up. Caleb seizes on it. "Listen to that, man." He starts slapping his knees in time. "You catch that?" He slaps harder. "No big drum crash. No drums! So spare! Just three, four people, live, in one room, but the way it's worked itself into everyone's psyche. The whole free world! Three, four guys! You'd think it was a fuckin'..."

"So you're a rockabilly diehard."

He scratches his scalp. His hair tousles obediently. "No, no. I'm not a clone of my old man. I went through my Motown phase. All bass players do. You think you're James Jamerson for, like, a year. And the Stones. All that. But Elvis, he's beyond rockabilly anyway."

And then he's really rolling. "Did you catch the Comeback Special in '68?" I reply that I did. "That's the best Elvis. Man, he's just the shit from start to finish! He's all sweaty, but he's trim, and he does all the right moves, and he's funny when he wants to be, and he sings out of tune at times, but I swear to ya, if he'd sung in tune it wouldn't be as good!"

Suddenly he's tearing through his CD carrying case. "There y'are!" he cries, and lunges at the stereo controls. Out pops pre-Army Elvis in mid-drawl. "Sorry, King," Caleb mutters as he slides his replacement into the slot.

He sits back in his seat and watches the right speaker for the first vibration. When it comes, the rush is visible on his cheek. He snaps his fingers and points to the speaker as if to cue the singer.

The version of 'Evil' that opens Elvis' hour-long TV special brims with so much pathos that I shiver at the first line. If we're looking for trouble, he tells us, we came to the right place.

"Fuck, listen to 'im!" Caleb rolls his window up to block out the sound of the Interstate. "He'd been doing all these shit movies, and everyone thought he was over. But here! He's out to prove he's still got it."

Elvis begins wailing, and I can hear that do-or-die urgency. He's evil, he wants us to know, and his middle name is Misery.

"So you saw this the first time?" he asks, in a tone that implies that this is an accomplishment. I take the credit. "Man," is all he can say as the pace triples and the crescendo builds. "Did you get the significance of it at the time?"

Significance. I suppress a smirk. "It was nice to see something familiar on TV." Which is true. At the close of 1968, after several painful months of a new life that was mercilessly foreign to me, seeing a face from my sheltered, structured adolescence was something akin to getting a postcard from home.

"Nice," says Caleb. While he digests my comment, Elvis fills the gap with a story of the road that moves at such a clip he half speaks to keep up. And the sheer abandon in his voice does find a way into my gut.

After a reverent minute, Caleb springs back to life. "See, he still had it! All those fuckin' sitcoms he'd been puttin' out, callin' 'em movies, that wasn't *him*." He pauses for breath. "He was bored as shit in those flicks, you could see it, but he *had* to do 'em." He's not talking about contracts. "He needed the *slump*."

The sermon that ensues has a crude beauty to it, as Caleb rescues it from parody with the naked passion of his belief. "Say you're a big success, you have your hits, then you go away, like retire, go find yourself in Tibet. You're throwing in the towel before the world can throw a punch."

The King has made it to Memphis by the second verse. He crams so many words into the ride from there to Macon that they melt into each other.

"You hang in there and go through a string of flops. Your career, your life, falls to shit." His fingers trace the lines in the air of something crumbling to dust. "You never do nothin' after that, I say the guy who gave up with the perfect track record ain't got *nothin'* on you, for all his hits. Fact, I say you're a notch above the other guy. Shit, even if you blow it all yourself, even if it kills ya, or you spend the rest of your life making a public ass of yourself, you got my respect, 'cause you're dealing with it, seeing how you take your lumps."

The King is down and out for the bridge of the song, but seems ready to turn things around when in the third line he hits Mobile.

"But man, if you go through what Elvis did, bein' a fuckin' laughingstock, grinding out shit for the Man, you got a bigger mountain to climb than if you're nothin', 'cause you're fuckin' *tainted goods*. You gotta be *better*'n you were before. You gotta blow 'em the fuck *away!*"

Sure enough, by the last verse Elvis is belting out his triumph, selling the song's story of finding a guitar-playing gig as though it's the climax to the Odyssey.

"And if you can do it, you're in a higher place just 'cause you carried the weight of having been in the trough." He brushes his wayward hair behind his ears. In my brief glance I see that he is just warming up.

"You do it the first time, it's all new, it's not your world, you're a visitor." The scene of our soundtrack switches to the show's famous, pared-down, 'Boxing Ring' segment. Elvis starts wailing the blues. "You hit the top again after being out, it's like comin' home." Caleb's voice drops to a mumble, disarming in its sudden solemnity. "Nothin' like comin' home."

"You should have been a preacher."

"Ah, well, there's the greatest comeback ever." He tugs at the collar of his T-shirt and frees a small wooden crucifix to dangle over it from a black string around his neck. Out of the blue he stabs at a button to advance the track. A gospel number bubbles up. "God made flesh. *Nobody* fell as hard as Jesus."

With the music rolling on and no interjection from the Reverend Porter, I let my eyes leave the road to take in the sight of a young man at pious peace. Eyelids drawn, he throws out his fingers in a fanlike motion with the downbeat. Gospel singers take the foreground and scat a moving bridge, and Reverend Presley starts to really testify. I can feel the Resurrection coming on.

The boy comes back to Earth to make his summation. "So when you're in the shit, you gotta wallow in it, like a fuckin' hog, 'cause if you get out...." To end it he just holds his hands up to the heavens. The gospel soundtrack carries on in a frenzy, climaxing in a chorus of *"I'm Saved!"* It falls silent, as do we for a minute, Caleb pondering the glories of the life after death God is to grant him, I thinking how nice it must be to believe in something.

The Comeback Special continues on its sweaty course. I steer the conversation back to him. "So what led you to become a musician?"

"A *musician?* Heh. Well, I dug the concept, wouldn't you? Kinda romantic life, don't you think? Travel the world, play to screaming fans. A girl in every port —" he snorts, "—and Porter in every girl!"

"And what does Jesus have to say about that?"

He doesn't take offense, but he does answer seriously. "I'll make it up to Him." After a breath for thought, "And I got Gabby anyway, so who am I really kidding?" He gives a grave little laugh. Suddenly fidgety, he cuts the CD off. Out pops Elvis, and in dives Jerry Lee Lewis, no stranger to sanctity and sin himself.

⌘

The computer-printed directions we've been issued bring us not to the Strip, but instead through the labyrinth of Sin Suburbs. The boys' van sits in the street in front of a great gaudy apartment building; Tim is walking down the path from the main entrance, alongside a skeleton in a Diamondbacks cap, as we pull up.

"Howdy motherfuckers!" the skeleton bellows as I cut the engine. "You're lookin' for Spike, right? That's me! Don't bring a fuckin' thing! Show me what you need upstairs right now and I'll bring it up." Spike grunts as he opens the rear door of the van and has to scramble to stop the small avalanche of equipment and luggage. "Shit, what is this, a van or a fuckin' shoebox?" He adds, "Who set you up with this? Fritz? Marty? Who'd he blow to get it? Wrong guy, for sure!" Only Caleb laughs.

We climb up one flight, a half-outdoor, stucco-encased staircase with desert plants in a great pot on the landing. Spike brings up the rear, directing us in terse barks, clutching four bags under his arms. Two steps above him, half-turned to offer introductory small-talk, I remark that the man's hairstyle (long, greasy, ponytailed), and attire (black sleeveless T-shirt, black jeans), don't immediately call to mind a moniker of 'Spike'. He flashes yellow teeth at me. "You wanna be the world's greatest roadie, don't exactly cut it if you're called Irwin. Spike just fit." Even armed with coherent syntax, who am I to argue?

Spike's apartment appears as one would expect when one enters it from a cheaply air-freshened hallway, through a glossy black door with only a spy-hole to distinguish it from a closet. Bright and airy in design by virtue of a large sliding glass door opposite the entry, this effect is thwarted by a dark red down comforter that droops across two thirds of it from clothespins on a sagging curtain rod. Scattered like debris over the stained, white carpet are a couch, a stereo on a stand, and, leaning against the left wall, a full-length mirror. Spike sees us all in, then walks to the sliding door and removes a clothespin from the makeshift curtain. Its left side comes down with a little tug, and the room brightens enough to reveal a new, lighter spatter on the carpet.

"Who's fer brews?" Our host dives into a waist-high refrigerator in the linoleum corner that I suppose we are meant to call the kitchen. A can of Coors hits my solar plexus in the next instant. "Take a seat, motherfuckers!"

Four bodies fall in twisting arcs to land side by side on the couch. I place my beer on the arm beside Caleb and make for the bathroom door. The room I enter has the rough dimensions of a small bathroom, but its central feature is a single bed, crammed in the space like a cork in a bottleneck, leaving just enough room for passage to the closet and toilet.

"So who gets to sleep in the bowl?" I inquire on returning to the living room.

Spike stifles a burp. "You can, if that's your thing, man. You're the only one sleepin' here." He assumes an air of beneficence as the boys exchange glances. "I've made arrangements," he says with a leer. "Tonight after the show, you lucky fucks each get a bed of your own—and a chick to keep you warm at no extra charge!"

Caleb yelps in delight; Tim looks straight ahead and feigns a heart attack; Joe's expression sharpens as though he's trying to re-decipher the roadie's English. Predictably though, Jack just nods, lifts a corner of his mouth at Spike, and drops it. His last glance in the silent second is at me.

"How much did that set you back?" I ask.

"Hey!" His face is scornful as he stabs at his chest with his thumb. "World's Greatest!" He takes off his hat and strokes his mane into place. "You know, there are plenty of chicks in this world — I mean a *shit*load — beautiful chicks — who've got legs like the Red Sea for a guy with a guitar. You just gotta move in those circles, ya know? Now, all I did is put the word out that there's L.A.'s finest rock band blastin' into town, an' the poor fucks got no place to park their peckers." Another snort from Caleb. "So we'll bring your overnight shit to the gig, I'll make sure you get paired off, and you can write your letters to *Penthouse* over lunch."

As the time for sound check nears, the boys gather up their things and make for the door, but my feet take me only to the couch. I find it convenient to claim the need to hunker down and tap out the day's events. The underlying truth is that once again I am utterly beat.

Of course, minds are elsewhere, and only Tim gives an earnest wave as my companions leave. As I let my head loll and then come to rest on the back of the couch, I feel the first pangs of an old man's worry. I have already logged well over three hundred miles behind the wheel. I needed rest in the desert yesterday—my goodness, it was only *yesterday*? Am I to spend this tour daily killing myself?

I drift off on a raft of resolutions. My driving partner will have to start sharing the helm. I'll need to skip a show here and there. Must write less. Say your piece and get out. Yes, that's it, and darling, stay on the sidewalk, just another second, and oh hell....

I awake to quiet darkness with a resolve greater than my energy should permit. In this fleetingly peaceful time and space I power up my computer and by its light alone I catch up on my blog. I take pride in the sheer volume of my output while trying to see past its rather hopeless tone. Then, with a two-hour catharsis behind me, I wrestle a bit with my work-issued cell phone, finally managing to punch in the Fan's number.

"Who's that?" The groggy slur in his diction gives me a jab of guilt for accidentally waking him, but his excitement at my voice coaxes him awake. "How are they? How's Jack?"

"Keeping out of trouble."

"Good. Tell Jack I emailed him today. Tim gave me his address, at the studio. I told him he's gonna be big! Number One!"

"I'm sure he'll appreciate it. How's the House of Barclay?" I query about the group home of which the Fan fancies himself patriarch.

"Good. Tell Jack about my email! Number One!"

"Number One."

And now, to sleep. The couch folds out into a passable bed, though with no sheets, I must sleep in my clothes and a light sweater. There was a time when I would take satisfaction in such a situation, akin to an outdoorsman roughing it in a tent and sleeping bag. I wonder precisely when that foolish zeal for hardship was extinguished from my being.

My eyes open like clockwork at two. With age my talent for sound sleep has diminished. The dread of lying awake, too exhausted in body to will myself to my feet, too alert in mind to go back to sleep, tilts me upright. The momentum of rising propels me to the quilt-curtained sliding door. Through the glass and over the tiny balcony beyond, a bright quarter moon stabs at the darkness, upstaged by the streetlamps below. Out front sits the van, the sight of which jogs my sleeping memory. Spike has come back in from the gig. Did he commit the crime of waking me? A cough emits as if on cue from the next room to signal the roadie's guilt.

My stomach growls. When did I last eat? A shared chicken wrap with Caleb in early afternoon; was that it? I open Spike's refrigerator and peer in on rows of beer cans and an array of takeout leftovers.

An irrational urgency, amplified by the dark silence of the room, tells me I must go out and get something to put my hunger to bed. I have no key, but this inconvenience fails to dull my impulse. I slide my laptop under the sofa-bed, then, making sure I have my wallet with me, I head out, leaving the front door unlocked. I doubt that Spike would notice anything missing after a break-in.

I march in the direction from which we arrived this afternoon, remembering a large gas station nearby where I might find a sandwich. A crumpled plastic package is all that remains of my purchase by the time I arrive back at Spike's building. I am cutting across the front lawn when something raises my eyebrow: upright on the sidewalk, just behind the rear door of the Flak Jackets' van, stands an empty beer bottle. I turn toward the van, and with the trepidation of one who feels himself a snoop, I strain to see past the street light reflected in the window.

A dark mass in the rough shape of a human body lies curled in the rear bench seat. Frequent jerking adjustments of the figure's limbs tell me that it is still getting settled, but the head never lifts and the eyes never look toward me. I enjoy playing with the idea that a vagrant has chosen the band's wheels as a flophouse, but the truth is obvious: one of the boys and his hostess have parted company early.

⌘

March 24, 2003

Over a table at a Denny's restaurant the tales of conquest fly. Caleb gets his arms into describing the time he spent with his girl, she of the glorious legs. The story calls to Spike's mind a dozen yarns of enterprising nymphets who have seen him as a rung on the ladder to one star or another on the various tours he's roadied. Tim has little to say regarding his tryst, except to call last night "one for the ages," and to thank Spike at every opportunity for setting them all up. He and Joe, who divulges nothing, sport matching green beaded bracelets, presumably mementoes of a night well spent.

Jack keeps cocking his head as though trying to unkink his neck. Halfway through his coffee, Caleb asks him, "She work you hard, man?"

The kid rubs his neck and mumbles, "Somethin' like that." Caleb cajoles him some, but the kid refuses to elaborate.

In the parking lot outside, squinting in the morning sunlight, we say our goodbyes to Spike. "Remember me, boys," the roadie says. "Think of your stay here as a free trial." He frees his sunglasses from the neck of his black muscle shirt. "You make enough dough to cover my meager unselfish salary..." he flips the shades on, "you'll get the royal treatment." With that, he saunters off down the sidewalk.

"What a character," says Tim as he watches the roadie's diminishing figure.

"Yeah," agrees Caleb. "They should put him in the rock museum in Cleveland. 'Roadie, Seventies to Nineties'."

We make for our cars. Without a word from anyone, Joe appears at my passenger door. I extend the keys to him over the roof of the car. "You drive?"

"Yeah." He fidgets, doesn't take the keys. "But my license expired." So much for that idea.

And so now here is Joe, from Tokyo. Let's examine him in his unnatural, naked state, without a guitar attached to his torso. Look at that abdomen, covered only by a dirty white T-shirt and an open denim jacket. His midsection looks concave, as though awaiting an instrument to slot into it and make it whole. As I steer toward the freeway, his left hand rests, palm up, on his thigh. At a stoplight I glance down, and see a hint of twitchy clutching motion in his bony fingers. I read a beat in the miniscule nods of his black-mopped head.

I tap the stereo. "You can put in a CD if you'd like."

"Oh. Thank you." After a quick rummage in his backpack, his hand emerges with a record. In a few seconds a jagged guitar rhythm conjures an image of calloused black fingers on steel strings, and an aged croak chimes in within a few bars to tell their story. "Lightning Hopkins," says Joe in his careful English.

For some time only the mumble and moan of Mister Hopkins drowns the hum of the freeway. I'm reluctant to press Joe with questions; each answer he gives is a complex contraption of English enunciation and syntax, which he must construct using mismatched Japanese tools. But as we zoom up the flat desert freeway, I do manage over the next hour to put together a backstory from his murmurs.

Joe the Guitar Player, from Tokyo, is actually Jiro, the son of a Japanese-American father and a native Japanese mother. His father's origins in San Francisco explain his ability to live Stateside (he apparently has a U.S. passport), but they beg the question: why is his English so poor? "We spoke Japanese at home," is his only answer. He can communicate the love he feels for American music, though. His parents reared him on Elvis, and his older brother brought blues to their home, bequeathing to young Jiro a sizeable collection of records ("lots records — lots of records"), upon leaving home.

Joe left school early. In his life he has worked only menial jobs, and it would appear the yen and dollars they brought him have gone to only three things: a one-way ticket from Tokyo to L.A. (a move which, if I'm understanding him, cost him his Japanese citizenship), a hovel to sleep in somewhere in the Valley, and the yellow and black guitar ("a Silvertone—Harmony—very special") that he so sorely misses right now. Certainly none of his money has gone toward food.

Lightnin' gives way to Jimmy Reed. I gather more facts. Jack met Joe at the gig of a mutual friend, a show at which Joe played a guest spot. "Jack liked my guitar." They are quite close as bandmates, but Joe knows little about his bandleader. "He sings good," is the only definitive statement he can make.

I open my window an inch. Over the hissing air, I hear only Mister Reed's loudest wails. It occurs to me to ask what a Southern Negro from forty-plus years ago has to offer a kid from across the Pacific.

"I get the words," he replies. "And when he's...not make sense...you...

know." In mild frustration he wiggles his fingers in front of his mouth. "The *way* he..." An instrumental break saves him. "And the guitar."

"Do a lot of Japanese get the blues?"

"You mean music? Or feel bad?"

"Either, I suppose."

After a moment of thought, he answers, "Yeah, we feel bad. Sometimes a girl...or you got little money...." After some fumbling, he sums it up: "We show it different there. But we feel same things." I glance over; he's staring at his knees. "I like the way they show." A hint of pink colors his chickpea cheek.

⌘

March 25, 2003

"Gee." Tim hefts the first of his drums off the stage, fifteen minutes after his last cymbal crash of the evening. "Was it just me, or were those the same people who saw us in Joshua Tree?"

"Ha!" Caleb hops down beside him, bass case in hand. "Yeah, twelve people drove all the way up to Salt Lake City to sleep through our set again."

Tim nods at Joe, scooting past us, cradling his amplifier. "And wasn't Joe on fire? He deserved more than just those few claps."

"You know it. What do *you* think, Mister Uncle H?" He continues before I can agree. "I gotta say, I wouldn'ta minded seeing another doofus call out for 'Wild Horses'. Give Jack some bait."

Tim squints at the horizon under the lights of the parking lot as we pass through the open back door. "Hah. I was expecting to see that field of Joshua trees in the distance."

"Shit." Caleb's shakes his head. "I didn't know the days would start running into each other so soon."

⌘

March 26, 2003

The kid is stoically brave when his number finally comes up. Faced with a slog to Reno, he gives a smirking nod at me as he breaks from the band around the van and approaches my Sephia. "I can drive," he offers when I open the driver door. I hand him the key with relief.

Gripping the wheel with both hands, he scans with faithful eye from side mirror, straight ahead, to rear-view, to passenger mirror. At every stop sign from the hotel parking lot to the Interstate, he comes to a complete stop.

I start to ask: "What did you think of the club last—"

"How far on this street?"

"Just a few hundred yards," I remind him. The freeway overpass looms large across our path up ahead.

"Got it." His eye tracks back through its points. With pedantic motion, as though I'm his driving instructor, he prepares to turn onto the ramp: mirror, blind spot, signal, mirror, blind spot. As he accelerates evenly up the ramp, I ask, "Where are you from?"

"Hold it." He's checking his side mirror. "Gotta merge." He slides into the empty lane. Two silent minutes ensue while he scans the light traffic. Finally he answers, "Back East."

"Oh, well, I'm from Connecticut," I offer.

"Really. Which town?"

"Winsted."

"Winsted." He leans back into his seat. "Near Hartford?"

"It's not far. Closer to Waterbury. You know Hartford?"

"Capital, right?" He smirks. "'S what they told us in school."

"Where did you go to school?"

"Oh, they'll tell you that anywhere." The smirk grows more crooked. "Anywhere in the U.S.A. Take a seat in Geography class, raise your hand, 'What's the capital of Connecticut?' No matter where you are, 'Hartford.' Doesn't change."

"Have you ever been to New York?"

"Yeah, I been."

"I lived there for ten years."

"Oh. Is that where you had your son?"

"Yes. We lived on the Upper East Side."

"Near Central Park?"

"Just a few blocks. Do you like New York?"

He shrugs. "Yeah, it's all good. Big City, all that."

"Different from where you grew up?"

"Hold it. Gotta change lanes." Mirror, blind spot, signal, mirror, blind spot. The lane we leave is empty, a mile ahead and behind. "So, your son."

"My son?" He nods. "Patrick."

"Patrick. He's got, uh..."

"Down Syndrome," I finish, shifting in my seat.

"Down Syndrome." Side mirror. Straight ahead. Rear-view. "Genetic?"

"No. Pure luck."

"So he's mentally, uh, you know..."

"Retarded. I know."

"Retarded." He keeps his eyes straight ahead for an extended moment. "Huh." The rush of the tires on the asphalt rises in my ears. A brief flicker of light, the reflection of the desert sun off a highway sign, splashes across the kid's face. He flinches and, like an idle machine switched on again, resumes his even scan.

Again his nervous eye catches mine. He shifts in his seat. "CD player's working, right?" Already his finger is gliding over the stereo buttons like he's reading Braille.

"Oh, yes."

"Tell you what," he says. "Grab my bag behind you?" In a Houdini-esque feat of contortion, I reach into the backseat and manage to grab the kid's knapsack. "Front pouch there," he says. As I unzip the pocket, he shoots his right hand into it, pulls out a disc and tosses it into my lap. "What'd I get?" he asks, returning his hand to the steering wheel.

I look at the disc. "Rolling Stones. *Sticky Fingers*."

"That'll do."

And so I watch the Utah desolation give way to Nevada desolation at sixty-four miles an hour with Mick Jagger bawling in my ear. A self-imposed etiquette prevents me from turning the volume down. Besides, the way the kid pounds the wheel gives me the first open window into his mind.

The kid's lips move subtly with the words. He puts his head back against the headrest. His grip on the wheel loosens; he even leans an elbow against his window. The second song is a sloppy largo, and by the third track, a ballad, I, too, start to relax.

"I know this one," I venture at the chorus. "Early seventies, right?" In my mind, the song is the red-orange motif of our East-Sixties apartment, the taste of brandy Alexanders in my mouth and the faint smell of feces ever-present on our fingertips. I can see it coming out of our woodgrain-framed radio in the living room on Cherie's day off.

"Seventy-one, it came out. They recorded it in sixty-nine." Jack bangs the wheel with a tom-tom roll. "Right when they hit their stride." He's talking at the windshield, but his voice projects like he's addressing a class. "This is what that old hippie called out for in Joshua Tree."

"'Wild Horses'."

"They wrote this for Gram. Parsons. You know, the guy who died out there. Or they gave it to him, anyway. Some people say his version's better—Tim, even."

"What do you think?"

"Can't come close to the Stones. Mick's a little, you know." He raises a hand from the wheel, and lets it fall limp at the wrist. "But who cares? He *feels* it. You hear this, it brings you somewhere. When I've been down, it's taken me to a better place."

"And what might bring someone like you down?"

"Hold it." I sit in chastened silence as (mirror, blind spot, signal, etc.) he edges from one empty lane to another. "Works when you're up, too." He taps the wheel at the start of a bar. "When you're on a high, you might forget to *feel*, you know?" He points to the player. "This'll give you depth."

"And what gives you a high?"

Halfway through the sentence, he's talking over it. "You dug the Stones? Like, when they were new?"

"I appreciated them."

"Were you Beatles or Stones?"

"I was twenty-four."

He looks sidelong at me. "What's that mean?"

"Well, *you're* over twenty, correct?"

"Yeah."

"What's *your* favorite record in the Top Ten these days?"

He scoffs. "That's different. You had stuff worth listening to." And he repeats, "So, Beatles or Stones?"

I sigh. "I suppose I was Stones. I liked 'Satisfaction'."

"Right, and 'Get Off My Cloud', and all that?"

"Yes," I allow. "But I'd moved on from seeking new music." I point to the player. "Your parents, did they expose you to this music?"

As before, two words reach his ears before he starts talking over me. "Your kid, he likes music?"

"He loves music."

"They tend to, right?"

"People without Down Syndrome tend to as well."

"Right." He looks away, and starts to scan anew.

Jagger wails on. I catch fewer and fewer words, but still I listen. In silence we absorb a long instrumental passage, followed by a rustic blues. The sun reaches its zenith, pouring light past sparse white clouds, and I begin to drift off. My vision alternates between the blue sky, the brown landscape of passing Nevada, and the black that glows red inside my eyelids. At one point a green Dodge passes us, and the sight of the driver hits my pupils as my eyes are closing. She has a delicate profile, a slender nose, and dark hair that flows in auburn waves from her head.

The SUV has moved past when my eyes snap back open. The image I caught rests in my mind, and I find words leaving my lips. "That was a pretty young lady who came to see you at the Mint show."

The car swerves abruptly into the right lane. The kid brakes hard and slaps on his turn signal. We careen onto an off-ramp and in seconds come to a stomach-turning halt beside a vacant pump at the roadside gas station I had not known was coming up. "Gotta fill up," the kid says, snatching the keys from the ignition and opening the door. At my frankly shaken stare he explains, "Third of a tank," and when my eyebrows rise in surprise he adds, "Desert, right? Never know when we'll get another chance."

⌘

"Jack Hackett, what's your all-time favorite record?"

This opener is Take Four of the band's 'radio' interview. Tim has given me a run-down of what we are doing: "It's an *online* radio show. We record it here, and then people can listen to it later, on a website. That and your blog, it's the wave of the future!"

It's a good thing this isn't live. Three times our jockey has tried to open with innocent questions about the kid's background. Only now, after being beaten back with acid-tongued one-liners, has he gained the insight to hand the kid his list of questions with a red pen.

The few items that escape the bold red stroke are adolescent questions, which the kid swats down with one-word answers. Favorite record? The one he and I enjoyed on the way here: the Rolling Stones' *Sticky Fingers*. The first rock record he ever got? *Born in the U.S.A.* Most overrated band ever? The Doors. That's it; no explanations, no qualifications.

It therefore comes as a huge relief for our hapless host to open the floor to the rest of the band and watch Caleb in particular fill the void to capacity with his complicated set of opinions and anecdotes. Tim compliments these with attempts at wit. Joe, like Jack, speaks only when spoken to, but even he is more generous with his tongue, describing the Japanese music scene and comparing aspects of American life to his home country.

In terms of insight, of course, the discussion is painfully inadequate. Listen more closely, though. Hear our host's halting speech when he ventures a thought, in language as sloppy as the room we occupy. Keep your ears open for the sucking sound his breathing makes, at a volume equal to his speaking voice, during the awkward pauses. And if that doesn't tell you anything, consider our surroundings.

We are 'broadcasting' from the basement of a cookie-cutter house, in a residential neighborhood. Our host wears a baggy T-shirt and khaki shorts; his thinning hair is pulled back in a ponytail with a rubber band. The Flak Jackets huddle around his microphone, seated variously in office chairs, on a coffee table, and on an ottoman. Upstairs in the kitchen sits the man's mother, middle-aged, middle-weight, middle-American, who greeted us at the door and led our party down here to "Richie's room." I wondered, as

I settled into the overstuffed couch near Richie's open bedroom door, if Mom had glanced in there and seen, as I had, her son's bed so spectacularly unmade. And I still wonder what she thinks of the fellow, her age at least, who has tagged along with her boy's little friends.

In the half hour of small talk that follows the recording, Richie points to the notebook that rests closed on my lap. "You writing about this?"

A grunt of amusement emits from Caleb. "I ain't seen him crack that thing open since we started!"

Caleb's observation underscores a tiny nagging in the back of my mind, an unquiet half-thought that has kept me from taking notes. I half thought it last night as I watched the boys put up posters in an exercise in futility, and as I watched the last two shows from a near-empty club floor. It tugs at me when Richie's Mom waves goodbye at us over her cup of coffee upon our exit.

Only as I get behind the wheel, and Caleb revs up his mouth for the stretch of road ahead, can I sweep it to the edge of conscious thought. I am glad, though, that it lingers there at least, so that when I do sit down and record the day's adventures, I can call on it, and put it down. And I can rest assured that in this way, before he surgically removes all evidence of it from this text, Marty will see it, and know that it is there.

⌘

Wheels turn. Highway signs count down the miles. We pull into motel parking lots adorned with the same neon enticements: cable, A/C, vacancy. We make small talk with reception at check-in, drop our bags just inside our doors, flop down on beds, flip on TVs to check in on Baghdad, stand back up far too soon, reconvene, make more small talk at reception while getting directions. The boys hop in the van.

Too often, a queer sense of duty impels me to endure the tedium of sound check. Bass drum? Thump, thump, thump. Snare? Bap, bap, bap. And so on, with floor tom, hi-hat, full kit, followed by bass, dum-dum-dum, guitar, ba-na-na, vocal, la-la-la. Okay, done, three hours to showtime.

Dinner, too much salt. Wander back to the venue, watch one or two other groups play to the half-full room. Watch the place empty out when the band before us winds up. Left with only a dozen bodies by the time the first chord is strummed. "Always twelve, ever notice that?" asks Caleb one dinnertime.

Tim drops his fork onto his plate. "I know! It's like some mathematical formula! Like, act from out of town, plus x open-minded locals, plus y lazy drunks..."

"Plus or minus one or two from weather," the bass player adds, "minus a couple if they promise any WMDs on the eleven o'clock news..."

The drummer snorts, "...equals, yep, twelve."

So, for the twelve: thump, bap, ba-da-da, dum-dum-dum, verse, chorus, verse, chorus. Repeat for forty minutes. And then pack up, head back to the motel. Sleep awaits those of us who are able, and after breakfast the wheels turn once more.

⌘

April 5, 2003

"To-*ga*! To-*ga*! To-*ga*!" The club tonight is flooded with flowing white. A nearby frat house has burst its banks, and the room is packed with enough bedsheet-clad followers of an asinine tradition to shake to its very foundation my belief in the value of higher education. The smacking sounds of flip-flops against bare heels fill the spaces between songs on the PA and chants from these galoots.

"To-*ga*! To-*ga*!" Flip, flop, flip, flop.

Eight of them sit at a row of tables pressed together against the stage. Every couple of minutes one of them calls something out. The remaining seven stamp their feet and chant something unintelligible that ends in "Hey!" Then it's bottoms up, and high fives all around. Empty beer mugs and shot glasses line their long trough like a row of trophies. When a barmaid tries to clear these, the frat boys shoo her away.

Some good-natured hoots from the crowd greet the Flak Jackets as they bound onto the stage. But Joe's opening riff is barely off of his fingertips before the mass exodus starts. A line of Caesars forms at the door to the terrace outside; by the time Jack comes on, the room is half empty. And though the band is a finely-tuned locomotive, by the end of the first song their audience numbers fewer than twenty. The eight contestants at Jack's feet, bloated and stagnant as their game takes its toll, lean back in their chairs and fold their arms against their chests. Two or three clap, two or three claps each.

Jack shuts them out. The band is tight and makes a hearty noise, and within their cocoon the kid can do what he wants. But after two more rockers, a flip-flop flutters into the air, landing by the drum riser. At the right end of the table, staring at the ceiling, the imp responsible wears his guilt in a self-satisfied smirk. Jack bites his lip, but ignores both the flip-flop and the culprit. Joe counts in a blues.

Harder to ignore is the volley of six more strips of fluorescent foam that fly onto the stage over the next minute. Jack flinches as one whizzes past his ear. He blinks, sets his sights on the far wall, and starts singing.

"Baby don't make me holler,
Baby don't make me moan."

A yellow one tumbles through the air and bounces off the base of Joe's guitar. A titter goes up among the frat boys. Caleb shakes his head and mouths the word 'assholes' at them. Jack ignores it. The more timid of the group lob their footwear at the very lip of the stage, where the things land like dead flies at the band's feet. These boys get pats on the back for their gumption.

The song swells to a final chorus. Caleb moves to the fore, wielding his bass like a machine gun, his lip curled into a snarl. Jack shuts his eyes, and so does not see the broad-shouldered Nero to the middle-left of the row. I first spy the brute as his head emerges from ducking under the table. He looks right, then left, flashes his teeth, and holds his own footwear, a pair of cork sandals, over his head.

Caleb sees what's coming. He stops playing and springs toward the frat boy, but is forced to duck as the two sandals rocket at the top of his head. The head of his bass pitches forward and hits the ground. Joining the resulting cough from the bass amp is the crash of the sandals, one following a split-second after the other, into Tim's cymbals. The song disintegrates. Tim rises from his seat, eyes wide and darting. Caleb takes another stride toward his attacker, but stops short when the kid's hand touches his shoulder.

The kid faces his opponents, his eyes narrow. He holds Caleb in place for a moment, then claps him on the back. He breaks into a smile, but his eyes keep their steely gleam. "It's all good," he says into the microphone.

Caleb retreats, and starts kicking the flip-flops scattered around his feet. They flutter from the stage, disappearing into the darkness of the club floor. With a crazed grin he mouths Jack's words, "It's all good!"

Joe starts hacking at his strings in a bluesy shuffle. Caleb follows suit. The frat boys all look to their burly friend, the one who hurled the sandals. Jack's gaze gravitates to this fellow as well. The kid's smile is winning. "Hail!" he barks.

Nero folds his arms against his chest again and pushes his chair back from his table. With a cocky eye on Jack he kicks his legs in the air and plants his heels on the tabletop. He holds Jack's stare while he wiggles his bare toes at the kid. One by one, the brothers copy the oaf's example, until eighty toes bask in the light that spills from the stage.

Eyes ever narrow, Jack surveys the stubby army before him. He ignores his cue for the verse; Joe throws out off-the-cuff guitar licks to fill the gaps his leader leaves. When the verse cycle concludes, the kid moves in to the mic stand. Slowly he picks up the stand while he sings, and sidesteps his way to the end of the row. There he stops, eyes once again on the hefty instigator. And, as the band changes keys with a cymbal crash, he unleashes his fury in a quick burst.

With a whoop he pivots to face center stage. The base of the mic stand sweeps out over the table and brushes against an empty glass. The glass teeters, tips, then drops brim-first to the floor.

The eight exchange glances before agreeing on a sneer to pour out at Jack. A few roll their eyes and shake their heads, perhaps thinking the kid is just clumsy. The stocky lady tending bar seems to suspect an accident as well; she signals to the waitress and gestures with a flippant wave at the table. Jack maintains a scowl of concentration.

"The devil's come to call,
If she stands me up I'll fall."

He strolls to the right and pivots again. Though a floor-to-ceiling pillar shields the end of the table from my view, the uniform straightening of the frat boys in their seats suggests that the kid hit his mark a second time.

Though the shattering of glass has visibly rattled the frat boys, their heels remain planted on the tabletops. The guy nearest to Jack uncrosses his arms to free his middle finger. Another plants the back of his hand against his forehead, with his thumb and forefinger extended in an *L*.

Caleb purses his lips and steps back to the very side of the stage. Tim, chained to his drum kit, cranes his neck over his crash cymbal to keep his eye on the kid. Joe never looks up, but glides with a stray guitar lick deeper into his corner. Jack shifts gears, singing softly, *"Do you know what's coming?"* Not one of the inebriated fools grasps the threat.

Jack's last line hangs in the air. The guitar swells, the bass throbs. The kid upends his mic stand, swinging the mic down in front of Nero's chin, like he's offering a carrot to a grizzly bear. His maniacally friendly grin seems to urge the jackass to sing along. The brute opens his mouth. The word "Fuck" takes up the end of a bar, but drops in volume as the kid swings the mic down and away from the brute's grabbing paws.

The frat boy's half-full beer glass shatters right on the first beat of the chorus. A deafening squeal of feedback follows. Beer drips from the table's edge and from the side of the frat boy's bed sheet.

The bartender's gruff bellow clears even the booming of the chorus. She leaps through the gap in the bar and charges rhino-like at the stage. The group of eight are slower on the uptake. That is their undoing, for the kid's trap is just about set. He looks his opponent in the eye, steals a glance at the approaching bartender, and with a quick tug reels the mic stand in. His staccato cry of "Hail!" quells the feedback before he sets the spring.

The frat boys take their feet off the tables and venture to stand. At that instant, Jack plays his glissando grace note. The butt of the mic stand sweeps back into view. One by one the glasses glint in the footlights as the metal disc touches them. Then they disappear into the gaps, between the frat boys, between the tables and the lip of the stage. The bombast of the song's finale drowns out the clatter of more shattering glass.

The frat boys stare for a few beats, in as much shock as the alcohol will allow—all but their leader. Glaring, Nero lets his feet drop and leans forward to spring from his chair. Alas, if drink does not slow a man down, it can still trip him up. A sober man, even in a fit of rage, would piece together two convergent circumstances: that he is barefoot and that the floor is covered now with broken glass. His howl adds a sweet dissonance to the song's closing chord.

Jack stands for a second to view the wreckage. The barmaid, momentarily stunned, resumes her charge with a roar. The frat boys blink together and gaze at the floor like squirrels caught in a cage. Together they turn inward to take in their leader's writhing agony. And as one they break from their trance and stagger to stand in their chairs when the one direction out of their trap becomes apparent.

"Hail!" calls the kid once more, and before the reverb has died from his microphone, he is airborne between the side of the stage and the backstage doorway. The barmaid's cry of "Come back here!" is a bugle blare to the frat boys. In company they lunge forward, stumbling over their tables, past the monitors and onto the stage. In their practiced way, though, Joe and Caleb have closed ranks.

Somehow the two bandmates avoid coming to blows with any of the furious seven. Caleb crosses his arms and looks each would-be assailant straight on with a fatalistic smirk. Joe can only do what he always does: he spreads his hands, palms up, in front of him. He speaks, no doubt in his cautious, clumsy English, of having nothing to do with this.

Tim, meanwhile, has leaped from his drum stool and skirted the onstage hoopla. We meet with a crunch of broken glass beneath our shoes and turn together to face the charging barmaid.

"Evening," I say to her.

"Who the hell are you?" Her nostrils flare as she speaks. Her head comes up to my shoulders, and I find my abdomen tensing as she stands before me.

"This is Henry Barclay." Tim waits an excruciating second before adding, "The writer."

"What the fuck does that do for me?" she barks. My abdomen tenses further.

"I'm in charge of this group," I say through a smile. "Call me Jack's babysitter."

"You oughta have a bullwhip if you're babysitting that fucker!" Her bark is still fierce, but she leans just a little bit back, and a ghost of a smile floats past her mouth. "Look at the damage here!" She crushes a shard of glass under her toe.

Tim looks over the wench's shoulder, then flashes a broad smile at her. "Tell you what! We'll clean it up!" The waitress is approaching with a broom, a dustpan and a garbage pail. Tim throws a look of excited benevolence at her and yanks her implements from her. Startled but amused, the waitress whirls around to look at the barmaid. She turns and dashes off when her superior gives her a weary nod.

The barmaid turns back on me with renewed menace. "Now what about the stuff you broke? You're talking seventy, eighty bucks right there!"

"You can deduct the damage from the band's pay."

"Now what the fuck makes you think you're getting paid? We book a band, they gotta draw! We have a twenty person minimum!"

"But there were forty people here!" I say.

"Hah!" She just about pops in exclamation. "See those togas? That's Delta Chi Epsilon, not your fuckin' Jack's Hackers!" She shakes her little head. "And they're all out on my terrace! Twelve people watchin' this show, they play five songs, break my shit, you're expecting *I* pay *you*?"

Tim is already emptying the first panful of glass into the pail.

"You owe me! You got that?" She leans toward me, bringing a strange musk to my nostrils. My abdomen crunches up so that I emit a small groan.

Sixty dollars in twenties cling to my thigh at this very moment. I can feel their grip slipping. In desperation I pull one of the bills from my pocket in a pre-emptive gambit to save the other two. "Here's twenty dollars! Can we call it even?"

Her very scowl is an act of violence. My body braces for an assault from beyond the hand that holds out the twenty, until Tim pulls himself up by his broom and sidles up to break the stalemate.

"Here, ma'am," he says, holding out his hand alongside mine. "I feel just sick about this, too." I glance at the bill in his hand—a five. "Will you take that, too, and call it even? I know it's not much, but...."

With one sweeping motion she relieves us of our money. "Just get that mess cleaned up and get out!" She charges off, turning the bills over in front of her face. Tim wipes his hand dramatically across his brow.

Onstage, Caleb and Joe gather their equipment while fielding over their shoulders the diminishing abuse from a few remaining frat boys. One of the Epsilons has found his flip-flops, and has retrieved the remaining ones for his cohorts. Two of the remaining three louts give up their haranguing, flip the bird at our boys, and storm off. At a booth in the stage-right corner, the great Nero holds a wad of napkins to his right foot. His expression is pitiable.

Tim shrugs at me and hunkers back down to work. I pull the row of chairs and tables out around the patch of glass. The PA music cranks a notch louder. In twos and threes, members of the patio crowd filter back in. Each group takes a minute to figure out what they missed, gawking at this crime scene over the police line I have fashioned out of the furniture. Tim rises to my ear and cocks his head at the onlookers. "*Now* they show up," he murmurs. "Next time, though," he adds, "they'll want to stick around for Jack."

Tim is shoveling more shards into the pail as the last remaining frat boy hops down from stage right, holding his bedsheet above his kneecaps to keep from tripping over it. The fellow lands just beyond my barrier. Tim looks up. Their eyes meet. I see the word 'Sorry!' within Tim's winning smile. The frat boy's face darkens; Tim takes the hint and turns back to his work.

The frat boy stares at Tim's back. I start moving toward them when I see the little Caesar gathering phlegm in his open mouth. Sadly, I am too far away to stop the assault. A second later, Tim is putting his hand to a slimy wet patch on the back of his hair, and the frat boy is scurrying to the corner booth to laugh with his leader. Tim brings his soiled hand to his face to inspect it. It trembles before him. He rubs his eyes with his clean hand. The glasses I project onto him are left askew. "What did he...?" He looks with glassy eyes over to the crew in the corner booth, then back at his shaking hand.

I reach for a cocktail napkin at a nearby table. "Here." I pass it to him, wondering whether it will go to his hair or to his eyes.

Tim starts dabbing at the back of his scalp. "What a jerk!" he whines. "I didn't do...." He crumples up the napkin, and his eyes well up some more.

But a moment later, through his near-tears he suddenly bursts out in a defiant, triumphant laugh. "Boy," he declares, "Jack sure got 'em good tonight!"

⌘

April 10, 2003

Marty's call wakes me. "Change in plans," he says as a greeting. "Before the hotel this afternoon, you go to SFO. Airport." He gives me a flight number. "I just reeled in a big fish," he says. "So you're getting a couple of new staff. The boys'll thank me. *Jack*'ll thank me."

And so after a truncated run, I hook up with the boys for a hurried breakfast and tell them the news. Their delight is matched by their intrigue.

"It's Spike," says Caleb, gnawing at a rock-hard roll.

"Yeah, but who else?" Tim wonders.

A chunk of the roll breaks loose. Caleb takes a full minute to chew on it. When he speaks again, he still battles with it in his mouth. "Maybe one of Spike's girls is coming to do laundry."

The road from San Jose to San Francisco Airport is straight and wide, but nonetheless we crawl there in traffic that moves like snails over honey. Arriving late, we are perplexed to learn that the flight is from Los Angeles and not Las Vegas. Maybe we aren't in fact going to find the roadie here. On we go to baggage claim 3 to answer this riddle.

The baggage claim area is sparsely populated, its conveyer littered with a few small suitcases. A few passengers are making their way past the belt, carrying only briefcases. "Over here, motherfuckers!" Spike stands at the end of the conveyer, clad in ripped jeans and a muscle shirt, a suitcase at his side.

Caleb jogs over and gives him a soul shake. "I knew it! But who came with you?"

The roadie looks wryly at Jack approaching him. "Heh heh." He motions at the carousel. "That's who we're here for. *I* came from Vegas. I been here an hour and a half. Come on!" And picking up his suitcase, he points to the opposite entrance.

She's just come out when we approach. She wears a plain white blouse and a flowing, ivy-colored summer skirt. Her hair, tied up to fall in waves and curls from a fount at the top of her head, has tugged out of its tie just a little. It lists at an angle, and stray strands poke out. She looks around with a nervous face. I feel my feet tangle on seeing her, feel a startling swoon, and I must stop in my tracks to keep from tripping.

Tim is the first to find words. "Holy cow!" His exclamation draws her eye, which falls immediately on Jack. I hurry to catch up with the band.

The kid's face is slack, his mouth open. Only his bulging eyes betray any emotion. Gradually his lips turn up into a smile. She takes a hesitant step toward him. "Hi," he says with a timid step of his own.

They stop a foot apart from each other. She looks up into his eyes as she adjusts the strap of the jute carry-on bag over her shoulder. They hold this position. Jack's chest rises and falls. He speaks softly. "I didn't know."

"Your manager—Marty? He offered for me to come. Are you...?"

His smile redoubles. "Oh, no, I'm glad you...." He looks at his bandmates and the roadie crowding around him. He glances at me. Hesitantly, he reaches for her hand, takes it with his fingertips, holds it with both his hands. After another glance around he moves in again. His lips tap her cheek, and he pulls away, grinning awkwardly. "You brought a suitcase?" he asks.

She nods. "Marty said I could ride along for the rest of the tour." A pause. "Is that all right?"

Here he doesn't hesitate. "That's wonderful!" His eyes dart at me, at his friends, as his cheeks go red.

He leads her to the carousel; we follow. Spike nudges past me. "How nice," he grunts under his breath. "How wholesome." His tooth-baring grin straddles sweetness and disgust.

⌘

Once we've checked into our hotel, it's down a steep grade to Fisherman's Wharf, where we exceed our per diem on a celebratory meal. "Some celebration," mumbles Caleb to Joe as we wait for a table. "I mean, Jack's happy, and we got a roadie now, but the gigs sure as hell didn't bring that on." With only a genial shrug from Joe, he directs his venting at me. "Marty just managed to con another old rich dude."

Happily, though, Spike's colorful barking, a mammoth plate of fish and chips, and a couple of tall drinks lighten Caleb's mood. By dessert he's matching the roadie wisecrack for wisecrack, laughing through teeth mortared with tiramisu.

"I quit my job to come here," the girl says with an air of astonishment at herself. "My parents think I'm crazy."

Spike speaks over a cup of black coffee. "Don't worry, Princess. Jack here'll put ya to work."

"I'm gonna whip this operation into shape," the roadie declares, balling his napkin in his fist while we wait for the check. "With you guys doin' everything yourselves, driving, carrying shit, you wipe yourselves out before you hit the stage. And over time, you just perform worse and worse. I know you ain't got an itinerary worth shit." He shoots a glance at Caleb. "But with me doing the heavy lifting, you guys can focus on puttin' on a good show—and that'll get the best outta this opportunity." Caleb gives a heartened nod.

"As for you..." The roadie levels his gaze on Jack, who sits with his chair angled at Wendy's place. "You got it made now. You got a babysitter," he pats his chest, then holds out a hand to the girl, "and guaranteed action every night. You won't have to scour every town for pussy like these poor fucks." Jack squirms in his seat. Wendy looks down at her plate. "So all that sweat you save, you use it well, my friend. And be glad you've got it." The kid just nods. He looks relieved to see our waitress arrive with the check.

⌘

April 11, 2003

Before departing for Sacramento in the morning, we take a detour and climb the steep sidewalks to the top of Lombard Street. As we near the summit, I catch sight of the multicolored flowerbeds that make the winding block so famous. An image from my memory, a line of station wagons and Volkswagen Beetles, superimposes itself over the current scene, a winding wall of SUVs snaking down the twisting red-brick path. The two images mash together, making such a clutter on my senses that I must look away. But this view, the beds of flowers, the line of cars, the hillside that tumbles toward San Francisco Bay, we have come here precisely for all of these things.

At the mouth of the river of cars we stand in wait. The Flak Jackets shuffle in place, looking around at the surrounding buildings and down at the bay, which glows green under a blue sky flocked with cumulus clouds.

"You guys lucked out today," says Spike. "Shit weather's the norm here."

"I can't see that we're all that lucky unless this photographer chick shows up soon," answers Caleb. He pulls back his jean-jacket cuff to check his watch.

Wendy stands outside of the band's circle, staring somewhere between the kid's ragged black canvas sneakers and her own black sandals. When she turns to look out at the bay, the kid breaks from the huddle. He slides his toes toward her and waits. The girl spins around. Their eyes meet, and Jack brings his body in line with his foot, six inches away from her. They peer into each other's faces, until as one their eyes fall, and each stares for a time at the other's shoes.

"We could be doing something else," grumbles Caleb. "I mean, come on, *this* band? In front of *flowers*? And Ford Explorers? We're not gonna use these pictures."

"You never know," counters Tim. "One of these could end up as the album cover."

"A tourist photo from San Francisco for a live album recorded in L.A.?" He sneers. "And that's if this chick even shows up."

Wendy murmurs something to the kid, motioning at the view down the hill. Both gaze down the sloping rows of rooftops. Jack's hand emerges from his blue-jeans pocket. It hovers by his hip. His eye jumps back and forth from the cityscape below to his girl, who stands with hands clasped, not catching his gaze.

Caleb scans the faces of pedestrians milling up and down the street. "Lotta Asians."

The kid takes a long look at Wendy's profile and bites his lip. His hand flies out and comes to rest with his palm against the small of her back, above where her flower-patterned, peach blouse tucks into her flowing green skirt. The girl's gaze falls for a second, but she makes no other motion, and soon both are back to watching the city street flow below them.

"There," says Caleb. "Halfway down. Right side." He points. "Asian chick. Alone. Blue polo shirt, with a camera."

The figure down the hill waves her camera at us as she leans into the slope and jogs up the final fifty yards. "Whew!" she says once in earshot. "My boss left me alone behind the counter. I had to wait for a replacement." She wipes imaginary sweat from her brow. "So, I was thinking, we could shoot you near the top there, with the flowers right behind you, or just looking out down the hill."

The photographer trudges up the stone steps ahead of us. A few steps up she wheels around and calls back, "Come on, up we go. I'm on my lunch break."

At the top the boys gather and assume poses of feigned indifference. I stand back between Spike and Wendy at the side of the sidewalk. The roadie stands with his arms crossed, wearing a face that wouldn't look out of place in front of the camera. The girl looks on with an absent smile, her hands clasped behind her back. Pedestrians pass in front of us, giving the Flak Jackets and their photographer wide berth.

The boys stand looking downhill. They face the cars that wait their turn to crawl down the flower-lined block. Tim and Joe squat down between Jack and Caleb. They turn their heads in various directions, rarely facing the camera, never making eye contact with each other.

Throughout this ritual the photographer jumps around them, holding her camera to her eye, letting it drop to give the band stage directions, bringing it back up for a few more shots. After a few repetitions she looks at her watch. "Gettin' late," she says. I check my own watch. She has been with us for fifteen minutes. "Hmm. How about a change, you know, to shake things up?"

Caleb frowns. "Like what?"

The photographer just shrugs. Caleb shakes his head.

"Wait a sec!" Tim jumps up from his squatting position. "Ever seen any old sixties photos where the band poses with a model? Or remember the *Gilded Palace of Sin* album cover?"

Jack perks up. "Yeah," he says, and motions to Wendy. Tim's eyes are already on the girl, a broad smile on his face.

The girl straightens up, looks from side to side. "M-me?"

Caleb deadpans, "Well, Spike's a little under-dressed, and I don't think the old guy's legs'll pass muster."

She looks down at her outfit. "But I'm not wearing...."

Jack steps toward her. "No, it'll be good. You're very pretty!" He holds out his hand, lets it hang there. Standing in the middle of the walkway, he blocks the path of a trio of tourists, who stop and cast glances of annoyance at one another. Finally the girl relents, taking his hand and crossing to stand with the band.

It takes a few shots for her to shake her embarrassed grin. She stands first to the left of the group, looking down the hill after the photographer directs her away from the camera lens. The Flak Jackets assume various expressions of aloofness, all looking vaguely in her direction. Caleb wears an outright scowl. As the photographer snaps away, pausing with increasing frequency to look at her watch, the boys turn, face the girl, and then gather around her.

Spike's arms are still crossed as he growls sidelong at me, "Shit, you know, these might make some good shots."

"Now all together." The photographer makes a squeezing motion with both hands. The Flak Jackets step up around Jack and Wendy. Jack stays put, a foot behind the girl. "Closer," orders the photographer. "Arms around her, or something."

"Um." The kid's back stiffens. He looks at his right hand, then watches it move until it rests gingerly above the girl's hip. The photographer grabs a few shots. The girl's face reddens. They remain a foot apart.

"Christ," Spike hisses. "Jack! Arms around your woman!" A few heads turn among the milling strangers. "A shoot in San Francisco, and you're touching her like she's got malaria? People'll think you're queer!" Several more heads turn. The roadie's voice lowers to a mumble. "What the fuck kind of rock star is he supposed to be, afraid of a fuckin' *woman*?"

The girl takes the initiative. Taking his hand at her hip, she pulls him in behind her until he stands against her back. His forearm she places across her midriff. The kid's awkward gape turns to a surprised grin, which he wipes from his face in favor of a cool stare when the photographer brings the camera to her eye.

"Like you mean it!" shouts Spike. The kid relaxes, and stoops a little to fit himself closer around the contour of her back. His left arm snakes around her waist to join his right. The girl turns her head toward the camera, eyes closed. Jack's arms tighten around her. His forearms rise until they just about press up underneath her breasts. For a moment his back stiffens again; his grip slackens and his arms drop an inch. But the girl loosens him up again, wrapping her arms around his and squeezing them.

They linger like this for a long minute, he with his face half-buried in her hair, she with her eyes still closed and a smile slowly spreading across her lips. The band members stand frozen throughout, their faces unwavering masks of rock 'n' roll boredom while the photographer snaps away.

"Oh my God! That's it!" the photographer gasps when she looks at her watch again. "My boss is gonna string me up!" She drops the camera to her side and makes ready to dash away.

"Wait!" the girl calls out. The kid is about to pull his arms away, but she holds him fast. "Could we get just one of us...like this?" She looks over to the other Flak Jackets. All three get her meaning and step away.

"Can you cover my salary when I get fired?" But the photographer is already bringing the camera once more to her face.

In an instant, Jack snaps out of his practiced stare. His eyes widen, his lips spread, and his cheeks bunch up. After four weeks of watching him, I learn that Jack Hackett has dimples. Wendy loses her tentative look and casts a glow with her broad smile. Her hair tosses lightly in the breeze, and a few more curls fall into Jack's face. He laughs, brushes them aside, and as I watch I hope that these pictures capture a modicum of what the poses reveal to me.

The shots fail to reach the roadie in quite the same way. "How sweet." His tone is saccharine. "A nice photo for the Hackett family album."

"Nice." The photographer looks at the small screen under her camera's viewfinder. "Yeah." Then without a second's further pause she rushes down the stairs. "I'll email some of these to Marty! Hope you like 'em!" Her straight black ponytail bounces after her like the tail of a galloping stallion.

The kid disengages slowly from the girl, as though he's just finished a conjugal act. He descends the hill beside her, head down, staring at the steps. At the bottom of the winding brick portion of the street, he reaches for her hand. She is gazing dreamily at the bay; as soon as his fingers touch hers, her eyes drop to the sidewalk. Her hand clasps his.

Spike trudges beside me, glaring at this spectacle from uphill. He lifts a palm at the two of them. "This ain't rock 'n' roll."

⌘

As Road Manager, Spike declares himself van driver. It comes as a relief to me; Caleb's driving makes me nervous.

Another edict: "M'lady," Spike tells Wendy, sliding the side door open, "you'll be ridin' with Old Man Barclay."

Jack protests, but the roadie's logic is unassailable. "Think about it, kid. It's my job to get you to the gig every night." He points at the Kia. "So what do I do if one of you, or one of your amps, is in that piece of plastic when it dies fifty miles behind us? No, I want the whole band in the same place, for as much of this trip as I can get! You afraid this senior citizen's gonna make a move on your chick while you're gone?" He looks me over with a wicked smile. "Sure, he looks good—for his age, you know—but no matter how you look, after a certain amount of years, a man's gotta tape a number two pencil to his pecker to keep it stiff."

So with a reluctant goodbye kiss from her guy, Wendy accompanies me to the Kia. I have to mute the trill in my heart as I sit in the driver's seat. "Welcome aboard," I say lamely. "The CD player is at your disposal."

"Thanks," she says. She pulls her selection from her suitcase in the backseat. We turn into traffic to the sounds of a classical guitar.

A doleful female voice begins a quiet lament in French. "Françoise Hardy," is her answer to my inquisitive glance. And though I understand not a word of the chanteuse's song, the spare music and her soft voice have me feeling wistful all the same.

We cross the Bay Bridge and make our way up the 80. Between industrial eyesores, the driver's side offers an intermittent view of the bay, faintly sparkling in the sunshine.

"I'm from New Hampshire," she says in the first half hour. "I guess that's one of the things Jack and I have in common—you know, New Hampshire, Vermont." She laughs. "The way he says 'Jeezum Crow!' I bet I'm the only one who's ever heard that saying before." She lets her smile linger for a while before going on. "And *my* dad's a teacher, too."

Sitting straight in her chair, her hands in her lap, she takes in the view with a small, quiet awe. Long pauses in our talk have none of the awkwardness that might fill Tim with panic. The girl just gazes at the passing bay, her head bobbing with the cadence of the French songstress.

We cross a long, high bridge with the bay on either side of us. A sunbeam glints off the water; the flash in my eye sets my lips in motion. "I'm from Connecticut," I hear myself saying. "You don't get views like this on Long Island Sound."

"No. Not even off Cape Cod." She rolls down her window. Curls sway and bounce around her head. She bats them away from her face for a spell, then gives up and lets them bounce, setting her hands down to touch the hem of her skirt around her knees. "I've learned to love sunsets since I moved to L.A." In the very corner of my field of vision as I watch the road, I can make out her slender wrist peeking out from her peach, silk sleeve. "How long have you lived there?" she asks. Her skin is that lightest of pinks, a smooth strawberry milk; her wristbone is that perfect curve that juts out a fraction of an inch, so that her joint tapers in below her thumb in the shape of an hourglass.

"Almost thirty years," I answer. "You?"

She tugs her skirt hem over her knees. Her fingers move with a delicate poise, then come to rest again just within my view. "Since January." A hand disappears to gather her wayward hair behind her head. "It took me till March to find a job." Her hand settles back with the other and absently traces her hem. "And now I've quit. My parents weren't too impressed."

Before I put my next thought into words, she continues: "My dad said how he hoped I wasn't 'frittering away' the gains I'd made since I moved."

"That's parents for you, I suppose."

"I guess. But—" She exhales sharply. "Well, there *are* no gains. I mean, I found work and all, but...." She throws up her hands. "I don't know. I haven't made any friends, really. I was hoping...." Her hands come to rest, fingers interlocked, on her knees. "And then, before the band left, Jack came over. And we went for a walk. And he was really sweet, you know? And everything I said, he seemed genuinely fascinated by it." I glance over at her; she's smiling at the horizon. "It just felt *so good*." She pauses; when she resumes, her words are pointed at her lap. "And then he had to go, and I felt lonely again." She looks back up. "So then Marty called last week, and he went on and on like he had to sell this trip to me. But I didn't need persuading. As soon as I said yes, I went back to feeling good."

"You have a place to go back to after this, I hope."

"I have a, um, special arrangement," she says. "And Marty is covering my expenses here. He's very generous."

"Do you suppose you'll move in with Jack when the tour is over?"

"I don't know." I can hear a warm blush in her voice. "It's a big commitment."

"Well." I laugh awkwardly. "For all intents and purposes, you *are* living together—at least for now."

She murmurs, "Yes, I guess we are," and lifts her hands from her knee. Her right arm leans against the window ledge, while her left forefinger starts its run along her collarbone.

⌘

April 12, 2003

"I dunno what Marty thinks we're gonna get out of doing an in-store," Caleb complains to me in the Sacramento record store's tiny parking lot, a half hour before today's first appearance. The van and my Kia are the only two vehicles in the lot. "Much less an in-store with a fuckin' day's notice!"

Indeed, Marty and Fritz have taken us by surprise, Marty having phoned me only yesterday with the strangely triumphant proclamation that we would grace a makeshift stage at Stylus Records, "the biggest indie record store in Sacramento!" When I demanded to know why my recent emails had gone unanswered, and about the status of the website and blog, still blank pages with 'Under Construction' headers the last time I visited an internet café, he replied only, "It's all coming together! Now lemme speak to Spike, I gotta give him instructions for tomorrow."

"No one's gonna show up!" Caleb whines. Cars roll by in both directions on the wide street. None turn in at the store. Inside Spike is working out the PA system while the others browse the racks.

"It's still early," I offer. "People go shopping on a Saturday afternoon."

"Who cares?" He directs his grievance at the blue sky. "What're they gonna shop for? We don't have a fucking record to sell them. We're not even gonna get 'em to come to the show tonight. Why spend eight dollars to see a band play the same set you just caught for free?"

I raise my eyebrows hopefully when a yellow convertible swings into the lot, but with the fellow in the Giants cap climbing out from behind the wheel and walking into the store alone, such hope does seem misplaced.

"One person." Caleb leans against the brick wall of the shop and crosses his arms. "Ya know, they only got this 'cause Fritz knows the manager."

"Is that so?"

"They sit around," his rant continues, "doin', you know, what they do." Here he taps the side of his nose. "And then one of 'em jumps up and says, 'Hey! I got a friend in Sacramento, owns a record store!' or 'I got a buddy in Reno who does internet radio!' And they call it tour planning."

"Well, I suppose—"

"Did you notice the signs for Salinas on the highway two days ago? Tim's hometown, right? Oughta get at least his parents in to pad the crowd some. Did you notice which town we *didn't* stop at?"

An SUV pulls in. As its lone occupant jumps out, a dwarf in a 'Def Leppard' T-shirt comes off the sidewalk toward us. They reach the entrance at the same time. "That's three," I say. The SUV driver, a tubby kid with a scraggly moustache, opens the door and motions for the dwarf to enter first. As he does, the Giants fan shoots out between them and jumps back into his convertible.

"Two," Caleb deadpans. He pauses. "One and a half. And no one in a Def Leppard T-shirt is gonna go for this band."

Inside, a half hour later, the numbers have changed. The mustached SUV driver has shopped and left, though the dwarf remains, chatting with the cashier and looking with some interest at the stage that blocks the middle aisle. To that net gain of one, we can add eight more patrons of varying ages and images, who rifle through bins of records with such single-minded collector's purpose I'm not sure they even notice the live band tuning up in their midst.

"Ladies and gentlemen," the store manager declares over a stab of feedback from his microphone. "I'd like to introduce a great band, all the way up from L.A." He pauses to scratch his bald head. "They're playing tonight at Elmo's on J Street." He darts away from the microphone and confers with Caleb, who groans and turns away. Tim murmurs over his tom-toms. The manager leaps back to the mic. "So let's hear it for Jack Hackett and the Flak Jackets!"

Jack hops out from behind a speaker to take center stage as the music starts. Three or four heads look up from their browsing. The girl peeks out from behind the speakers and watches the kid's back. One verse in, Caleb wears a smirk that has already written off this appearance. The sound is a bass-heavy, incoherent noise, made all the more appalling by its oddly low volume. Jack works some strained emotion into the chorus, but the song is doomed.

Spike twiddles a few knobs on a console by the stage. When nothing changes, he sneers at it and storms away. Two more songs garner a distracted patter. Standing near the cashier fifteen feet away, I clear my throat during 'Hollerin' Blues' and think I catch Joe looking up at the outburst.

Wendy inches out from behind the speakers, and tries to skirt the stage to the front. The little platform is wedged snugly between 'Prog Rock N-Z' and 'Hardcore A-Z' though, and she must circle an entire row of record bins to get around.

Settling at my right, Spike crosses his arms at the store manager, who huddles by a fire exit on the far side of the room. "This wouldn't be such a fucking waste of time if the PA was any good." He emits a sighing grunt. "That fuck told Fritz he does this stuff all the time, and he gets half of Sacramento's rock scene in and outta this place on a Saturday." He grunts again. "Some fuckin' rock scene."

The girl squeezes between two record bins into the aisle in front of the stage. She leaves a ten-foot gap between herself and the band, a buffer zone occupied by only a stout, pimple-faced forty-year-old in shorts who stands stubbornly at Joe's feet, sifting through 'Prog Rock A-M'.

"You with them?" asks a tenor voice somewhere below my shoulders. The little person sporting Leppard is watching the band from my left.

"I am." I don't have to raise my voice to overcome the sludge from the stage.

He strokes his chin with stubby fingers. "They're good," he says. He watches Jack wail for a moment, as he tucks the record he's just bought under his arm. "Best of luck to 'em." With that, he drifts past me and the roadie. Spike puts a five-by-seven flyer with the show time scrawled with marker into the man's hand before the fellow makes it out the door.

The kid shuts his eyes to the scene and works as much feel as I suspect he can into his delivery. Words seep out of the sonic mire: *"kickin'"*, *"lonesome"*, and *"pride"*. But they don't slap at me the way they have in the past. His bandmates press at his flanks on the soapbox that serves as a stage, and he comes across as a caged hamster.

Midway through a chugging boogie he opens his eyes. They come to rest on the girl; in the next instant he's messing up his line: *"Call me what you—damn."* But from that moment, his voice begins to cut through the soup, projecting the songs so that at least they sound complete. A familiar line in one of the slower numbers materializes in my ear: *"... share the whispers when I dream."* Viewing the girl's figure from behind, I watch her lift her hand to reach her neck, and I know her finger is tracing its familiar path.

Spike makes sure that each patron receives a flyer. He leaves a sizeable stack at the register and growls at the cashier to put a flyer in every bag. The band is on Elmo's stage at nine. Leaning against the bar, I breathe in air soaked in alcohol and five-years-stale tobacco ash and scan the floor for a dwarf in a Def Leppard T-shirt who never shows up. Two songs in, Caleb leans over the stage toward me and mouths the word "Twelve." For the rest of the set, he slumps over his bass and looks on the night's dozen with the glare of a prophet.

⌘

April 15, 2003

From Northern California into Oregon, the wheels keep turning. The days flash by like the pages of a flipbook, the same ride-eat-play-sleep cycle repeating over and over.

The color of the tour has shifted. Already the desert browns of Los Angeles and Las Vegas have bled away, the landscape turning green and wood-brown in their stead. Damp has seeped into my bones, stiffening my frame during my morning runs, sealing the sweat against my skin so that I feel slimy on the surface when I return to take my shower.

"All right, motherfuckers." Outside last night's motel, Spike holds up a bulging white canvas bag with both arms. "Laundry Day. Who's up?"

"Like fuck," says Caleb when the roadie's eye falls on him. "And remind me why the four of *us* still have to take turns when we've got *two* people in the Kia these days?"

"Well, shit." The roadie raises his eyebrows. "I guess chivalry *is* dead. I thought it was fair for you to take turns. But okay. The old man's already said he's doin' the blog at an internet place across the street. If you wanna let Princess spend two hours on her own getting the cum-stains outta *your* briefs, I won't argue."

Caleb sniggers. "A woman's place... Right?"

"Ha ha. Ho ho." Jack smirks at the bass player as he steps past him to grab the bag. "I'll be up this time."

Wendy touches his arm as he hefts the bag toward the Kia. "You don't have to do it every time, you know."

"I know." He drops the bag by the car and opens the driver-side door. "But I'm up for it." As he tips the driver's seat forward and grabs the top of the bag to heave it in back, he adds, "You know you're not here for laundry duty, right?"

"I know."

"You know Caleb's an asshole, right?"

"No, he's your friend."

"Well, if he's my friend, he'll start being nicer to you."

Standing at the passenger side for the whole conversation, I'm surprised it takes Jack until now to look over and see me. He freezes for a second, then re-affixes the scowl to his face and says to me: "Hey, uh, you don't record these stretches, right?"

"With just Wendy? Never."

"So you're not gonna record now?"

"I don't even know where the recorder is."

"Then gimme the keys, and let's go."

We drive a block to the Laundromat. I cross the street and send a new blog entry to Marty. I come back to find them watching the cotton, polyester, and denim tumble.

In the driver's seat again, Jack holds up a CD in each hand. "You pick." Wendy lets her index finger hover over each one for a second, then taps the one in his right hand. He flips it to see the title: "*Sticky Fingers* again. You're okay with that, right?" he says to me through the rearview mirror. He turns the ignition and has the stereo loading before I can nod my approval.

For some time Mick Jagger does the lion's share of the speaking. From the backseat I catch Jack's eye a couple of times; neither of us says a word. As he glides onto the freeway, the sun comes out from behind a cloud, and the glare of the early afternoon intensifies. I shut my eyes and tilt my head back to find some shade. A few seconds later, I hear Jack murmuring to Wendy.

"You know how many kids that guy has? Mick, I mean."

My eyes stay shut.

"How many?"

"Seven."

"Well! That must be quite a handful."

"I think it's four different mothers, so there's a division of labor there."

"Could you handle seven kids?" she says.

"Jeezum Crow! Seven? No." Mick gets in a few lines before Jack muses: "*Maybe* one."

"Just maybe?"

"Maybe-probably." Mick raises his voice for the bridge to his song. "You?" I barely hear Jack ask.

"Yeah, I had thought about *working* with kids before, so...." She giggles softly. "Maybe-probably."

The tempo drops on the stereo. Acoustic guitars replace the electrics, and Jagger's voice comes down from its usual bark to a gentler coo. I let a verse go by before feigning a wake-up stretch and opening my eyes, in time to watch as the kid's right hand floats down from the steering wheel to rest on the girl's knee. The girl doesn't clasp his hand, doesn't turn her soft gaze on him. She only leans her head an inch or so toward him.

For three verses it lasts, neither of them saying a word. But a couple of times, when the kid looks to his right-side mirror, I catch his expression. And behold, gone is the paranoid suspicion he normally directs at me, gone is the smirk he projects in all his monosyllabic conversations. In their place hangs a dumb grin, and a giddy gleam lights his eye.

And then, slowly, as one would withdraw from a baby who had just gone to sleep, he lifts his hand from her knee and returns it to the wheel. His back straightens, his smile fades, and he squints against the glare. But his knuckles don't blanch, and from behind I can see one cheek still bunched up. The wheels roll on, the car sucks up the dotted freeway lines under the hood and shoots them out the back, and as the kid's waning glow reaches its ebb, I start waiting for Jagger to coo again.

⌘

April 20, 2003

We're halfway to Hood when the van weaves into the right lane ahead of us. Out the driver window, Spike waves over his roof at a sign for the next rest stop. Tim nudges up the Kia's turn signal, and we glide into the exit behind the others.

The sounds and smells of impending summer greet me outside the Kia door. We've missed a morning rain; the asphalt remains dark in patches, and the dew is still heavy on the grass and picnic tables in the shade of the nearby trees. But through a gap in the whitening clouds, the sun radiates a cheery warmth that has already dried several benches sitting in the open. Contorting themselves in exaggerated stretching moves, the group migrates across the grass to a table.

Spike leaves the party for the shack that houses the men's room. "You fellas try to keep it in your little heads to go too, since that's what we're here for," he says as he walks away.

Sliding behind the table, Caleb whips something small and white from the pocket of his windbreaker. "Shall we partake?" The joint lodges itself between his lips while with both hands he pats himself down in search of a lighter. Wendy and the band take places around him. A sense of propriety keeps me standing, looking innocuously over Caleb's shoulder as he lights up.

"What's it like?" The girl bites her smiling lip, her eyebrows raised to make way for an expression that knows its own naïveté.

Caleb, holding in his first puff, lets it out in a chuckle. "'What's it like?'" The joint moves to Joe; Caleb turns to Jack. "You, my friend, have picked a real winner." To the girl, he qualifies, "I mean that in the nicest way."

The joint has made its way to Tim. "It really depends on the person," he tells the girl. "Me, I tend to brainstorm." The joint hovers in front of him. He turns hopeful eyes at me, and I realize that I am being drafted to return behind the wheel when our break is over. I nod gamely—let no one accuse me of spoiling a party.

"You got something against it?" Caleb asks the girl.

She shakes her head. "I just never got around to it, I guess." She puts her hand across the open top buttons of her blouse.

Jack is drawing from the joint now. "You gonna pass that to your girl?" Caleb asks him, and then to the girl herself, "Why not try it? Solve the mystery yourself."

At this moment, as she drops her defensive hand from her collar, the top of her blouse billows out a fraction of an inch.

She reaches out, hesitantly, ever the good girl even as she transgresses, to take the joint. Her blouse tips further open, an imperceptible inch to her seated companions, but enough from my vantage point to open a line of sight to where the white lace center of her brassiere lies just barely exposed between her breasts. Before my eyes have a chance to focus, I feel the reflex of an old man's shame, which kicks in with swiftly mounting force to tear my gaze away and fix it first on her face, and then on to some random, neutral spot on the horizon.

Sadly, my shame, though strong, is too slow. When it finally sets my eyes on her face, that face is looking into mine. An explosion inside me forces my eyes shut. I turn away and reopen them on the wall of trees that encloses the rest stop on three sides.

The next voice to speak is the girl's. "What do you do?" My guilty mind first registers this as accusatory, some rhetorical aside to her companions, as in: 'What do you do when some creep gropes you with his eyes?'

Caleb answers her before I can formulate an apology. "Just suck it in—don't breathe it in yet."

I look back at the table. Wendy is examining the rolled piece of paper, charred at one end, pinched between her thumb and forefinger. As though sensing my eyes on her again, she glances at me. It's a glance that knows what I've just done, but it is not hard, offended or alarmed. She makes no move to close her blouse. When, a second later, she returns to the object in her hand, I have the feeling that I've just been forgiven.

"Like this?" she says, and plunges the thing into her lips. She draws in her cheeks. Her eyes widen. The joint leaves her mouth, coming to rest at the level of her chest. She looks at it for a beat, then at Caleb.

"Now breathe it in," directs Caleb, "and hold it."

Her chest rises. Her eyes widen more.

"Now let go," he says, like a yoga instructor talking her through a new stretch. "Do you feel it?"

"I think so," she answers softly. Her face takes a few seconds to fall, millimeter by millimeter. "Maybe not," she confesses at length.

"Well, pass it on," and the edge is back in Caleb's voice, "to those of us that do!"

⌘

May 3, 2003

"Boy," says Tim after a loud gulp at breakfast, "I'd like to get eggs that don't *cool* my tongue sometime." He picks a second chunk out of the yellow mass on his plate.

Caleb pats him on the back. "Come on, pal. You've been moping ever since we won the war." He picks up a newspaper, two or three days old, that some other hotel guest has left on the table. "Here. This'll cheer you up." He points at the large color photo of Dear Leader, standing in full flight suit on that aircraft carrier runway. "Heh. Check him out below-deck."

Finally, the forlorn veneer over Tim's face breaks. "Heh heh," he ventures. "Presidential pocket rocket."

"I bet he approves of *USA Today*'s coverage!" Caleb flashes teeth caked with half-chewed toast and jam. "Am I right, Joe?"

"I guess so," answers Joe. "Heh heh."

Jack and Wendy enter the dining area, side by side. Spike towers behind them like a shepherd over two straggling sheep. The girl looks ashen. A somber-faced Jack holds her hand. Caleb, facing away from them, is still cracking wise ("You think a suit like that oughta come with a codpiece?"), while the two collect their food. Spike stalks off to tend to our checkout. The two are in under the wire; a staffer snatches each platter of food off the buffet the instant both have moved away from it.

At the table, the kid holds a chair out for his girl. Seeing them for the first time, Caleb points at the paper. "You see this?"

The girl bows her head. While she stares at my half-full glass of orange juice, Jack answers, "Yeah, funny," with a curt nod.

"Well? Why so down? It's over."

The girl gives a hollow laugh. "Yeah. Over."

I sense a disconnect. "Are we all talking about the same subject?"

"Likely not," the kid answers. He looks down at the girl's hands. Her right turns a roll over, again and again, in its plate. Her left she holds closed at the edge of the table, near her heart. The kid watches the roll turn over a few times before reaching out and touching her left hand. She lets him take it, lets him gently uncurl her fingers, lets him take the coin from her palm.

I share wary glances with Caleb and Tim. "What's that?" asks Caleb.

The kid places the coin, a quarter, tails-up between the trays in the center of the tabletop. Caleb picks it up and examines it. "Oh, *that* story. Heh. You had me worried there!" He passes it to me. 'New Hampshire', it reads under an engraved image of the state's symbol, the Old Man of the Mountain.

Seeing my still-puzzled expression, Jack tells me, "It fell down." At these words, Wendy closes her eyes.

It takes a moment for an image to form in my brain. The view of the famous rock face, clear in my memory from a family vacation circa 1950, comes into focus in time for Jack's next remark, "Fell apart overnight," to smash it to pieces. I can't explain, but neither can I deny the pang of shock, nor the wave of loss that follows.

"Yeah, that's heavy." Tim says solemnly. "They said it's been there thousands of years."

"Wait," says Caleb. "We're talking about a bunch of rocks on a hillside?"

Wendy opens her eyes, shrugs, and smiles wanly. Jack shoots lightning bolts from his eyes at the jerk. After a few moments the girl finds words. "My family used to go hiking around there."

Caleb smiles half-heartedly at the girl, with one eye on Jack. "Okay," he says, "that's great. But, hey, it's not quite the Twin Towers."

"I think I get it, Caleb," offers Tim. "My family has a bunch of photo albums back home. They go all the way back to my parents' wedding. I haven't looked at them for years. But if my mom called and said they'd been lost in a fire, I'd sure be sad. Is that it, Wendy?"

"All right, fair enough. Wendy, I'm sorry for your loss." Caleb injects just enough genuine sympathy into his condolence to drain the ice from the kid's stare. Jack takes back the quarter I've been holding all this time and puts it back in the girl's hand. She stashes it away in a tiny leather change purse. We resume our breakfast routine. Throughout it, though, I battle the urge to pull out my cell phone, call my father and ask him if on this sad day he's holding himself together.

⌘

May 16, 2003

"June Carter died," Tim says before my door is all the way open.

"Who?"

"The Carter Family. Johnny Cash's wife. It was just on the news." He bows his head as I stand aside to show him into my room. "Poor Johnny Cash."

"How did she die?"

"Some operation. She was in recovery." He sits on the bed and looks out the window onto the hotel parking lot. And he repeats, "Poor Johnny Cash."

"She saved Cash's life, ya know," says Caleb when we convene in the lobby. "Brought him back to Jesus—helped him be born again."

"Have you read his book?" Tim lets the question float out to anyone in earshot. "He goes on and on about her. No man loved a woman like Johnny Cash loved June."

"I like Johnny Cash," says Joe.

Jack comes down the stairs, his arm around Wendy's shoulders. As the two set down their bags and enter our circle, his hand sneaks out and takes hers.

"Bad news, Jack," Tim intones.

"June?" Jack assumes an appropriately solemn frown.

"You saw the news, then?" Tim tries to match his friend's expression. "She wrote 'Ring of Fire', you know."

"We all know that, Tim," says Caleb. I didn't know that.

"And 'The Kneeling Drunkard's Plea', that's a Carter Family song."

Spike has pulled the van up to the curb at the entrance. In he struts as usual, until Tim calls out to him, "Spike, d'ya hear about June Carter?" At that he slows up, his eyes turn questioning and his step becomes reverential as he joins us. "She died," Tim finishes.

"Shit." The roadie winces. "An' Johnny bein' the way he is these days, he ain't long for this world no more."

Reverend Caleb lifts both hands. "A man like Johnny Cash is on his way to a better world." At that I catch Wendy, heretofore looking on friendly and sweet, stifle a laugh. Oblivious, Caleb preaches some more. "Blessed are those who mourn, for they shall be comforted. He's got a lot of family, they'll pull him through." He shrugs. "And like you said, Spike, we won't have him here much longer. Now she'll be there to greet him in the Great Hereafter." Wendy turns to share a head-shaking look with Jack which, with his eyes to the Hereafter, Caleb once again fails to catch.

Spike rounds up suitcases. We follow him out to the parking lot, where he puts the last piece of baggage into the back, then grabs the laundry bag. He looks at each band member in turn, then suddenly thrusts the bag like a medicine ball into Caleb's gut. "Your turn, you lucky fuck."

⌘

Piling whites and coloreds into machines, pouring powders into basins, we watch little red digits count down to zero. The Laundromat radio overhead is tuned to a country station. Midway through the final spin, we get a break from the synthesized sounds of modern Nashville for the obligatory death-day tribute to dear Mrs. Carter Cash.

"'Peace in the Valley'!" Caleb bursts before Mister Cash can get past the song's first line. And when June's voice floats over Cash's low-key testifying, the bass player gets the spirit.

"There will be peace in the valley for me someday..."

"See, there's the Lord, right there." He slaps his knee—actually slaps his knee. "There's two people who're goin' to Heaven."

Wendy holds a hand over her incredulous grin. Now, finally, Caleb notices her reaction.

"What?" he asks.

"You're not serious, are you?"

"Of course I'm serious. What, you're an atheist or something?"

"As a matter of fact!"

I feel an inexplicable pang in my heart.

"My father teaches a college paleontology class. He has to spend his first two classes each semester debunking Intelligent Design for the believers before he can get down to the subject he came to teach."

The coloreds' machine reaches zero. I spring forward to grab a wheelie basket and begin unloading the clothes. I shut my ears to the debate unfolding behind me, even knocking the back of my hand into the inside of the drum so that I can focus on the clang it makes. I divide my attention between the synth-country tune that lays June Carter to rest and the squeak of the wheels as I roll the basket to the dryer. Wendy has just brought up the inevitable comparison of God to Santa Claus.

I load everything in and slam the portal shut. The machine waits politely for five quarters; in all of my pockets I can only find three. A sign over on the change machine tells me that it's broken, to please consult the attendant. I haven't seen a soul since we came in.

"I'm out of change." I point to the sign on the change machine. The two rummage in their pockets. They come up with only a pile of nickels and dimes between them.

Wendy pulls a five dollar bill from her pocket. "I'll try next door."

I pull my wallet out and fish for a bill. "Don't use your own money."

"It's okay. I want to get something from the deli anyway." Off she goes, leaving Caleb shaking his head.

"That's the first time I've ever heard a peep outta her," he marvels. "And such a good girl otherwise." He leans over to help me with the last handful of whites. "You see the smile they always get when they bring up Santa Claus? Like they've outsmarted God?" I am getting nauseous.

The conversation resets itself on Wendy's return. We chat about the next couple of dates, the Pacific Northwest, and nothing else in particular. Soon Caleb finds a magazine, Wendy a paperback, and both go silent.

We're on a straight stretch of the 5, listening to Caleb's *Johnny Cash at Folsom Prison* CD, when the last song triggers the debate again.

The girl is in the passenger seat beside me; Caleb is in back. At the words 'the Lord,' the tousled top of his head creeps into my rear-view mirror. As the first verse, about a prison chapel, passes into the refrain, he muses, "Beautiful song." From the corner of my eye I see his hand reach out and nudge Wendy's shoulder. "Don't ya think?"

She shifts around to face him. "So's 'Rudolph the Red-Nosed Reindeer'."

I let them argue, fixing my eyes on the horizon. I clench my teeth and roll my tongue tightly into the side of my mouth, building my resolve not to take a side and voice a belief that it cuts me too deeply to hear from my own lips.

"Look at all the beautiful things in the world. You really believe they just happened by chance?"

Stare on, Henry. I have beheld many things in my life. Some things I have found beautiful, some terrible. But most things simply *are*; they sit idly in space and time, serving no purpose. Fifty million drops of rain fall in a thunderstorm. Take away any one, any ten, any ten thousand, and the ground is still wet, the plants still get watered, the people still scurry for shelter. Take them all away and let the crops wither, double them and see them wash away;

all those trillions of raindrops working in tandem won't alter the course of the Earth around the sun, the sun around the galaxy, the billions of galaxies falling, themselves like raindrops, through eternity.

"Everything has a purpose. Everything has a reason."

You honestly buy that, do you? Go ahead then, flip a coin to solve your next big life decision. Throw the dice, consult the I Ching, surrender to that great cosmic jigsaw puzzle of random events. See how well the will of God treats you.

"What about all the suffering in the world? What about the little kids in Iraq being blown up right now? How can there be a good God who would allow that?"

You tell him, young lady. A young man of questionable strength and integrity learns that his newborn has a 'condition'. He swallows hard and soldiers on, but the blow has made a crack in him. He needs a crutch, so he leans on a bottle, and on his wife. And the going is rough on him, on her—and on the little one, who never did any harm to anybody, nothing to deserve the hurdles that clutter his path where others move with ease.

"You know, there's a line in the Bible that talks about this. It goes..."

And the wife tries to shoulder this whole burden for years, until one day she realizes that she needs to cut loose the dead weight to move any further. And so, though she doesn't want to, she takes the kid, leaves the man, tells him to start putting his weight on both legs and maybe she'll walk with him again.

"Forget all the resurrection hocus-pocus—can you show me one bit of proof that Jesus even *existed?*"

And the man gets the message, cleans himself up, visits with his boy, starts to make things right. His wife starts to believe in him again, and one day decides he's proven himself: a routine phone call to discuss the boy's needs ends, unexpectedly, with her soft, sweet command, "Honey, come home."

"Maybe that's why they call it 'faith'. Did you ever consider that?"

And three hours later, before he can carry out her orders, she is dead. Hit by a car. No drunk driver, no nut behind the wheel, just a law-abiding citizen driving within the speed limit, in front of whose car she just happened to trip off the curb, and whose life is also marked by tragedy for no conceivable reason.

"You know why you believe in all that? It's because you can't come to terms with death."

And it hurts like hell, and it's one more injustice served on a boy who's already paid the dues of a lifetime or two, and wouldn't it be great to have a proper plot to the narrative, with the surprise twist in the final pages that can tie up all the loose ends and serve up that perfect happy ending? Or at least to have some hack you can blame for giving up at the first draft of your life, leaving you to deal with all the inconsistencies and the damned illogic that pervade such a work, born of naked inspiration, un-reared by second thoughts?

"Maybe you can't come to terms with sin. Ever thought of that?"

Alas, a man of reason puts all the pieces together, takes a step back, and sees not the face of God in mosaic, but an enormous mass of nonsense—a Rorschach test that's pretty if you cock your head right and block out parts of it, but of no practical use, and too easily shattered and swept away like so much dust.

"God doesn't exist."

"He does too."

"Does not."

"Ha. Does too. But don't worry, Wendy—my God loves you. Henry, you got any Ray Charles to listen to?"

And you, Wendy, you're brave enough to call it like I see it, and I'm proud of you. But still, what a punch to the gut to hear you say it.

⌘

May 23, 2003

"I've finished the book I was reading," Wendy says with a sense of loss over breakfast.

"You need something to read?" Jack asks. "I've got a magazine!" And so before we pile into the vehicles, the kid rummages through his bag and pulls out the promised magazine, *American History Monthly*.

She laughs when she sees the cover, with its heroic painting of Robert E. Lee. But she is gracious. "Thank you, sweetie," she coos as if she'll treasure it always.

Under Caleb's mocking stare, the kid mumbles, "Well, it's nothing, really. I'm done with it. You can throw it out when you've finished."

We snake up the 5 Freeway, I at the wheel, the girl leafing through a reassessment of General Lee, and our Parisian belle crooning softly for us over a lush bed of strings. Wendy tosses the pages over as though browsing through a catalog. Before she reaches the middle she flips the magazine shut and sets it in her lap. "I don't really like the Civil War."

"Does Jack?"

She shrugs. "He doesn't ever talk about it, but I guess it's in his blood—you know, his dad teaching history and all." She taps the post strip on the bottom corner of the magazine cover. "I think that's where his parents live." She opens the magazine again, leafs a little further. "But maybe he likes it. I don't know everything about him yet." She closes it again and stuffs it into the glove compartment. "After all, you don't see me reading *Scientific American* because of *my* dad."

The road brings us by a river lined with evergreens. Françoise moans on, and for some time we let her. The words "*Je t'aime*" leap out at me, and I feel a small thrill at knowing their meaning.

A question comes to me out of nowhere, such an obvious one that I marvel that it hasn't occurred to me before. "How did someone like you discover this music?" I tap the dashboard over the CD deck. "A French singer from the sixties? I'd say you're a little young for that."

She flips down her visor and starts fussing with her bangs. "I had a French teacher in high school. He used music to keep us interested."

"*Voilà*," says Françoise, and a section of violins answers her.

"I guess he got through to at least one of you."

She snaps her visor up. "Well," she says, and holds her tongue for a long moment. "He didn't get through as far as he wanted." She looks down at her lap. "Not with me."

I find words a full verse and chorus later. "Do you mean what I think you mean?"

"He tried to make a pass at me after class one day."

"Oh, cripes."

"It wasn't that bad. He kissed me, and I pushed him away." She turns up her palms. "That was all. And he was really apologetic—he even cried a little. He *was* a very nice man." She lets out something like a chuckle, then clears her throat.

"Surely you reported him!"

Her voice takes on baggage. "I told some friends. That was it."

"What did your friends say?"

She chuckles some more. "They thought I should have, uh, gone with him."

"Really."

She examines her fingernails. "Well, he *was* good-looking. Everybody thought so. With that accent and all. And I *was* a senior." She drops her hands back into her lap. "I just couldn't...." She exhales to finish the sentence. Even spoken in the silence that follows the fade-out of the song, her confession, "I guess I'm funny that way," almost gets swallowed up in the low noise of the car.

Françoise is mournful once more. A lone acoustic guitar accompanies her in a minor key. I let the songstress go for a verse. "At least," I venture at length, "you came away with your honor." I point at the CD deck. "And some great music."

Her laugh is rueful. "She is great." She shrugs. "And I'm not damaged or anything."

"I'm glad," I say, and let the record play. Miss Hardy sounds dolorous over an orchestral waltz, wistful over a go-go beat, remorseful as she sings a word that sounds like '*regret*'. We let her do these things without interruption.

⌘

May 28, 2003

My phone is dead. The battery works, it recharges, but I can't dial out. I call the number from my room phone, to learn that it has been disconnected. I call the *Upsetter* office. A girl's voice tells me in monotone that her boss is out today, to try back tomorrow.

We zoom up into the Northwest. The Portland show stands out; a minor squabble between Jack and Caleb beforehand, over a Snickers bar, heats up the kid's blood and sharpens his tone in a way the soothing sight of his girl can't quite dull.

I call my son the Fan and his social worker daily. These essential calls now begin to go on my credit card. Over three days I call the office at different hours, and always the secretary's monotone asks that I try back tomorrow.

⌘

June 2, 2003

Tim has finished my book. "I really liked it!" he gushes during a laundry run. "Really, Wendy, you should read it!"

"What's it about?"

"Well...." Tim looks at me as if asking my permission. "This guy is born with stigmata—you know, where a person bleeds from his hands, like Jesus on the cross? So he goes around doing carnival shows, you know, *bleeding* for people." The back-cover synopsis didn't make it sound much better.

"And what happens?"

Tim takes a few seconds loading a machine. "Well, not a *whole* lot," he admits finally. That's it. Two years inception and writing, months of editing, my magnum opus, and not a whole lot happens in it.

She looks at me. "Is that so?"

I shrug. "He read it more recently than I did."

"Wait a second." Tim's hands are flapping in the air. "It's not about what *happens*." His eye searches my face, begging for approval. "See, he has to keep doing this show, and he's gotta bleed more and more each show to keep the crowds coming, and he's getting paler and weaker each time. So you gotta really feel for the guy." He has to use both hands to slide the coin tray in the second washer. "But he doesn't do a whole lot of different things. That's what I meant!"

"I'll have to read it," says the girl, and I feel heat in my cheeks.

"I can see why Marty asked you to cover this tour." Tim gives me that obsequious smile.

I shrug again. "I don't think his list of candidates was very long."

"No, don't you see?" He reaches into his knapsack on a chair beside him, pulls out the trashed paperback, and holds it up as Exhibit A. "The hero in your book—it's Jack!" He sees me hold back a groan. "No, really! Jack goes out there every night, and with the kind of songs he sings, he's gotta eat his heart out to do 'em justice—you know, he's gotta bleed." He claps his hand against the cover. "Just like this guy."

"You're assuming Marty's actually read the whole book."

The girl speaks up again. "What happens to the hero?"

"I, uh, guess you'll have to read it to find out." Tim bites his lip.

"May I borrow your copy?"

Tim beams as he thrusts the old paperback at her with both hands. "Here! Take it! It's great! I actually, honest-to-goodness started *re-reading* parts of it last night!" With the book safely in her grasp, he raises both thumbs at me.

I find myself struggling to keep from cringing and feel the need to tell Wendy not to listen to this fellow, who clearly has no idea what he's talking about.

The girl flips the book over and squints at the tiny back-cover headshot of me, bleached out and blurry on the bottom corner. She then looks up at the fallen features of man in front of her. "You've kept your looks," she says with a sweet smile, and I must laugh heartily, if only to offer an excuse for my face turning scarlet.

We drive for three hours. Tim expends most of his oxygen intake raving about my work from the backseat. The girl takes no notice. Her head stays bowed over my book, nestled in the folds of her flowing skirt, and her eyes never leave its pages.

⌘

June 3, 2003

The band plays Eugene, in a wood-paneled room with Christmas lights strung along the rafters. Jack's mic stand knocks out a few bulbs, a crowd of fourteen yells for more, and Caleb snags a petite redhead to bring back to the hotel.

The next morning we drive inland from the Oregon coast, through rain that falls in curtains across the highway. Dense forests of massive trees surround the road. At intervals the trees have been clear-cut, leaving swathes of hillside stubbled with stumps.

Wendy lets the hills roll by without once lifting her head. Her unrelenting focus on my book gives my palms a film of sweat and turns my tongue to sandpaper. She nears the middle by late morning, and I curse my younger self for having written that ridiculous, loveless sex scene. More than one review called my story edgy, pointing to that implausible scenario as evidence. But my wife had called it correctly, raising her eyebrows as she read the manuscript, and asking, "All that blood, sweetie?" Has the girl reached that part yet? She might be reading it now, holding her features steady but inwardly crossing herself and labeling me a pervert.

I sit through our communal lunch in embarrassed silence. Rejoining the road, I very nearly ask the girl to stop reading, though she's three quarters of the way through and the damage is certainly done.

As we come off the freeway at our destination, however, she shuts the book by its back cover and muses, "How sad for your character." Ignoring the hiss of air I let out at her comment, she goes on. "I mean, to have this same performance, this meaningless show, and then to die like he does, onstage and all." She looks out on the strip mall that rises to greet us at the end of the off-ramp. Before I can respond, before I can thank her for seeing past dull prose and wooden dialog to the heart of my story, before I can beg her to forget that depraved scene—before I can do anything but take in a deep breath—she asks, "Why was Frank Sinatra at his last show?"

I give her the bland truth that a hundred critics missed: "I like Frank Sinatra." And before she can formulate a follow-up, I exclaim, "Look at that hillside! Those trees! You've been missing quite a view!"

⌘

"I like that girl Serenity," she says halfway to Salem. My fingers, thus far tapping the steering wheel to Françoise's gentle rhythm, drop to the wheel like birds shot dead. "From your book," she clarifies when Miss Hardy's chorus dies down. "It's, um, *poignant*, the way she just sweeps out of nowhere, and then mysteriously disappears."

I mumble my thanks.

"And then of course, she's an actress, and what with me being an actress…"

"I didn't know you were an actress."

She laughs that pleasant lilt, tilting her head forward and stirring up her jasmine scent. "It's kind of on hold right now anyway, isn't it?" I draw great gulps of jasmine into my lungs. "Not that there's that much theater work in Hollywood. In three months I've only gotten work as an extra on game shows."

"You mean standing beside the shiny new car?"

"Worse. You sit in the audience and clap when the red light goes on."

"Easy money."

"I don't know about that. There's a reason they're paying people to sit and clap."

"Why Los Angeles, then? Wouldn't New York be better for the theater?"

"I thought of New York. It's closer to home, too. But I couldn't afford it." She opens her window a third of the way. Her jasmine flares up again, then vanishes. "My uncle owns a building in Burbank. He's letting me use one of the apartments there for free—until I find my own place."

"Convenient."

"Yeah, especially for my dad. He likes the idea that his brother can keep an eye on me." She sweeps imaginary dust from her long, green, summer skirt. "He wasn't too happy about *this* trip."

I feel the urge to speak up for a fellow father, but a second later, she's talking again. "Jack feels bad about me missing work," she says. "He's really encouraging. He says if they do a video I should be in it. He likes the way I look."

"Obviously so."

"Even not seeing—would you listen to me?" She grins into her hands. "Jack wouldn't like me talking like this, would he?"

⌘

June 6, 2003

Tim is twenty-three today. An awful feeling of immaturity-by-association grips me when Caleb relays this news to me. I live, work, socialize these days among a peer group whose members came into being as my son passed into teen-age.

A lull in bookings leaves us two days to get from the Dalles to Walla Walla. Spike vows in the morning to find us a perfect eatery for celebrating Tim's big day. Somehow he does it: just before Hermiston, at precisely the minute my evening hunger sets in, the caravan turns off the freeway and into the designated restaurant's parking lot.

Service is swift, and we are soon diving into a communal platter of nachos, a boisterous party of seven pressed into a corner booth meant for five. The arrangement won't work, but such is the sense of camaraderie that none among us mentions the tight squeeze until our orders arrive. At that point, plates begin to overlap, and I am moved to a chair that takes on the appearance of head of the table. My first instinct is to bow my head as my father does: *Our heavenly Father, we thank thee for this food. Would thou bless it to our use, and us to thy service. Amen.* I don't speak them, but the words play in my head despite me. It falls to Spike to say the benediction: "Chow down, motherfuckers."

The food is good, a variety of American fare and the odd exotic piece, allowing me to enjoy my chicken salad while Tim digs into what he dubs his "Birthday Burrito." Spike has done it again, and when I commend him on his achievement, my motion is strongly seconded all around.

"Yes, yes." The roadie strokes his ponytail over his shoulder. "You ride with me, you're a lucky fuck."

Caleb keeps it going. "'Course, this can't match the girls in Vegas."

The comment sits between us like a gun on the table. It is harmless enough on its own; it is the chain of events that now unfolds that loads it, cocks it, and points it at Jack's temple.

Tim makes the first blunder. He gives a horrified, horrifying look at Wendy. The placid smile the girl has thus far displayed takes on an air of slight confusion. "Girls in Vegas?" she asks.

When Caleb clarifies offhandedly, "Just four chicks Spike found for us to stay the night with — his apartment was too small for us," it could be an attempt to make matters seem more innocent. But he must realize how loaded this explanation sounds. And he uses the number four.

The girl bows her head, looks up again, and turns to Jack. "I didn't hear that story," she murmurs.

Jack has the look of a cornered animal. He opens his mouth, shiftily glances at me, then shuts it. He swallows, and then chases the tension from his face. "Relax, sweetheart. I'll explain later." This he says with his eye on me.

She's still smiling, somehow, but her brow furrows. She grabs at a ringlet of her hair, tugs it straight. She leans in to Jack's ear. "Did you..." she begins softly, confidentially save for the five other people within obvious earshot.

Jack looks mournfully at me again, and I want to hit him. I can see the gears spinning behind his pupils, the frantic brainstorm that wants to try a hundred responses but that jams him up instead. Meanwhile, my companions sit similarly immobilized. Tim's jaw hangs open; Caleb's full fork hovers over his plate. Only Joe plows on, through the apple crumble he ordered as his main course.

"Don't get all worked up, Princess." Spike takes a casual sip of his soda. "Jack's only human, ya know."

The girl wears an expression so taken aback it has neglected to drop its smile.

"You joined this crew as Jack's girl, right? So when a musician's on the road, he needs a *vent*, ya know? Now, I seen the cot they sneak in for you whenever your hotel room don't have two beds." At this, even Joe raises his eyebrows. The roadie continues, "You know, you ain't doin' Jack any favors keepin' your fuckin' *virtue*."

Wendy looks ready to pour tears over that stubborn smile. Her boyfriend looks at Spike with similar shock, but remains silent. "Look at 'im," says the roadie through a bite of hamburger. "He's flesh and blood. I don't care what he may tell you in private, but a guy joins a band to get *laid*."

Finally, the girl finds her voice. Her words come out in a near whisper, but she looks him in the eye. "You think you know Jack?"

The roadie chuckles. "Well, Princess, I been around Jack, what, two months?" He puts a napkin to his mouth. He puckers his lips into it as he wipes. "And of course, I ain't fucked 'im or nothin'." He jams the napkin into the puddle of ketchup on his plate. "But, far as I can tell, there's no one at this table who's got that over me." He leans back in the booth, grinning.

Tim's face has turned a distressed, embarrassed red. "Whoa there, Spike," he says, at about half the volume he would need to give his comment weight. "Pick on someone your own size!"

"Listen, sister, I'm doin' you a *favor* here, all right?" Spike waves a hand at Jack. "My boy here is only gonna wait so long. Look at 'im!" Jack sucks in his lips, begins drumming on the table with his fingertips. But still he remains mute. "He's a good-looking kid, right? Don't you think he's had his way with a few lookers already? Hey, you're a fair piece yourself, but it seems to me like you've got a fuckin' padlock on your cherry. So as it is, I'd say there's a gap between your résumés."

She reaches for the kid's drumming hand. He pulls it in and hides it under the table. He stares straight at Spike, through him, at some point a mile away. His mouth opens, he inhales, closes it. She clutches his upper arm, then after a short second lets it go. Her hands float before her, drifting without anchor.

"All I'm sayin', ya know, is get over your hang-ups, is all." Spike gives a shrug. "Then you'll both be happier."

I count five in my head before I speak. As I do I watch Wendy's face redden. I watch Jack raise his eyebrows and bite his lip, and fritter away his last chance to come to his damsel's defense.

"You know, Spike," I say at last, "you're an asshole."

"Fuck you," he says, still smiling.

"And, you know, we can't all be assholes. Where would that leave you? Now maybe you'd like to drill up a girl's skirt at the first opportunity. But forgive me if I'd want to get into her head and heart first."

"Suit yourself, pal," the roadie replies. "See how long Jack can keep up that 'higher mind' shit."

Jack's head sags, and he sighs his humiliation. But still he holds his tongue.

"All right, let's stop talking about this young lady as if she has a sell-by date," I say. "You think she has hang-ups? Let her have hang-ups. Give her a month—give her a year. If it means Jack gets to spend his evenings fully-clothed with a beautiful, intelligent girl like that, I still say he's the luckiest man at this table."

This seems to settle our embarrassing dispute. Silence reigns for a time as we stab at small morsels left on our plates. Finally, Tim pipes up: "Happy birthday to me!" He gets a chuckle and a pat on the back from Caleb. We go on from this point as if a happy birthday is all today has been.

⌘

She knocks on my motel room door after midnight. Seeing those wide eyes as I open the door, I am thankful that I'm still in jeans and my collared shirt, grateful that my laptop sits open with its screen half-full of fresh new type on the table at the foot of the bed.

"Hi," she says. She stands for a few seconds, looking at me without blinking. Those eyes. Her hair is pinned back so that the few locks that tumble from her untidy bun dangle at her shoulders. Her baggy green T-shirt ends halfway down her thighs, covering almost completely her knee-length, satin pajama shorts. Those brown eyes, staring.

"Wendy, come in," I say once my labored brain registers the chill of the night air on the walkway. "You must be freezing."

She replies with a little shake of her head that sets free another lock from her bun. Still fixed on my face, she steps in, and I shut the door behind her. When she breaks her stare, it is to step two paces past me and take a seat on the side of my bed. There she sits for a long moment, lips pursed, looking down at the floor. "Thank you," she says finally, more to the faded motel-room carpet than to me.

"For this afternoon? Forget it." I pull the chair from the desk and sit down.

"No, it meant a lot." Again at the floor, softer and slightly bitter, she adds,

"Jack didn't stick up for me." She crosses her legs, meets my gaze, and leans against her arm toward the foot of the bed. She is two feet away.

I feel myself straightening my back and planting both feet on the floor. "Well, you know how my poison pen scares Jack." I lean back. "Heaven forbid he might open his mouth and give me any insight."

She furrows her brow. Her lower lip begins to quiver. For a moment I think she is going to cry, until she bites the offending lip and holds it with her front teeth. She takes a deep breath, staring at her sandals. "The cot...Jack sleeps—well, he seemed to want it that way, too—I never told him...." As her voice floats away, she turns her face to me, and her eyes widen. "I never knew...." Her voice breaks; she sucks in a sob and closes her eyes.

I move to the foot of the bed, take up her hand, and sit down beside her. Forcing from my mind any thought of the warmth that radiates from her body, the faint remnant of the sweet jasmine scent that so intoxicates me, I look her square in the face. "Hey," I say. "Jack is a kid."

She's staring at me. Those sad, brown eyes. She lifts her hand, about to answer me, but lets it drop into her lap when the words fail to come. She casts her eyes down, gazes in silence at the carpet. Speechless myself, I bite my lip and listen to the sound of two people breathing.

A charge starts building in my core as I contemplate the soft contour of her cheekbone. At the same time, my mind starts following a peculiar train of thought. This feeling I have, an inner voice muses, it would take so little to tell it to her. Just a few short words, less than a single breath. And wouldn't those words make her feel better? Wouldn't we both feel better? And as the charge grows ever stronger, my musing gels into a certainty, and I feel my lungs fill with air. My mouth opens. She lifts her head. My breathing crests. Her eyes meet mine.

Those sad, sad, brown eyes. "He loves you."

At this the tears erupt. Burying her face in my chest, she begins softly sobbing. Though she must feel my heart hammer against her cheek, I speak evenly as though wholly unmoved. "He told you nothing happened," I surmise aloud. She nods into my shirt. "And you don't believe him," I say, "do you?"

The jag that clenches her hands and pulls a tiny cry from her mouth confirms my suspicion. And now I find my fatherly voice. "Well my dear, would you believe *me* if *I* told you the same story?" I let her cry a few more seconds, then give her verbatim the kid's airtight alibi, the one that has him cramped in the bench seat of a minivan under the eyes of a convenient witness on the night in question. Her face emerges from my shirt, awestruck. "And let me repeat," I conclude, "he loves you."

Her tears still flow in slender ribbons down her cheeks, but the sobbing has stopped. I reach down into my suitcase lying open on the floor by the chair. As I ferret around and pull out my handkerchief for her, I add some more fatherly wisdom. "You two take things at your own pace. He's a kid. He makes mistakes. But he knows he's found someone special. That'll grow him up nice and quick." My folksy character astonishes me.

She dabs away the tears and pinches at her nose with the handkerchief. "You think so?"

I let my soothing paternal gaze be my answer. "Now try not to wake him when you get back."

The girl leans in close again, squeezes both of my hands to set off my insides anew. Standing, she sets my handkerchief down on the nightstand. I rise and open the door for her. Before leaving, she stands on tiptoe and plants a soft, dry kiss on my cheek. I send her off with a wise, virtuous smile.

Back at my computer, I save and close the blog entry I've been composing. In its place I open a new document, and stare for a moment at the white screen. The charge is still buzzing somewhere behind my diaphragm, but I think I know how to quell it. It takes just a second to type those few words I meant to say, just another moment's pause to read them back to myself. With that the charge surges and dies away. Relieved, I close the document without saving, shut the computer, and collapse onto the bed.

⌘

June 11, 2003

Seattle is rainy and smells like fish. The gig here isn't until tomorrow, and I'm looking forward to an early night, but an anomaly occurs at check-in when the hotel clerk goes to authorize the credit card: she tries it three times, and thrice the terminal spits it back. I call the customer service number on the back of the card. A chirpy operator breaks to me what I have been dreading for some time: that we've maxed out.

It's no use calling Marty; nonetheless, call him I do, on the friendly young clerk's phone. And as I fully expect, the same robotic secretary asks me to try back tomorrow. I ask her, *demand* of her, to get an urgent message to him from Henry.

"Last name?"

"He knows who I am!" I take a breath and conclude: "With the band."

"And what band is that?"

I look up to see my face glowing crimson in a mirror on the far wall. After a second to compose myself, I dictate to her a two-word message for Marty: "Maxed out." I have little confidence he'll receive it.

My own credit card, pushed to the breaking point already by my phone use, might just about cover a single night's stay. Spike puts that unpleasant idea to rest. "You put your money in, you won't get it back." Without another word he takes my briefcase, opens it on the counter and retrieves the envelope that holds our per diem bundle. Shaking his head, he counts out two hundred and fifty dollars and slides the bills across the counter to the waiting clerk. He closes the envelope and wags it in the air. It flaps limply, thin and only slightly weighted. "That's three days' food gone. We're gonna crash and burn if Marty doesn't get his shit together."

"How's that golf cart of yours for gas right now?" asks the roadie as we cart our bags to our rooms.

"Down to about a quarter tank, as I recall." A nervous tension presses my chest.

"I can't fill up the van on that cash—we go a day or two more, even on what's in that envelope, and Marty don't come through? We'll never get back to L.A." We're climbing a flight of stairs to the second floor. Every word Spike utters is a weight that makes each step a little bit harder to clear.

Caleb leaps past us two steps at a time. He waits for us at the top, nostrils flaring. "You see what I mean about them?" he says. "They don't know what the fuck they're doing!"

"Hey," says Tim from two steps below me, "this is probably a temporary snag, right?" He looks up at Spike. "Maybe I can get in touch with my folks. My Dad's cool. He may front us a bit to sustain us, you know, till Marty clears things up."

"Fuck that." Spike stops beside Caleb at the top of the stairs and addresses all of us like he's rallying troops into a rout. "This tour's already pissed away a shitload of other people's money. Marty ain't gonna clear nothin' up. He can't even make it to his office to talk to his company's only asset." He spurs himself into motion again, heading down the hall. "Nope. Unless Marty pays his bills by tomorrow, the tour's off."

Only Tim makes a sound in reaction, breathing a soft "No" at the roadie's executive decision. The roadie shoves his keycard into his door, yanks it out again and throws the door open. He gives no further instruction.

Tim rubs his eyes; I see those imaginary lenses push up toward the sky. "Well, that was fun while it lasted!" And for once he says no more.

I can forgive his despondence. I, of course, have much to return home to. I will see my son, slip back into my regular routine, and begin the process of finding work, so that I can pay off the months of rent which Marty was supposed to cover. But as we head to our rooms, I feel wistful at the thought that this is the last night I will put in an hour of typing, the last time I will struggle to put down for posterity the details of a night's work.

The log of our pathetic exploits reads back in a repetitive canon; each entry follows a predictable arc. But together they recount a process of *doing*, and their very recounting is such a process, one which had for too long been absent from my life. If I never speak to Marty again, or if I am carted away for trying to tear him limb from limb, he might one day look on my words and find within their final paragraphs my equally deserved thanks for the gift, however tarnished, of *doing*.

Marty will not come through. Tomorrow we will turn tail and retreat homeward in defeat. I will ride with Tim. I doubt there'll be much conversation. We will let Tim's hero Gram serenade us, and I will long for Françoise. We will stop at a roadside inn for the night, and possibly empty our per diem envelope there. If we're short, I suspect that shortfall will go on my credit card. And on we'll go the next morning, listening to sad songs, nursing feelings of exhaustion, relief, and longing, watching the road signs count down the miles until we take the final exit and the wheels stop turning.

Middle Eight

Minutes after my suitcase landed in my apartment doorway, I stormed past a startled-looking receptionist and threw open Marty's office door. My timing wasn't quite as I had hoped it would be: Marty was on the phone, standing facing the side window, not shoveling powder up his nose. There was, however, a crumpled tissue on the desk, speckled with red and brown. At the click of the opening door he turned, and said into the phone, "Shit—I'll call you back," in a pinched nasal squeak.

We stood still, his eyes wide and nervous like those of a panicked horse, my stare cold and piercing. His lips moved, but no words came. At length I pointed at his desk. "I see your phone's working."

His pupils darted around, to the phone, to me, to the window. When his voice returned to him, he gushed like a burst dam. "Yeah, oh God, just today we got it back. How are you? Oh, it's been a nightmare! When did you get back? I've been trying to–"

"You haven't tried anything."

"But your cell was down!"

"You couldn't call the hotels?"

"*My* phone was down!"

"Most people have phones. If you have no friends, and I can see why you might not, even a payphone can reach Seattle."

His voice was rising, in pitch and volume. "I didn't have the names of the hotels! It's—it was—it's in my email—our internet was down, too!"

Letting my glare work him like a looming hot iron, I closed the door and sat in the chair in front of his desk. The stony silence sucked the air from the room. Marty tugged at his white collar, ran his hand through his greasy mane, and then let his fingers rest splayed across his lips. I watched him fumble.

He started a series of halting sighs, and then sucked in a long, hissing breath. "Tour's fucked." I raised my eyebrows in mock surprise, and he continued. "My funding's dried up."

"And the record?"

He groaned. "Record's *beyond* fucked. Fritz disappeared a month ago. He could be in jail—or dead—for all I know."

"Your investors figured out where the money was going?" I shot an obvious glance at the bloodied tissue on his desk.

His jaw dropped as he followed my line of sight. He looked at the floor, and his voice became a dismissive mumble. "I don't know what you're talking about."

"*I* do." The painful memory was by now playing in my mind, running parallel to the unfolding scene. Familiar lines, long dormant in my brain, came back to me ("The money's run out." "We did all we could." "It's not our fault!"), and brought acid to my tongue. "It was easier to take from strangers."

With a face like I had convicted him of murder, Marty fell into his chair. From there he stared at the wilting potted fern in the corner, sniffling, grimacing, shaking his head. "It's not—" he started, then winced anew, pitched himself forward and cupped his hands over his face. "How can you—?" his muffled voice started through his trembling palms.

Old, bitter feelings poisoned each word that I spoke. "Marty, I believe you started this project with honest intentions. My old friends at Dominion Pictures did, too. They got all the way up to buying me in before they got other ideas. And if you're anything like them, you have nothing to be afraid of."

His red-rimmed eyes peeked over his fingertips; I went on. "They never even saw the county jail, not for embezzlement, not for drug use." At this last he emitted a defensive squeal. "I understand they went on to fleece a good deal more innocents of their wealth, under a whole new name."

"Fleece?" His hands dropped to his desk. "I never fleeced—you think this was all a front?"

"Wasn't it?" I demanded. "Tour dates arranged like you threw darts at a map? No advance work?" I chuckled. "The heart of your operation, and it came across like an afterthought."

"That's not true!" he bellowed at me, so loudly it made me start. "That's not true," he repeated in a whisper. He became still; silence blanketed the room.

I sat upright, my glare softening. I slid my chair forward and put my elbows on the desk. "Marty," I began, rubbing my eyes, "what were you expecting these past few weeks?" My fingers dropped. Marty was staring, eyes glazed, at his computer screen. "Did you think I'd never find you again?"

Marty sniffed suddenly. He clamped his eyelids shut and rocked in his chair. A fatherly pity welled up in me and held my tongue. "It was never gonna work," he whimpered. "The scene, the clubs, it's all different, now." He pressed his knuckles against his temple, then stuck his finger out to wipe a tear from his eye. "It's all dead out there." He sniffed again. "I *needed* to take the...to...." His eyes bulged in horror for a split-second. He recovered with a doozy: "Why did this have to happen to me?"

"To *you*?" A wave of righteous anger carried me to my feet. Even at full height I am not large or imposing, but a menacing scowl can grow a man. Marty rolled his chair back and sat with his hands braced on the armrests. His face turned from sadness to fear. My sanity prevailed, though, and I was able through force of will to break from this toxic exchange and make for the door.

As I turned the knob, Marty cried out at my back, "Oh, Uncle H, I'm all fucked up!"

I was halfway out. I turned to look at the wretch and worked to find my proper feelings for this specimen: crook, user, liar, but before it all my godson, almost flesh and blood. I found no anger left, no hurt, and no pity worth holding onto. I found only a scrap of inexplicable love, and I seized it. Gazing at this mess of a man, wringing out the dregs of this flimsy love, I managed only two words for him: "Get unfucked."

I closed the door, gave a pitying look to the stunned secretary, and shuffled out, exhausted. When I passed by his window, the curtain was drawn.

⌘

A week later I was on the phone with my father, begging, for the first time in my life, for money. Three weeks after that, I was on hand at the old man's burial. The first event, I am told, had nothing to do with the second. "You couldn't kill someone by asking him for cash," my sister Ruth would say to me over the brim of her coffee cup, on the eve of the funeral. Across her kitchen table, I would reply that you could if that someone was Old Hank Barclay. And the same three scenes, each set so neatly a week from the last, would turn in my mind again.

The first: my father's voice growing soft, distant, like our phone connection was fading. "Five thousand?" For a moment I could hear only his slow, contemplative breathing. That very pause spoke to me. The strong, self-reliant figure of my memory, he who would have countered my request with a lecture on frugality, was somehow shackled and gagged by the years. "Have you spoken to your sister?" His voice grew smaller still. Five thousand dollars would have stirred him before. Now, all it had done was hurt him.

I answered that Ruth had her own money problems and that he was my last resort. "Oh," he replied, his morose voice shrinking further. "I see." I felt a strange guilt then, as though I should have hit him up years ago, when he could have used his anger at the appalling prospect and grown stronger by it. I was about to tell him to forget I'd said anything, but he spoke again. "Should I mail you a check?" My voice cracked when I replied that, yes, a check would be fine.

The second scene, as the first, a Friday: Ruth's voice, grim and foreboding. "Come home, Henry. Dad's had a stroke." And just like that, a chunk of the sum that my father had sent me that week, that hadn't yet cleared the bank, went right back out. Patrick and I were on a plane four days later, landing in Hartford on a muggy Tuesday afternoon.

Gray and tired in a yellowed blouse and jeans, Ruth greeted us with a wan smile as we rounded up our bags. Patrick, used to a cheery, matronly fussing from his aunt, took her into his arms and tried heroically to squeeze the grief out of her. And then we were off to Donington, the home my father had settled into for his 'widower-years' after Mom had died eight years ago—off to put the period on a life I once thought invincible.

The third, another Friday, his last: a burst of coherence after three days of rambling nonsense. "Henvy," he said through the precipitous droop on the left side of his mouth. "About de boy." Patrick, until then dozing in his chair, sat up and edged his seat closer to his grandfather's bed.

Dad moved to shake his head but managed only to tilt it from side to side. "What I said. About de boy. Fuggeddit." His head gradually slumped into his chest, his eyes following the droop of his face until he stared at his drab, turquoise bedsheet. "Please. Fuggeddit."

"I already have, Dad."

Patrick retreated, his face showing that slackness it acquires when he is tired, and turned to the television that had been silently screening endless reels of stern Iraqi and military faces while we kept our vigil.

Ruth arrived a few minutes later to take over the watch. Patrick and I took the elevator down to Dad's apartment. My boy collapsed on the fold-out bed in the living room. I fell asleep gazing from Dad's little single bed at a framed, sepia-toned photo of my mother. Seated on a wrought-iron patio chair, young Mom smiled timidly at Dad, doubtless the one behind the camera, and the one who had lain in this bed and bid her image goodnight every night for eight years.

At two the apartment buzzer sounded, and Ruth brought in the news: Dad's second stroke had been massive, and his death had been swift.

⌘

Those three stages of Dad's defeat paraded before me as I sat in Ruth's kitchen. That evening she brought out Dad's slide projector and ran a parade of her own by me. Setting it up in her living room, she proceeded to show Patrick and me a selection of slides she had culled from Dad's vast collection. "I started gathering these a few months ago, when I started to notice him slipping," she said. "I hoped it would be longer before they came into use."

The archaic whirr of the machine, the smell of ozone, the bits of dust that glowed as they floated into the contraption's intense beam, all of these coalesced into each other as Ruth pulled down the white screen. I began to perceive them as one thing, not the machine but an entity it sustained. I started to feel its presence—*his* presence.

The slides ran in chronological order, punctuated by the clicking and whirring of the machine as each slide leaped from the projection slot to be replaced by the next. A faded sepia photo of Dad as a toddler, dressed in girlish white and looking impossibly small on my grandmother's knee, was followed by a high school photo for which he wore a suit and tie. Then came a wedding picture, Dad dwarfing Mom and looking strangely solemn.

Click-Click!

Color splashed onto the screen for the first time, and it was Highland Lake, just a short drive from our house. Despite Dad's absence from the shot, I could feel him in the way it was arranged. The bathers in the water, all faceless and small, served only to give perspective to this grand work of nature. God's Art, he called it, and his photography labored to give it glory. The result was that Highland Lake, no pond to be sure but certainly no Lake Superior, became an ocean, the tree-filled land in the background a great continent rising from its far shore.

The slide's setting reminded me of the day before. Patrick had insisted that we make a detour along our post-mortem errand route and go over the Highland Lake spillway. This strip of road along the lake's edge was flooded much of the time six or eight inches deep with the lake's runoff. As a child, I looked on the splashing water as the family Buick forded this stream as if it were the parting of the Red Sea. Patrick had gotten a similar kick out of it well into adulthood. But whether it was from the low summertime water level or the fact that it was never much to look at through adult eyes, the stream seemed a trickle when we tried it this time. The car made only a light splash, and I caught in his eye a glimmer of disappointment.

Click-Click!

Ruth and I joined Mom and Dad for the next picture: Summer of 1949. Gathered at the observation deck at the summit of Mount Washington, Mom, Ruth, and I huddled together; we had climbed rather than driven to the top, woefully underdressed for the cold we would encounter at the peak. But while we hunched into each other and hugged ourselves for warmth,

Dad stood triumphant, enormous even as he stooped to put both hands on my shoulders. And as with all the old man's outdoor shots, God's Art threatened to engulf us from behind. Visibility was exceptional on that day; endless waves of forested hills—all of New England, it appeared—filled the background, threatening to burst out of the top and sides of the screen.

Click-Click!

A twinge of unease pinched at my heart. Here was Dad in his Sunday clothes, his black hair thinning and streaked with white, in the autumn yellow and burgundy of our backyard. The trees seemed to squeeze into the foreground and crowd into him from beyond a picket fence that boxed him into a virtual pen. The blink of the screen came as a relief.

Click-Click!

Worse, a view of our dining room, the modest chandelier making a downward arrow from the top of the frame, looming over a cake with 'Happy 75th Dad' scrawled in icing between the candles. Mom and Ruth crowded in from the left. Patrick, watching the screen on the couch beside me, bounced in his seat and pointed to the right. There was my boy in shirt and tie, on the cusp of adulthood but beaming like a schoolboy. Behind him on-screen, I stood facing away with my right side cropped out. Dad was the only one sitting, looking colorless, hemmed in and already diminished in stature, bemused behind horn-rimmed glasses. My unease rushed back to squeeze my heart further. It gave ground to wistfulness when it occurred to me that my Cherie must have taken the snapshot.

Click-Click!

Now Dad sat alone in the frame, in a navy blue suit and cherry tie, looking stately as always but grizzled and white and somehow compressed in an armchair in his Donington apartment. The walls and ceiling glowed light blue in the camera's flash, pushing in on the room from three sides and making it appear as a little box. For all this encroachment around him, though, the old man in all his dignified power struggled to take up any of the space left to him.

Click-Click!

A brief flash of pure white projector light filled the screen before Ruth flicked a switch. The light went out and the buzz of the projector wound down. We sat for a moment in black, numbing silence.

Patrick stirred first, switching on the lamp beside him and asking Ruth, "Can I do the machine? Tomorrow?"

Ruth smiled her assent and turned to me. "What do you think?" Taking my thoughtful nod as my answer, she went on. "A friend of mine offered to put this all on some software, for some new-fangled computer projector." She looked into her lap, then patted the projector like an old friend. "I told her no. Dad would want it this way." I nodded but stayed mute.

"But then she said she could do text on-screen. I'd thought to end with a sort of epitaph—you know, 'Henry Barclay, Sr., 1912 to 2003', and then adding 'Lucky Man'."

Patrick gave a verdict of "That's nice." Still I did not speak.

"I thought, you know, ninety-one years. He was so terrified of dying. All those doctor's visits. And then to live so long, and not really have to be *all there*," she tapped at her forehead, "when the end was near."

I found my voice. "It's better this way," I said, and sighed.

She nodded at first, casting a glance at the projector. But then she stopped and looked me in the face. "But it *is* true, don't you think?"

"Yes it is," I answered. After another pause, three seconds of even more horrifying stillness, I added, pointing at the machine, "I like it better without."

They buried Dad in Winsted. The service was simple. The reverend, an old friend of Dad's, gave a heartfelt tribute to his "indomitable spirit" and "love of life." We sat amid a sea of white with splashes of silver. Though the numbers that had come filled out the room fairly nicely, my mind flirted with a juvenile thought: that the old man's draw would have been better if we'd put up posters.

My boy worked the projector with aplomb during Ruth's slideshow, advancing the slides on her cues over a soundtrack of Pachelbel's 'Canon in D'. The last picture hung on the screen until the musical passage wound to its conclusion. Dad's spirit vanished as she flipped the projector switch and the fan motor's hum faded away. His body, in a sleek black coffin, vanished under falling soil next to Mom within the hour.

It was as the last square inch of shiny black disappeared under earthy brown that, for the first time since Ruth had knocked on Dad's apartment door three days before, a tear escaped my eye. That night I sat at the edge of my folded-out bed in Ruth's office-cum-spare bedroom, and let another drop go as I stared for a small eternity at an old photo on her desk. Mom, Dad, Ruth and myself grinned back at me from the living room of my long-ago youth, and I felt small and old and utterly powerless against Time.

The following morning we piled back into Ruth's Corolla and headed once more to Donington. Ruth was making arrangements to get a moving truck to bring Dad's effects to a storage space in Winsted. We agreed that, for the day I had left in town, I could make myself useful by driving Dad's car back to Ruth's house. Once we had filled Ruth's trunk with small pieces from the apartment, I saw her and Patrick off at the gate. On my own, I ambled over to the apartment's covered garage and sank into the front seat of Dad's sky-blue Buick. Viewing the dashboard from the driver's side, I felt like an impostor.

I took the car over the river into West Hartford to get an estimate on it from a dealer there. I left with a paltry offer on a slip of paper. Sitting in the driver's seat before pulling out of the lot, I opened my briefcase to file the offer away. Robert E. Lee, looking noble, serious, and magazine-glossy, greeted me from atop a pile of my papers. The name printed on the magazine's bottom corner jogged my memory: 'John P. Hackett'. I closed the briefcase quickly, to dam back any recollections and feelings this memento might unleash.

I headed back over the bridge in search of the exit to Route 44, which would take me back to Winsted and matters important to the present day. But a sign over the empty right lane caught my eye and changed everything. '91 NORTH', it read. I didn't need to read the city name, 'Springfield', below it. I knew what lay beyond Springfield.

Suddenly as I cruised in the center-right lane, the dotted line that started streaking by on the passenger side bisected the world. I glanced down at my briefcase lying on the passenger seat. The corner of the magazine poked out on one side of the case; it glowed at the edge of my vision. The car inched to the right, and now I was hurtling toward the divider.

A surge of electricity rose in my chest. With a single thump of my heart in my throat, I found myself arcing right with the ramp to the I-91. The drab Hartford skyline that should have been gliding by on my left began retreating in my rear-view mirror. And with the river on my right, I felt suddenly like Huckleberry Finn hopping a raft and hightailing it down the Mississippi.

The sun pooled its rays through a gap in the gray-white cloud cover, shining down on the point where the Interstate reached the horizon. Over the next hour the hills around me grew to verdant mountains, the clouds grew light and parted, and God's Art opened itself up like a great pop-up book with the road ahead as its spine.

"Ruth, I just remembered something I have to do before we leave tomorrow," I told my sister's answering machine from a rest-stop payphone two hours later. And then I was back in the Buick.

The sun soared overhead, glinting off road signs and car windshields. I had to squint at times to mute its brilliance. Green signs flashed the names of nearby cities at me: White River Junction, St. Johnsbury, Newport. Twenty miles from the Canadian border I turned off the freeway and found a gas station.

"Marston?" The attendant crushed the *r* between his teeth when I asked about the town. "Well, you're just about *in* Marston. Just up the road there, you'll hit the Menard Market. That's really your center of town."

"And how about South Marston Road?"

His hand cut through the air like a slow-motion karate chop. "Down to the library—" he jerked his thumb, "—make a right. A mile down, at the lake, you're on South Marston."

A vague plan had been forming in my head as I drove up from Hartford. Pulling up to the shoulder of South Marston Road, I flipped open my briefcase to double-check the address on the magazine tag with the number on the great gray lake-house before me. This was it, 1359A, a two-story job with aluminum siding above a stone front, skirted on the side by a grand wooden deck. In my briefcase were my clipboard, some pens and an extra copy, blank, of the form for Dad's death certificate. I grabbed the form and slotted it into the clipboard. Then I carefully peeled the address off the magazine cover and clipped it over the top of the form. The little clip just covered the words 'Certificate of Death'. I pulled out a pen and stuck it behind my ear to complete the charade.

I strode up the driveway, past a dusty Ford wagon, my heart pounding in time with my footsteps. I rang the bell, and as I waited for an answer I looked down at myself. A pang of panic hit me when I noticed that my fly was open. There was a click, and the door flew open before I could reach down to zip up.

For a heartbeat, my panic at my open fly gripped me so that I could not bring myself to zip up. More startling was the sight of the man who greeted me with a questioning smile. His hair was thin and graying, smile lines dug deep around his mouth, and crow's feet grabbed at the corners of his eyes, which were magnified by large, frameless bifocals. But even trim and combed down in a side part, his hair would not sit still, and rose in a little tousle at the top. And his small, thin nose seemed to point down at his obtuse lips. "Hi there," he said when it became clear to him that I wouldn't speak first. His voice was light and reedy like an oboe. "What you doin'?"

I pushed the thought of my gaping fly to the back of my mind. "How are ya?" I waved my clipboard around, pointing at the seal in the top-left corner and tapping the tag with his name on it before tucking the thing tightly under my arm. "My name's Henry. I'm with the Census Follow-up." I pulled the clipboard out again, and read off the tag in a bureaucratic tone. "John Hackett?"

"Yup." His mouth clung stubbornly to his smile, but his right eyebrow rose. "Census Follow-up?"

"You remember last census," I said. "We all know about that one. This here—" I flashed the form on the clipboard again and then pressed it back against my ribcage, "—is a follow-up questionnaire. Your name was randomly selected for a more in-depth demographic study."

His eyebrow was still arched; his hand, at his side since he'd opened the door, moved back to grip the doorknob. My throat tightened, but I pressed ahead. "Various branches of the federal government will use your answers to better adapt to the changing dynamics of the population."

"Uh-huh." His tone was flat, his smile gone. His hand stayed on the doorknob while he screwed his face into a contemplative knot. With great effort I held my eyes level at him, maintaining a friendly grin. After a moment's thought, he looked me from head to toe as if sizing me up. Then he lifted his hand from the knob and pointed at my pants. "Heh. You're flying low."

I looked down, and the words came to me like a divine gift. "Jeezum Crow!" John Hackett wheezed a chuckle as I zipped up.

With that, the door swung wide open. "Sounds like you'll be awhile," he said. "May as well come in for it."

The elder Hackett led me through a small foyer into a large and airy living room. Giant windows let in the sunlight and a panoramic view of the lake. Forested foothills rose from the far shore, dotted with small, rustic cottages. "Have a seat." He motioned at a plush armchair that faced a long couch and a little potbellied stove.

As I sank into the armchair my eye settled on a framed photo on the table beside me. A firecracker burst in my gut. "Your son?" I tried to cover my apprehension by coughing the words out.

"That's Jackie, yes," a woman's voice answered me. Tall, slim and striking, she glided into the room with a dainty step that cried out for an evening gown rather than the sleeveless top and denim skirt she wore. Giving me a slow once-over, she asked her husband, "Who's our guest, dear?"

That photograph.

"This gentleman's from the Census Bureau," Mr. Hackett told her. They moved to the couch and perched themselves side by side on the edge of the seat.

The kid is younger in the shot — perhaps sixteen—but already his spirit has etched itself deep into his face. His hair is an epic mess, obviously an intentional flourish to compliment the blotches of black ash that stain his cheeks and chin.

"Seems we've hit a jackpot of sorts," Hackett went on to his wife. "Henry here—that is your name, right?"

"Yes. Henry."

"Henry. Henry here needs to ask us some more questions. We're like a snapshot of the American People, is that about right, Henry?" I wished the man would stop repeating my name.

His costume is a filthy-looking brown tunic, with a piece of rope tied around his waist for a belt. His body faces the left side of the frame, as he hunches over a booklet of some sort, which he holds in both hands. But that ruddy face is turned toward us; he's peering over his shoulder at something behind him.

I nodded yes to Mr. Hackett's assessment. "I'll be just a few minutes. A lot of these are repeat questions from the questionnaire three years ago. Forgive me, that's just the way the government works." I feigned reading from my clipboard. "Now, as of the year two thousand, I have two residents at this address." I looked up at them. "That's you two?"

Mrs. Hackett gave a nod, slow and regal. I made a check-mark on the margin of the form. "But you only lived here for..." I trailed off, and felt sucked right back into speaking by an unexpected silence. "I mean, there's no listing of this address in the 'ninety survey." I was taking a chance; the structure and décor looked so uniformly new, and the A-address seemed to reinforce the idea.

Mr. Hackett gave an encouraging "Yup."

I scribbled a line across 'Name of Deceased'. "And you come from...?"

He gave a confused frown. "You mean before here? Or where we were..." Before I could decide for myself which I wanted to mean, he volunteered, "We *were* in Middlebury. I taught history at the college. That was till ninety-nine. I'm *from* just up 'round Newport."

"I see." I scrawled 'Middlebury' in another box, and 'Newport' in the next.

I only had to look at Mrs. Hackett, and she spoke. "I'm from Providence." 'Mom, Providence, RI' overflowed from a box marked 'Date of Birth'.

"Now, to education." Why not? "What's your level of schooling?"

"Doctorate in American history," was Mr. Hackett's reply.

"I have a bachelor's degree," said his wife.

What would come next? "Ethnicity?" There was the faintest twitch in the wife's brow. I added quickly, "You can decline to state if you want to."

"What are we now?" he asked. "White? European American? Pigment deficient?" The face of his son leaped out at me when he gave a crooked smile.

"And religion?"

"You got a 'Decline to State' for that one?" He furrowed his brow, but held the wily smirk. As I nodded and jotted, he added, "'Cause I'm inclined to doubt about a Man Upstairs, but all these great men I owe my living to—" he made a sweeping motion at the tall bookcase behind him; my eye caught the names in bold text on the spines: Washington, Jefferson, Lincoln, King, "—they're just about unanimous on the subject." He shook his head. "Jeezum. Won't go on record against a roster like that."

"And, uh, political affiliation?"

"Decline," said Mrs. Hackett.

"You know this part of the state," Mr. Hackett said. "Ollie LaDuke, down the road, boy, I tell ya, in 2000 he called me a communist for votin' Gore. These days, I'm a terrorist for Dean."

"And you had one child in Middlebury." I pointed to the photo and was drawn to it again.

There, in his right hand, is a pen. He's writing in the book—or rather, *on* it. He's *signing* a program.

"Yup." Mr. Hackett motioned at the picture himself. "That's Jackie in high school. John Preston Hackett III, if you need to write it down."

And he's not hunched over. That's an illusion. Behind his shoulders rests a giant hump.

"Hunchback of Noter-Dayme," continued Hackett. "That's him in costume."

What is he looking at? The right side of the frame is a blur.

"That boy." Mrs. Hackett was shaking her head. "He never lets us take pictures. The only way to get a photo is for John to sneak up on him."

It's a whirl of white. He's intent on a whirl of white. And he's sucking in his lower lip on one side, biting it. His eyes are pleading and sad.

"So your boy moved out before you came here?" I backed off the photo.

"Moved out to college in ninety-nine."

"Outside the State of Vermont?" I felt a tug on my eyes from the side table.

"Got into NYU."

There's something extended out of the white blur, obscured outside the range of the flash. It's long, slender, tan—an arm. A girl's arm. Holding something. A circle of little discs reflects the flash's light. A tambourine.

"New...York...N...Y." I scribbled across another blank field. "So, child in New York State—"

"Oh, no." Of course Mrs. Hackett would interrupt me. "He left college —dropped out." Her eyes cast down for only a moment. "He moved to California last year."

Mr. Hackett chuckled. "Boy, I tell ya. I love that boy to death, but he can't finish a damn thing." His laughter doubled. "'Less it's a girl involved. Then he'll give it all the time in the world."

He's looking back at a girl with a tambourine. Someone is getting his autograph. His sad eyes are pleading for a girl with a tambourine.

"A lothario, huh?" I gave a short laugh of my own. "Sounds like *my* son." A lie of course, but a small one, all things considered.

It was Mrs. Hackett's turn to giggle. "Not quite. He's a bit awkward, poor dear."

Mr. Hackett nodded. "It's pining he's got a knack for."

Pining. Pining eyes stare forlornly at the girl with the tambourine.

"So for his migration pattern, I put..." My pen began to scratch almost randomly at the page. "...New York...to...California...."

Mrs. Hackett repeated, "California." She glanced again at the photograph. "Off after some Esmeralda, I'll bet."

Pining. His eyes pull at this young lady with all their might, but she remains a blur at the side of the frame.

"Oh my. We've jumped ahead. Mr. Hackett, you said your occupation was a professor?"

"Yup."

"And Mrs. Hackett?"

She brought her fingertips to her chin and shook her head. "What do the forms say these days? Homemaker? Carer? I suppose housewife is terribly out of fashion."

He is not a great actor. But as Quasimodo he has dazzled. A kid is getting his autograph, certain it will be worth something someday.

"I'd put down 'Mother'. Ain't that right, Sue?"

"Mother'll do," I said, and wrote the word in the margin. "A noble profession."

And he cares not a lick. How sad for young John Preston 'Jackie' Hackett, that *his* eyes plead for *her*, and not vice versa.

"Although," Mrs. Hackett was reticent about letting a technicality slide, far less so about exploding my concept of the kid's psychology, "I'm not sure it's a valid term, since he's not *my* son."

I flipped the sheet over the top of the clipboard, holding it down tightly so that it wouldn't float back up and give any glimpse of my fraud. I clamped my face down just as hard, into a look of benign interest. "Oh," I blurted. "I have to fill out a different box for that." I felt suddenly warm. "Mr. Hackett, I assume he is *your* son."

"Yup." The man had every right to refuse to answer. He had every reason to be suspicious. But on he went. "Had Jackie with my first wife."

"And she..." My face was a wall of bland friendliness, holding back a rising wave of shame. I hoped, against myself, that he would put up a hand to stop me.

He chose to aid and abet. "Some folks can't admit they're not made for children." His lip curled up on one side, and I saw the kid in him anew. "Give that woman credit for one thing: she admitted it."

Poor John Preston Hackett, playing Quasimodo and nailing the part.

"John." The stepmother's voice tried to rein the man in with that one syllable. With a few quick glances in too-rapid succession, I searched her face for the suspicion I knew must be festering. John Hackett would not be reined in, though, and beyond that one word, she held her peace.

"When your Illinois or Ohio counterparts track her down, you tell 'em to give her my best." The elder Hackett's half smile could have cut through steel.

I scribbled some more. "Divorced, then? What year?"

"Ninety-three."

"Remarried? When?"

"Ninety-six."

Pity Jackie Hackett. Bleeding from his adolescent heart, and they call it acting.

The man was silent. I looked back over at his wife. She sat there, prim and elegant, with something still resembling a smile on her face. Her eyes seemed friendly enough. Nonetheless, nervousness grew into outright fear inside of me. Those friendly eyes were on my clipboard.

"Mr. and Mrs. Hackett, I've gotten what I needed."

⌘

Settled in West Hollywood again, I eased back into a familiar routine. I paid my regular visits to Patrick's group home. We went to movies, or watched baseball on television. With the last out of any game, the remote would be in my hand, and the TV would go dark before local newscasters could edge in with the latest on California's brewing recall election. I began the task, now unavoidable, of dusting off my résumé and looking for work. I ran most mornings.

For Patrick's thirty-fifth birthday we drove up to Malibu. "Tim emailed me!" he gushed at me as we ate take-out fish and chips on the beach. "Things are happening!" I didn't bother to ask what those things were.

A week later, I came home one afternoon to a message on my answering machine: "Uncle H, it's me. Call me right away." Marty gave a new number that I didn't write down.

Time passed. I zeroed in on work as a telemarketer for a limousine service. I anticipated holding that job for the two years it would take the lawyers back East to extricate my inheritance from the labyrinth of Connecticut law. And between phone calls to businesses across the Southland, I allowed myself a healthy measure of self-pity.

I don't know how long Marty waited after his phone message before seeking me out in person. An L.A. summer gives no markers to measure the passage of time. Whatever the date, he hit me in the morning, calling out "Uncle H!" as my sneakers hit the sidewalk and the building's steel front gate clicked shut.

"Hello, Marty." I barely looked at him before my legs started pumping.

In motion, I thanked myself for having done my stretches inside. But hardly twenty paces in, he was at my side and matching me step for step.

"You've spoken to Patrick?" he huffed.

"I have," I replied, and turned left on the corner at the end of the block. At my right, on the outside track, Marty had to lunge forward a few steps to keep up with me.

"He's told you?"

"There's a new tour, I hear." I floated over a familiar square of sidewalk that a tree root had pushed up. Marty stumbled over it and had to hustle again to get back in step.

"New tour, and bigger." He was starting to pant. "And I'm off the stuff." I looked at our feet slapping the sidewalk. Marty was wearing bright, shiny sneakers.

"Well, congratulations," I allowed him, "if it's true."

"It is." The slapping of his sneakers grew louder as he flagged. "Listen." He started making a soft "hoo!" sound with each breath. "Come up to my new—hoo!—office. Hoo! Things are better—hoo!—you'll see. Hoo! And you'll want in. Hoo!"

"Why would I want in?" I started to pant as well; I was turning my usual morning jog into a sprint.

"You've worked hard," he gasped. "You deserve—hoo!—a piece—" He gulped and let his sentence end there.

A stitch began to dig into my right side. We jogged on for a while, exchanging only puffing breaths as we gathered sweat. I leaned in an awkward arc away from my stitch and lumbered more than jogged. Two blocks later, Marty folded. "I gotta...you go...call me!" He slapped a damp business card into my palm and fell away from my side.

I sped up despite the stabbing in my abdomen and rounded the next corner without looking back. I ran halfway down that block before I stopped for a breather. As I panted I examined Marty's card. '*Farley Management*'. It looked professional enough. I resolved to do him the courtesy of a visit in the next few days. Then I limped home; the bastard had gotten me off to a bad start, and I'm not the type who can recover.

⌘

"I had to ditch the last location," Marty told me as I sank into the cushy leather couch. "I would've been evicted soon, anyway." At four ornate desks before me, three of Marty's new colleagues typed at sleek black computer keyboards. Marty leaned over me on the arm of the couch. "This all happened just in time."

Speaking in a hushed tone, he laid out what had happened, how the Flak Jackets had landed a better deal, the massive organization that was now behind them, and how he'd used that to parley his way into his new position here at Farley. Though his narrative was impressive, his murmuring was modest. "You sound like your father," I quipped when he had brought me up to date. "It suits you."

"I'll tell you what else suits me," he replied. "Sobriety." He straightened up. Looking out the wide office window onto the Melrose Avenue sidewalk, he broke into a grin. "I owe this whole fresh start to you. I flushed everything I had on me after you left last time. I haven't touched a thing since." He turned to me, and his smile curled up further. "I got unfucked."

Suddenly he leaped to his feet. "And now I can welcome you back to the tour! I've read through the blog entries you sent me. They're fucking great! They really capture the feel of the tour!"

"They must make depressing reading."

"That's just it! You've got the angst, the struggling, the defeat, down! Now you can record the triumph, the success. You'll set down their victory lap." He paused for me to respond; I let the clatter of keyboards fill the space. "Uncle H." He used his trump card. "You need this, if only for a paycheck."

"Oh, no," I protested. "You're wrong there. I've joined the workforce."

He frowned. "Who you writing for?"

"I am a man of many talents."

His smile returned, an incredulous smirk. "What are you, a greeter at Wal-mart?"

Cornered, I drew my pity card. "My father died last month."

The smirk melted away. "I'm sorry. You went back to Winsted? How's Patrick?"

"Patrick's fine." I steered him into talk about the town, telling him which stores had appeared and disappeared from Main Street since he'd last been there. He inquired about old friends of his father.

And then suddenly he was back on form. "Wendy's going with them again." His tone of voice was a wink and a nudge in itself. "She's asked about you a couple times." His eyes narrowed on me. "Uncle H, everyone—the record company, the people in this office, Da Capo Press..." He put special emphasis on that one. "Everyone is excited about giving you the scoop on the biggest rock 'n' roll story of the decade." He lowered his voice. "And it'll pay. Better'n a busboy's job, whatever you got. Ten times what I offered you in spring."

Weariness crept into my bones. "Let me think about it." And I got up to leave.

His face glowed, but he humbled himself. "Tour starts September first.

We would be thrilled and honored to welcome you back."

My hand was on the doorknob. "We'll see what happens." And I drove home to give a week's thought to the offer. But each moment's cogitation seemed a waste. I knew the answer already.

Chorus

September 1, 2003

Whether by Marty's flair for the dramatic or by his new employers' sense of economy, a stretch limousine arrives at my door around sunrise this Labor Day to take me, along with the resurrected Flak Jackets, to Long Beach Airport. I join the others in a row facing an empty bar. They've piled the backseat high with guitar cases; Tim's enormous bass drum is wedged in the well, pushing his legs into Joe's beside him.

"Couldn't fit everything in the trunk," Tim tells me, nudging Joe over to make space for me between them. "It may be a limo, but the trunk's like a sedan's. This driver's a great packer though! How are you, by the way?"

I'm fine. My muscles ache at the thought of the grind ahead, but my heart warms at the sight of them—of the kid and his girl, sitting side by side between Joe and Caleb. She holds his hand in her lap. They nod at me in greeting, he with his wicked, impenetrable smirk, she with her radiant smile. He's dressed better, buttoned into a short-sleeved, collared shirt, his jeans no longer threadbare at the knees. His hair is trimmed a bit, though it still misbehaves, leaping up in the same tuft atop his head. Sideburns have crawled halfway to his earlobes.

The girl is better turned out as well. Her standard white-blouse top is now a shimmering satin, embroidered with sequins. Her navy skirt hugs her thighs and ends neatly over her knees. Her hair is pulled back at the top, where it sits in a little bun over the torrent of auburn that flows down past her shoulders, somehow fuller and more lustrous than the work of art I remember.

"Who'da thought, last time we saw you, that we'd meet again in a limo?" bubbles Tim.

"They could've stocked the bar," says Caleb, scanning the rows of empty glasses and the tub that could have held champagne on ice.

"At six in the morning?"

"What, you went to sleep last night?" Caleb retorts.

Tim pushes back the bangs that have grown past his eyebrows. "Anyway, it just goes to show, you never know what's in store."

"Wouldn't it be nice? Jack? Joe? To sit back with a cool drink and watch the freeway roll by sideways?"

"I mean, an opening slot for the Torinos reunion is a pretty big deal." With nobody else giving any sign of listening, except for Wendy's faint smile, Tim lowers his voice and directs his speech at me. "It's not the Rolling Stones, but the T-nos were pretty big in their day."

And who among them was it, I ask, that caught our show in Stockton and was moved to track the Flak Jackets down?

"Enrique Love, their guitar player—that's just his stage name. He said we can call him Nick." He smiles. "It's funny," he says. "None of us can remember the Stockton show. But Nick said Jack was wild—like an animal. Was that the show where Jack was swinging off the lighting rig?" I confess that I don't know. "Well, anyway," he continues, "he passed our name along to their people, and now, here we are."

Here we are. The limo swings onto the 405 on-ramp and picks up speed. The smell of air freshener begins to turn my stomach. Tim raises his voice to overcome the freeway's roar. "So, I've been hearing from your son."

"Have you." The Fan and his pen pals.

"We all have." He laughs. "Well, all but one. Henry's son doesn't write to you, does he, Joe?"

Joe gives one of his friendly shrugs. "I don't do the email."

"I think Jack gets the most," says Tim. "Isn't that right, Jack? From Patrick? Don't you get an email from him just about every day?" The kid nods. Tim elaborates. "He just sends us well wishes. Likes to tell us we're Number One. He was real happy when I emailed him that we were back in business. Sent me a long reply, all caps: '*YIPPEE!*' E's for, like, twenty lines, and then about a hundred exclamation points." That's my boy.

We're unloading the limo at the drop-off point at Long Beach Airport when I see two more familiar faces. Fifteen feet up the curb from us, Spike and Marty heave heavy-duty equipment cases from the back of an SUV and lay them on a porter's cart. Marty hefts a case quickly with his head bowed. When the roadie points at an empty space on the cart, he shoots over and deposits the case with the concentration of a beaver plugging a dam. I wait for someone else to call out to them; I'm enjoying the scene too much to interrupt it myself.

"Hey, motherfucker!" Caleb calls to Spike.

The roadie looks up. His eyebrows clench over his black sunglasses; this action alone serves as his greeting. Two more cases pile onto his cart, and he dismisses Marty. He turns, throws his weight behind the thing and wheels it past us to the terminal entrance, counting the cases on it as he does. He breaks his stride long enough only to twitch his lip at us before disappearing behind the glare on the sliding glass doors.

"Hard at work already," quips Tim. "A credit to the firm!"

"Boys." Marty has closed the back of his hulking vehicle and made his way over to us. The swagger has returned to his step. "I'm proud of you. You've earned this tour."

Caleb cuts him off. "You gave us this speech already, Mart. Remember backstage at the T-nos show?"

Marty gives him a wink. "I repeat it for emphasis. You go back East and you knock 'em dead! You steal every show you've got with the Torinos, and each side date you've got on your own, you play like it's your last on this Earth. When you come back and do the live record in November, there'll be such a buzz behind it you'll hit the top without breaking a sweat." He points his finger like a pistol at the band members. "Number One!" And he winks again.

"Oh, so he's sending *you* emails too?"

Caleb's crack will not dampen Marty's mood. With handshakes all around, he sends the band off. As they cart their bags through the terminal entrance, he drops the arrogant lines from his face and pulls me into a bear hug. "This is it, Uncle H." His words are muffled against my shoulder.

⌘

The flight is a six-hour slog. Dark blue leather seats with flashy consoles that play cable television can't quite distract from the fact that we get no in-flight meal. Still, an airplane ride speaks far better of success than a Kia Sephia. Beside my aisle seat, Joe listens through earphones to CD after CD. Over in the window seat, Tim divides his attention between his paperback and the cloud formations below us. Ahead of me, Spike and Caleb exchange banter across the aisle. The high seatbacks in front of my knees block any view of Jack and Wendy. I steal glimpses of them as I stand to go to the toilet. Each glance offers the same picture: two young people leaning into each other, arms entwined and fingers interlocked on the armrest between them. I make a couple of bathroom trips on an empty bladder.

⌘

"What a shithole!" Half an hour after checking into our hotel, Caleb is complaining to Spike beside the brochure rack at reception. Oddly, he's smiling. "We coulda stayed at the Chelsea!"

"The Chelsea's a shithole!" snaps the roadie. "That's the fuckin' shithole to end all shitholes!"

"Okay, but it's still got history. Sid and Nancy, and all that."

Tim bounces into the room, into the conversation. "And Bob Dylan, and Leonard Cohen. Dylan Thomas, too."

Spike jams a Big Apple Tours brochure he's been toying with back into its slot. "Yeah, and when we get to Virginia we'll stay in a fuckin' log cabin—I hear George Washington slept there! Listen. Marty don't run the show no more—and shit, it's a good thing! This ain't some family vacation. This tour has to make money. You fucks work your asses off for long enough, things'll start to pay off, you can come back and fuckin' *live* at the Chelsea."

Joe, Jack and Wendy aren't much longer in coming. Together we set out on foot to find someplace to fill our empty stomachs. Jack walks a few feet behind his bandmates, his arm around Wendy's waist. Tim's legs stagger forward without guidance from his head. His eyes swing like a compass needle pulled on by a thousand magnets. Twice he bumps into Joe, who is doing his share of looking but takes more care to pick out his path. When he tries to be sensible and sets himself apart from our roving posse, he finds himself walking into a lamppost instead.

When a red neon hand blocks our way, we turn down 16th Street, stopping halfway up the block to let Spike read a menu in a restaurant doorway. "Huh," he grunts. "Bit pricey, but we could use a solid meal to cover the lunch we missed." Why, I ask, does the normally all-knowing roadie have to look around for a spot to eat? He growls. "Half of Manhattan is gone!"

Back outside an hour later, the light is fast fading from the narrow column of sky overhead. I am ready to put my head down with the sun, but the boys are loath to waste any of their precious time here on sleep. While I turn to follow Spike to the right in the direction of the hotel ("Tomorrow's a big workday for me. Gotta rest up," says the roadie), the band and Wendy go left, toward Union Square, aiming ultimately for St. Marks Place. I look back at them until they round the corner.

Spike turns indignant. "What the fuck happened to this city?"

"I don't follow," I confess after enduring his expectant stare.

"It's so fuckin' clean! Spotless!" He points to a curbside where the Henry Barclay of 1975 would expect to see heaps of trash, where now stands a lone trashcan. The scene is hardly spotless. Flattened wads of gum dot the sidewalk, and the gauze of New York City grit covers every surface. But the change from all-out cesspool is marked, and I must sheepishly admit that I like it.

"What are you, a fuckin' Republican?" He turns on me like I've declared my fealty to Mussolini. "That Giuliani killed this city. Sold it up the river to

Walt fuckin' Disney! Fucks with the numbers to say he's brought the crime rate down, then opens the doors to all the assholes who wanna turn the place into a damn country club! And Bloomberg's no better!" He spits on the sidewalk, a loud, phlegmy ball that leaves a grimy spatter on the cement. "Gotta put some of the slime back in her, man." He empties his mouth again. "Just doin' my part."

⌘

September 2, 2003

There is some comfort in going to sleep with the sound of traffic below my window and to waking up to hear it unchanged. The city rolls on, a mighty river with a million currents pulling this way and that. I feel lifting from my shoulders a certain weight: whereas elsewhere I must be an agent of action, here I feel I might just place myself on the sidewalk and let one of the scores of currents take me, to be turned around, knocked down, flipped over and towed under by every eddy that I pass.

It's a day for me to do exactly that, for while Spike takes care of our van and equipment rental, while the band book a rehearsal space on Thirtieth Street to make sure their chops have followed them to the East Coast, I have no assignment. I stroll out the front door in my usual jogging attire, with the vague idea of running up Seventh Avenue and into Central Park. But as the soles of my sneakers start beating the sidewalk, the city's currents turn me sideways. At each corner, the northward light is red. Not wanting to stop, at each Don't Walk signal I follow the green light to the east. I have it in mind to double back if the lights carry me past Fifth Avenue before I reach Central Park South, and to enter the park across from the Plaza Hotel. But at the corner of Fifth and Fifty-Seventh Street, crossing to the southeast side, I ignore the change in signals that opens the path up the avenue. I opt instead to continue dodging between oncoming pedestrians and the curbside. Another destination becomes apparent.

I'm soon at Sixty-First and Lexington. Up the avenue I go, and inhale deeply the smell of flowers and produce outside a corner deli. My airway starts to burn as I hustle up Sixty-Fifth, and my footfalls slow as Third Avenue comes into view. I am reduced to walking, staggering slightly, when beneath my feet Third Avenue rises toward Sixty-Sixth—yes, that's right, my feet do remember an uphill climb here. Just another block.

With each step down Sixty-Sixth, past one, two, three apartment building entrances, the years strip away like layers of skin, until I reach the old front step. Here I am, as near as I will get.

The concrete steps and metal rail of my address are painted black. Both cry out for a new coat, the rail peeling in spots and the concrete dull and fading. I crane my neck and peer through the cage-like fire escape, up at the third floor window. Potted spider plants line the sill, providing the only inkling to the current tenant's taste in décor. I look on the spindly leaves and ask myself, *Would she approve?*

Fatigue pulls me to sit on the second step. I rest my arm awkwardly on the rail beside me. It feels alien, probably an inferior replacement to the one that we had in our time. But despite it, despite the late-nineties sedan and shining new Lincoln Navigator parked in front of me, the years roll back. From the sill where rational thought tells me spider plants still sit, I hear her radio.

A rollicking bass-line, chugging guitar and a smooth, operatic voice. Jackie Wilson. '(Your Love Keeps Lifting Me) Higher and Higher'.

1968. Nineteen Sixty-Eight, and the smell of Johnson's baby powder supplanting the old scents of perfumes in the living room. Nineteen Sixty-Eight and the dim cracking of gunfire shooting out of our TV speaker, drowned out by the gurgling cry of a small creature in a yellow bassinet in the nearby bedroom. Nineteen Sixty-Eight and the warmth of a new mother's bosom as her blouse absorbs the tears from my cheek, its softness drawing moisture to my tongue, dulling the new taste of white wine in my mouth. Nineteen Sixty-Eight and the feeling of hell on earth that has aged and fermented through the decades and now seeps into my 2003 bloodstream like ambrosia.

And all at once my body lurches forward and I am walking, this time down the slope toward Second Avenue. I stroll up Second for a block, turn down Sixty-Seventh, and pass by the entrance to the elementary school. I slow but don't stop to observe mothers and children enjoying the public playground that borders First Avenue. I am glad to see a few fathers interspersed among the crowd. My gladness is dampened by the realization that I have only ever looked on a scene such as this from the angle of the sidewalk.

Circling the park up First, I lurch right and turn down Sixty-Eighth toward York Avenue. Though my mind has no part in the decision, I know where my legs are taking me next.

The hospital has the same box shape, the same height, and the same leafy trees scattered around its base. At York and Seventy-Second I plant my feet side by side on the ground. I stand and stare and feel close enough.

Here it comes again, as I have expected. 1968. Nineteen Sixty-Eight and her strangled screams as she gave one final push. Nineteen Sixty-Eight and the wizened face of the doctor eking out a few extra wrinkles with his grin and declaring it a boy.

Nineteen Sixty-Eight and his smile vanishing, giving way to a look of grave concern. My brand-new boy making a croak as his bottom got tapped. Nineteen Sixty-Eight and the doc's knowing glances at two nurses who took the new arrival to be cleaned, dried, and swaddled. And the look of foreboding in his lip-biting as he pulled his horn-rimmed glasses down from his forehead and gathered my wife and me together with his eyes.

"We think that the child has Down Syndrome."

And my wife's gasp, "Oh, God!" And her tears turning from a trickle to a river.

And the flinching jolt through my system as a door behind me slammed irrevocably shut.

Nineteen Sixty-Eight and a nurse, calling the doc back to the child's side, for the child, who they thought had Down Syndrome, had swallowed its meconium. That first bowel movement, which generally comes after the child has been born, had occurred in the birth canal. And the doctor stepping over without another word to attend to the child, who they thought had Down Syndrome.

Nineteen Sixty-Eight and awful thoughts swirling as I listened to the child, who they thought had Down Syndrome, struggling to breathe. Nineteen Sixty-Eight and how appropriate that here he is, in his first seconds of life, eating shit. Nineteen Sixty-Eight and maybe they should step away from the child, who they thought had Down Syndrome, and just let it die. Nineteen Sixty-Eight and my rational mind growing irrational, turning on myself and thinking that perhaps I should be the one to die, for having such ideas.

Nineteen Sixty-Eight and the sounds of the child, who they thought had Down Syndrome, turning from a choke, to a cough, to a cry, and the doc's assessment: "He can breathe now, but we need to take him to Intensive Care."

Nineteen Sixty-Eight and my wife as they began to wheel the bassinet with the child, who they thought had Down Syndrome, out the door. Nineteen Sixty-Eight and the urgent need of a new mother. My darling swallowing her welling grief, hardening every fiber of her spent soul, steeling it against the sense of calamity within her, to summon up in its place the strength of will to cry out, "Wait! Please! I want to hold my baby!" And the doc stopping short in the doorway, staying the bassinet, giving eyes that said to the nurses, 'A minute won't hurt it.'

Nineteen Sixty-Eight and my darling wife pulling the freshly wrapped child, who they thought had Down Syndrome, from the nurse's starched, white arms, taking it—him—to her breast. Nineteen Sixty-Eight and my girl smearing sweat from her palms over his forehead, planting saliva from her lips on his tiny cheek, and pouring her tears over his face. My sweetheart anointing her child, who they thought had Down Syndrome, and whispering to him, "I love you," with eyes that said 'I'm sorry I made you this way.'

Nineteen Sixty-Eight and our tears mingling on her hospital gown, the child taken from her and gone to another ward. Nineteen Sixty-Eight and the doctor back at the bedside, offering condolence instead of congratulations, and then a choice: "You don't have to be saddled with this." *Saddled with this.* "The child can go to a home, and be taken care of." *Taken care of.* "You can visit. And then you can try again." *Try again.*

And the look of shocked horror on my darling's open jaw. And the cringing gasp that followed when she was able to harness some emotion, the gasp which screamed 'I can't face this talk! Oh, God, help me!' And the voice inside telling me, *It's up to you. You're the man. You must be strong for her.*

Nineteen Sixty-Eight and my eyes burning, my head throbbing, my heart pounding and my throat parched. My whole being marshaling every iota of its strength to answer this call, to answer those words the doctor was using to comfort us, but which I knew by my darling's sobs must be a gauntlet thrown at my feet.

And my body, spirit, my entire being, falling so far short. "I think we need to be alone to think about this," where there should have been a snarl.

Nineteen Sixty-Eight and two bodies huddled where there should have been three. Nineteen Sixty-Eight and the third somewhere down the halls, being stabilized, set up for observation, beginning its life being monitored by strangers, those strangers' faces cold and clinical, or worse, only pitying.

Nineteen Sixty-Eight and a waiting room, and my mother biting her trembling lip as her son delivered the news. Nineteen Sixty-Eight and my father taking it with a stoic squint through his new horn-rims. And the old man lifting his face to look at the white ceiling, perhaps to tip the tears back down into their ducts, and saying, "Well, son, this is God's will." And those words so strangely comforting that they loosened my tongue, so that I heard the doctor's offer float out to their ears.

And Dad's reply. "Of course." *Of course.* "He'll be cared for, and you won't be held back." *Held back.*

And my feeble reply when I dug for the strength to knock the old man down: "I think Cherie wants to keep him."

Nineteen Sixty-Eight and Dad's brow furrowing, the sickening silence as he put together a rebuttal. "Cherie's tired. She's had an emotional day. Once she gets some rest, she'll see things more clearly. A child like this is better off…"

Nineteen Sixty-Eight and my blood simmering when it should have boiled. My new paternal instincts kicking in and finally pushing from my lips words which contradicted the old man. "I think *I* want to keep him." Words that I wished, then as now, could have been served in a roar instead of a murmur.

Nineteen Sixty-Eight and these words between the old man and me, these words which I would not repeat to my darling, but whose echoes she might have heard in the days ahead. Did she see these words reflected in the old man's bifocal lenses as he gazed down on the child, who they thought had Down Syndrome, for the first time? Did she hear them in my sudden acquiescence to her wishes ("You know, honey, I think Patrick Barclay *does* sound better than Henry Barclay III after all.")? If she did, she forgave him, and if she heard those echoes in my voice, that would resonate in a dull hum for so many years to come, she forgave me too. Nineteen Sixty-Eight and off she trotted down the path of letdown and forgiveness, thirty years long.

My cell phone buzzes against my thigh. My time-traveling illusion collapses like a sand castle with its vibration. I'm back in 2003, and my presence is requested somewhere in the now. It's just as well—I'm not sure how much more of 1968 I could take.

⌘

"I thought you might want to hear the new improved Flak Jackets," Tim tells me on my arrival outside the West Thirtieth Street building where the band is rehearsing. "We're tighter, and we've got a couple new songs." He leads me inside, into a rickety elevator, and presses a button.

When the elevator slides open, Wendy is emerging into the hall from the ladies' room. Her pale face draws from me the question: "Last night's meal not agree with you?" She works up a tired smile.

We walk across a navy carpet past a water cooler and coffee maker and into the band's room. "Nice digs, huh?" Tim enthuses. Caleb and Joe twiddle knobs on their shoulder-height amplifiers on a stage that takes up a third of the room, facing a floor-to-ceiling mirror on the opposite wall. Tim scurries behind the drum kit, set on a riser a further foot above stage-level. Jack lounges on a black leather couch in the far corner. Seeing us, he sits up and drapes his arm over the back. Wendy walks over and seats herself with his arm as her headrest.

Tim taps his hi-hat. "Let's show Henry some new stuff!"

Joe starts an arpeggiated guitar passage I've never heard. Tim taps a few cymbals now and then, and looks out at Jack, who stays put with his girl under his arm.

Caleb stands idle with both hands resting on the body of his bass. The dreamy ballad goes on as an instrumental for another minute before he leans into his microphone and barks, "Hey! Jack! Anytime!"

The kid gives his girl a peck on her pale cheek and gently pulls his arm from behind her head. He stands, climbs onstage to his microphone, and waits for Joe to come back to his cue. Satisfied, Caleb steps back and leans against the side of his enormous amp. After watching Joe toss out a couple of country licks, the kid mouths his count-in to himself, 'One, two, three, four.' He winks over the microphone at his girl, and takes a breath.

"To know you're there, waiting, behind me,
If I'm lost, to know that you'll find me."
He closes his eyes, takes another, deeper breath.
"To know that Death, grimly reaping,
Would pass through me and leave you weeping."

His pitch and volume are perfect. His tone is nasal and sweet, and it surprises me that for all its warmth, it leaves me dead cold. Maybe there's a conduit misfiring in my heart, but I cannot make a connection.

"To know your kisses are never far away,
To know I share with you every night and day."

I bring my hand to my mouth to mask my groan as a suppressed burp. But behind the kid, Tim beams over his sticks. Caleb lends the first legato bass notes to the mix with a smile of his own. Wendy sits up and leans slowly forward. Her face passes under the soft lighting to reveal her blushing.

"It's better to smile than to cry,
But the tears can run over a smile,
And they do, and I bleed my eyes dry,
To know that you're there for awhile."

The kid opens his eyes in the break before the next verse. He fixes on his girl, winks at her, and his face melts into his broad, dumb grin. His eye strays for a moment to me.

I offer only a benign poker face. It therefore comes as another surprise to me when the kid abruptly pulls away from the microphone, and flaps his hand at his bandmates behind him as though dispersing a bad smell. "Ah, fuck it," the microphone only barely picks up. He hops down and flops back on the couch, leaving the song to collapse in his wake.

Tim thumps on a tom to make a clear end to their take. He scratches his temple with a drumstick. "What was wrong with that?"

The kid scowls at the floor. "Just forget it."

"But shouldn't we...?" The drummer's plea stalls, and when neither Joe nor Caleb helps him jump-start it, he abandons it for another suggestion. "How about we try 'A Cradle for my Heart'?"

Before the title has left Tim's mouth, the kid is shaking his head. "Forget it. Forget the new stuff." He touches his throat as he looks around the room. His eyes make great leaps to avoid looking at me. "Jeezum, I'm thirsty. Is anyone else thirsty?"

Caleb nods. "Hear, hear!"

"I can make you coffee outside," offers Wendy. "Or maybe tea? Or is water better for your throat?"

"I'll go you one better," says Caleb. "Lemme run downstairs. I'm sure there's a place on the corner where I can get us some beer." He is already unslinging his bass; in a minute he is out the door. He bursts in ten minutes later, a bottle of beer already out, poised to pass to Jack's waiting hand.

Bottles tip, limbs loosen, faces broaden. Jack takes the stage, leaving his seat on the couch to me, and the band runs through the favorites. For 'Fifth Wheel/Third Rail', the kid uses his beer as a prop to wave around. He punctuates each line with a swig, so that the bottle is nearly empty by the song's end.

The kid fills 'Hollerin' Blues' with swaggering visual flourishes. Vocally, his tone shifts, if not into the song's agonized wail then at least into a cry that conjures its memory. Before the band kicks out the last chord Jack flings his empty bottle like a tomahawk at the trash can in the corner. The bottle spins in a blur and hits the can's rim with a thud. Only the light padding of the can's plastic lining keeps the brown glass from shattering before gravity pulls it to the bottom.

The jarring thump jolts Wendy upright. Though she doesn't speak, her wide eyes fill the silence that follows the song's end.

Oblivious, Tim takes a small sip from his own bottle. "How about 'Poor Boy'?" he suggests.

Eyes on Wendy, the kid answers the drummer, "Let's do it," while his cocky grin says 'Don't worry, my dear,' to his girl. As Tim counts in, Jack reaches down and pulls another bottle from the case at Caleb's feet.

The Flak Jackets hit their mark with laser-like precision on 'Poor Boy'. The hot-tempered rockabilly strut is taut and slick. Joe's incidental fills add a sparkling polish, and Tim's exuberant cymbal crashes snap Caleb's bass to attention as each verse gives way to the chorus.

Over such stellar playing, the kid lays an uneven cover. "*Stood up, shot down, Known all over town,*" he half-speaks. His pitch wavers as he leaps for the high notes.

"*As the guy who loves the ladies
Who won't let him mess around.*"

The beer has put marbles in his mouth, and he struggles now more to enunciate the swarm of words than to hold down the melody. Faced with such impairment, in the short spaces the chorus allows, the kid hoists his bottle and pours in more marbles.

"*I'm a Poor Boy, Can't get what I want,
I'm a Poor Boy, I'm just a Poor Boy.*"

For the guitar solo he leans on the mic stand, toying with the bottle cap in his right hand.

Speeding through the final verse, Tim stumbles on the tightrope of his drumbeat, holding the rhythm but escalating several bars early into a roll meant for the chorus.

"What the *fuck?*" Jack yells in the middle of his lyric, and in that moment the bottle cap flies from his hand. It bounces off the drummer's cheek to land behind the drums.

Tim drops his beat and brings his hand to his face. Caleb stops playing, then Joe. Jack turns his back on the girl and me to stare down his errant drummer. My ears, which just a second ago withstood a barrage of guitar and drums, suddenly smart against a vacuum of sound.

But Tim is not interested in a staring contest. His hand drops to reveal an unblemished cheek, and the look of hurt and panic drops away as well. He forces a good-natured laugh. "Sorry, chief."

"Sorry?" the kid repeats. "You gonna say that tomorrow when you do that in front of three thousand people? Sorry?"

Tim's jaw drops open. "No, Jack, it's all good," he pleads. "I never did that before, I just—"

Jack snorts. "Right, you never fucking did it before, you're gonna wait and start doing it now, when we've got people fucking watching?"

Wendy sits up at the edge of the couch. "Jack."

The kid wheels around to glare at her. As he does, he pauses on his image glowering back at him from the mirror. The sight must displease him. He looks down and away, and we get another spot of silence.

Caleb is the first to speak up. "It's all good, Jack," he coos, keeping his usual sarcasm in check. He bends down to grab another bottle. "Here." He offers the beer to his friend with both hands, label facing out, like a waiter presenting champagne. "You're on empty. Take it easy. No one's gonna screw up. Not tomorrow, not any night."

Without looking up the kid takes the beer and opens it. And in another minute they're back in the pesky last verse of 'Poor Boy'. Tim grimaces through the middle where he previously slipped. He then throws himself into knocking out the crescendo roll in its rightful place.

By the chorus Tim is laughing, Caleb is smirking and nodding, and even Joe has a grin on his face. Jack, though not approaching a smile, settles into a shrugging posture and lets his features grow placid. But beside me the girl, still perched at the edge of her seat, stares on with sad eyes and bites her lip. And when I turn my head to the side and catch my mirror image behind me, I am taken aback at just how much my own face has soured.

⌘

September 3, 2003

With an audience in the hundreds and a sixties soul number playing on the PA overhead, Spike darts around the theater's stage checking the band's equipment. Down a short maze of bare-brick corridors I find the band's dressing room. A dressing room: a lighted mirror, plush chairs, a couch. No backroom with stacks of broken chairs, no mountain of cardboard boxes restricting our movement. Joe plays along with a Stones number on the stereo. Wendy sits in Jack's lap on the couch.

Jack takes a swig from a bottle of spring water. Wendy watches him, then gives me a winning smile. The kid sets the plastic bottle on the arm of the couch and leans back, pulling the girl with him. She laughs an angelic tee-hee-hee.

The door swings open, bumping into my rear. Leaning into the room, Spike pays my pained yelp no notice. "Okay, motherfuckers, you're on!"

Joe stands and carts his Silvertone through the doorway with his usual gig face on. But for Jack, a directive we have heard dozens of times takes on an immense weight tonight. Setting Wendy down beside him, he rises from the couch with the slow, even motion of a defendant about to take the witness stand. He takes a breath, full and deep, before moving forward, takes one step, then stops and seizes Wendy's hand. "Come to the stage with me!"

"Of course, sweetie," she says, pulling herself up by his arm.

As they pass the arm of the couch the kid's hand shoots out again and grabs his water bottle. I hold the door for the party before taking the rear of the procession.

We greet the other two at the wing of the stage. Tim is talking to a lanky fellow with a pompadour and a silver silk shirt. The fellow breaks off his conversation with the drummer and moves to shake Jack's hand. "Good to see ya, brother!" He hooks his thumb with the kid's in a soul shake and pats him on the back. The kid nods his respect and returns to peering past the curtain at the crowd beyond.

"Stage fright, huh?" I recognize this man. I can see him in my mind's eye wielding an orange Gretsch guitar on a Torinos poster outside.

Jack lifts Wendy's hand and squeezes it. "Lot of people."

"Awww, that's nothin'!" The Torino slaps the kid's shoulder. "We got bigger crowds comin'. This is a warm-up. Tell you what!" He gets a devilish grin. "Drop by our dressing room after." His wandering eye falls on me. When he speaks again, leaning into the kid's ear, a new guitar riff from the PA smothers his words.

The house lights fall. A cheer goes up, fuller and more booming than I have heard before. Some unseen announcer calls out to the crowd: "Ladies and gentlemen, please welcome Jack Hackett!" The audience gives another, smaller cheer. A second later, the voice returns: "And the Flak Jackets!"

This stage is a vast plain. Joe seems to run a mile before reaching his amp and plugging in his guitar. It's another mile back to the front of the stage. Finally, lording over the back of them on a gigantic drum riser, Tim counts them in. Even the tap of his sticks echoes through the microphones and crackles through the hall like small-arms fire.

With the intro to 'Fifth Wheel/Third Rail' shaking the floorboards beneath us, Jack fidgets for a final minute. Then all of a sudden he takes Wendy by both shoulders, yanks her into him, and plants a kiss on her lips. "For luck!" He shuffles out the first few steps, before a small patter from the crowd grows his strides. At center stage he comes under a spotlight. A spotlight.

"Oh, you think you got me sorted out."

Spotlights cast a phosphorescent glow on each of them. It's a dazzling sight. Every few bars, Tim ducks into the shade of his cymbals, while Caleb nods his hair into his eyes.

"It comes to this my dear."

Jack throttles the microphone, tilts the stand, and steps to the right. The shaft of light follows him. I lean out from the wings to trace the beam back to its source. My aging eyes can't adjust to the dark around it, high up the far wall, where it meets with the other three.

"And it comes as quite a shock."

Below the beams, lit by the afterglow of the stage lighting, sit a good thousand people, halfway filling the great hall. Most of the faces I can pick out are twenty- and thirty-somethings. A few pockets of teenagers stick out; those kids would have been underage for any of the Flak Jackets' gigs up to this point.

"I'm feelin' like a fifth wheel..."

A pair of hands grabs my shoulders. "Stay off their turf, motherfucker." Spike jerks me back into the wings beside Wendy. "Unless you plan on playing rhythm guitar!" He moves over to stand, arms crossed, against a pillar next to the Torinos' guitar player.

Onstage, Joe takes a solo, standing way back near his amp, head down and eyes on his fretboard. After a few moments Caleb, leaning over the lip of the stage with one foot on his monitor, looks back at him. Shaking his head, he shoves off from the monitor and skirts around to the guitar player's side of the stage. Once there, he sticks the head of his bass like the butt of a rifle into Joe's back and marches him toward the audience. A ripple of laughter greets them at the end of their journey.

"Ahh, Fifth Wheel...

Ahh, Third Rail."

Ripples are the order of the evening. The cheers that greet the song's end are sincere but shallow, dying away before the band resumes playing. The awkward moment leaves the kid hanging on his mic. Into the silence he can only insert a deadpan "Thank you," and, a few seconds later, "Philadelphia."

For six more songs the kid holds back. Where I have seen him scream, he only shouts. Where we have gotten wails, we get only muted moans. Bursts of energy that would have given us defiant struts yield only half-hearted shuffling and a stomp here and there. And for his trouble he gets to leave the stage to a ripple.

Heat emanates from the Flak Jackets as they pass me. Jack shuffles into Wendy's arms and walks toward the backstage with her as his crutch. I close ranks behind them, joining a parade whose mood straddles between the triumphant and the funereal.

"Hey Jack! Wait up!" The Torino waves at the kid as he springs past me. "Follow me." The kid follows the Torino; we follow the kid. Spike heads out onstage to collect the band's gear.

We file down the hall, past the Flak Jackets' dressing room, coming to an open doorway from which loud music and a haze of smoke emanate. Tim calls out to the Torino, "Is that you guys in there, Nick?"

The Torino leers back. "Just follow your nose." His pace slows as we approach the doorway. "Great opener," I hear him tell the kid.

The kid mumbles his thanks. "I couldn't connect, though." He slows even more, until he's just inching forward. "They were so far away." Just outside the doorway he comes to a stop. I see the reason: the girl has been tugging him back, and finally, before they can enter the room, has planted her feet to the floor. She leans back to hold him in place.

"Jack." Her voice carries over the music and other din that pulse from the room. "Can we stay out here? I mean, the *smoke.*" Even out here, the smell of pot invades the nostrils.

But Jack has been invited into this great band's inner sanctum. I can't blame him when he unhooks his arm, kisses her cheek and holds up five fingers. "Five minutes, baby." In he goes. The others follow.

Wendy passes me on her way back to the Flak Jackets' dressing room. She fixes me with a melancholy look. I shrug, edging closer to the doorway. "Five minutes," I blurt. "What harm can it do?"

I enter the doorway but go no further, more out of courtesy than anything else. The boys amble deeper inside, sheepishly at first, as though concerned about disturbing royalty. They finally break out of their huddle when one of the Torinos holds out a joint. Caleb jumps at it with comical speed; Joe and Tim share a chuckle and take small drags in turn. Jack wades among the bodies toward the back, with Nick speaking into his ear.

I look in on a rather domestic scene. Four Torinos sit on two long couches, each with his arm around a well-dressed blonde. They lounge around a coffee table on which rests a solitary, half-full bottle of wine. Two of the ladies sip at their glasses; everyone else seems content with the marijuana.

Two of the Torinos stand to welcome the newcomers with fatherly smiles and pats on the back. The Flak Jackets immerse themselves in the scene. The pounding guitar rock that blares from a stereo washes over their conversation before their voices can reach me. Caleb is all ultra-cool winks and smirks as he revisits the circling joint and helps himself to a glass of wine. Tim keeps his eyebrows raised and his eyes wide while Joe maintains an affable grin.

A quick scan of the room finds the kid sitting in a folding chair in the far corner. Nick Torino sits on a tiny side table and speaks directly into his ear. I linger a few minutes, for as long as my tolerance for the smell of marijuana will allow. The flutter of contact high in my stomach tells me it's time to go. Before parting I glance one last time across the haze, just as the Torino slips a small envelope into the kid's palm. The kid, looking perplexed and not a little uncomfortable, nods and stands, putting the envelope in his pants pocket.

I turn from the scene and start down the hall to the Flak Jackets' dressing room. Before I reach the door I hear the scuffing of feet against the linoleum. I don't have to look behind me to know that the kid has kept his word.

The girl stands as I enter the room. Her eyes ask me what her man is up to. I am happy to step to my side and hold the door open for the kid himself. She sits back down and waits patiently for him to examine himself in the mirror. After a minute he shuffles over to flop down by her side. She holds back the worries behind her eyes, leans close against him, but doesn't embrace him. The kid waits a minute, looking between her and the floor. Then he pecks her cheek. "You look nice," he says.

The door flies open again. I have the presence of mind to dodge it this time. "All right, ya three-chord wonders," comes the roadie's sandpaper voice. "Let's get in the van. I got a schedule to keep." He enters the room and looks around. Coming up with only one Flak Jacket, his eyes come to rest with bemusement on me.

I point out the door. "They're with the Torinos."

"Still?" He shuts the door and looks at a sheet of paper taped to the back of it. "Well, they'll be out in just a sec. See?" He runs his finger down it, showing the schedule of events, neatly typed in bold capitals: '8:15 JACK HACKETT —9:00 THE TORINOS.' He points at a clock over the door.

The minute hand looks ready to pounce on the twelve. "This ain't the fuckin' Whiskey, 'showtime at ten but let's wait till more people show up.' This tour's for real. That band'll be comin' down that hall any second."

The door opens again. In walk Tim, Joe, and Caleb, reeking of pot-smoke and looking stoned-stupid. "They're on in a minute," Tim gathers the words to say. Outside I can hear the band's entourage moving past our door to take their places in the wings.

Spike claps Tim on the back, then with a disgusted sneer withdraws his hand and wipes it on the front of his jeans. "Well then, sweaty motherfucker, it's time for you all to get home to bed."

Tim looks crestfallen. "Can't we watch the show from the wings?" Caleb frowns behind him like a child denied dessert.

The roadie digs in his heels. "It's two hours back to New York. I gotta get you back to the hotel, then get you all up and out by eight."

"Maybe just one song?" asks Joe.

Caleb seizes on the offer. "Two! Just two!"

Spike glances at the clock: nine o'clock sharp. The boisterous voices of the Torinos, coming down the hall to take the stage, float through the door. He gives just a little. "A song and a half. Once Nick starts his solo on the second song, you vacate the premises. Anyone not in the van by the start of the third song is walkin' back to New York."

The boys hurry out. From the hall I hear Tim call out, "Go T-nos, have a great set!" I, feeling my age catching up with me again, opt to grab the keys from Spike and stake a claim to the front seat.

A bevy of loud guitars vibrates through the outside walls of the hall as I reach the back exit. I find myself holding the door for Wendy. "I never really got the Torinos," she confesses.

I open the door of the waiting van for her and hear myself entreating her to take the front seat. Now I know what will happen: the band will burst through the stage door and pile in, trapping me in my place behind the driver's seat. Wendy will leave the front seat to sit with Jack, and Caleb will scoot into the front. And yet I am equable.

"That was an okay show, right?"

"It was decent," I reply.

"Jack was fine tonight."

"He had a bit of trouble."

"But he sang well."

"He stayed on key."

"Isn't that the point?"

I spread my hands. "He'll get better again. Let him play a couple of club dates, and then give him time to learn to work a big stage."

We listen to the throb of guitar and bass that pulses through even the van. Wendy gazes out the side window as she twists the lanyard of her backstage pass.

"How was your summer?" she asks after a verse.

I consider telling her about the death of my father, before saying simply, "Eventful. Yours?"

The worry lines in her face melt behind her smile. "I wish life had a 'Repeat' button."

"You and Jack?"

She nods. Her fingers move from her lanyard to her collarbone.

"Still," I muse, "I've missed this."

She rolls her eyes and chuckles. "I'm not sure how much *I* have." Seeing my face fall, she lifts a hand and shakes her head. "Oh, not *this*." She tilts her palm out the window at the stage door. "I mean *that*."

"Ah, I get it." I glance out at the wall. "You're back to waiting in the wings."

"Hah," she says. "More like *wasting* in the wings."

"I see. Did you have acting work during the break?"

She laughs softly again. "To be fair, I should have made more of an attempt." She shrugs. "Jack tried to persuade me to get out there and try, but he kind of gave up after a while. The only offer I got was from my sister-in-law."

"You're sister-in-law is in casting?"

"No, she's near Concord. Back home. It's my brother Terry, his wife. She runs a drama school. She had an opening, teaching the preschoolers there."

"And would you settle for that?"

"I know what you think." She starts giggling. "Reciting nursery rhymes while herding a bunch of four year-olds around a stage?" Her laughter trails off. "But to be honest, it kind of got me excited. We might have said yes if Marty hadn't called the next day."

She lets me ponder her story for a minute. When she speaks again, her voice is soft. "Henry?"

I look up into those doe-eyes. She takes another moment, draws another breath. "I'm..." The rest comes out in a sigh, "...a bit overprotective. Aren't I?"

At this I laugh. She looks startled at the sudden blast. "Forgive me." I can't hold back the chuckle that riddles my speech. "But after seeing Jack work a crowd, I'd say he needs whatever protection he can get."

"You don't think he might leave me if I'm too..."

The chuckle rises in me again. "You'll still need a crowbar to pry him off."

The stage door clangs open; five bodies swarm around the doors. Wendy takes Jack's hand, and in the next moment they are sitting in the row behind me. Tim and Joe crowd in beside me after the opportunist Caleb scoots into the front seat. "Hey Wend, thanks for keepin' it warm!" Just as I predicted.

"All right, folks." Spike climbs into the driver's seat and plucks the key from my hand. From his mouth the word 'folks' sounds suspiciously like 'fucks'. "You've had your fun. Now everybody shut up for the ride." Minutes later the nighttime Philadelphia skyline recedes behind us.

The last words to be said, for the entire trip, are from Tim: "I didn't get to see the Liberty Bell." In the silent dark of the van we sit, lit only by the passing lamps over the Interstate and with only the highway noise for a soundtrack. Spike bears down on the wheel and the gas pedal; the Flak Jackets sit back in their seats and float down from the highs, natural and otherwise, of the evening. And there, too, sits the girl, in the dead calm of the back of the van, wide awake and clinging to the kid's arm as though to a kite-string in a gale.

⌘

September 4, 2003

Nick Torino is present at the Cornell University auditorium for sound check. He ducks backstage with his arm around the kid's shoulders. Wendy, in a plush front-row seat beside me, whispers, "I don't like that guy." She glides down the aisle, up a small staircase to the stage, and disappears behind a curtain.

Thirty minutes later, I walk into a dressing room in crisis. "I'm not going on." Jack rocks back and forth in his seat, his right knee pumping up, down, up, down. He bites his nails, runs his hands through his hair. "I can't do this. Look at us last night. I couldn't do it then, I can't do it now."

The girl tries to get close, but the kid's arm rises like a barrier between them. "Ah, Jeezum. It's not you, it's just...." He tries to convey the rest with dolorous eyes, but his pupils keep getting drawn away by movements in the room. The girl shifts an inch away from him, pursing her lips. After a motionless minute, she starts picking at the fabric of her pea-green skirt. Jack's eyes never stop moving.

Tim is standing by a water cooler. "Cheer up, Wendy. In thirty-five minutes, it'll all be over, and you'll have him—"

"I'm not going on!" the kid snarls.

"Aww, Jack." Caleb stands in a corner of the room, beer bottle in one hand while the other tries to find a radio station on the stereo. "Whatsa matter? You need attention? Having your full-time groupie ain't enough anymore?"

"You *fuck!*" Jack roars. "I oughta break that bottle over your fuckin' head!" His rocking ceases. Caleb holds his glare, gives it back to him. On the tiny stereo's digital screen behind him, the frequency numbers go up, up, up.

For several seconds Wendy stares at Caleb. "I'm not a groupie," she says finally.

"Yeah, Caleb," Tim seconds. "That wasn't very nice."

Caleb pays Tim no attention. But he does soften his face, nod and blink at her, gestures I take as some sort of apology. When he turns back to staring down his singer though, his jaw clenches again.

The wordless space, silent but for the hiss of the stereo speakers and Joe's pre-show guitar picking, stretches on until the door swings open. Spike knocks at it after the fact. "Okay, boys and girls—Caleb, I'm talkin' to you, heh, heh—time to earn those pesos!"

Jack reaches his feet just as Caleb passes him. Their faces come within inches of each other; their eyes shoot their daggers. Caleb moves off, a sneer curling his upper lip. And without another word about his nerves, Jack storms out with the others.

Wendy stares solemnly down at her skirt again. I hold out my hand for her; she takes it, forcing a smile as she pulls herself to her feet.

⌘

Coming offstage thirty minutes later, Caleb claps the kid on the back. "A good show, my friend!"

"Yeah, good." The kid puffs his cheeks. He puts an arm around Caleb's shoulder. They stagger together toward the dressing room.

Wendy is left to follow with me. "He was good tonight."

Smothering in my mind the creeping hoarseness in the kid's voice and his frantic reeling from one side of the stage to the other, I stretch the truth just a touch. "Yes, he was."

⌘

September 6, 2003

The band's first night in Buffalo is a step back: a short set among an assembly line of bands, in a small club, for an even smaller crowd. It's a blow to morale, but for Night Two we're back with the Torinos, in a good-sized theater on the other side of town.

I let the band clear the dressing room when the time comes and sit alone in atmospheric semi-darkness for a time, suddenly craving a few minutes on my own. But at a certain point I realize that I am taking up my sacred meditative minutes pondering furniture, and fish my cell phone from my pocket.

"They're playing the Red Sox." The Fan has barely heard me say hello.

"What are *you* up to?" I ask.

"It's on TV here." His voice is a distracted monotone.

"The band is on right now."

"Really?" His voice regains some life. "Where are you? How are they?"

"They're doing well."

"How's Jack? They love him, right?"

"Well, they're mostly opening these Torinos shows—"

"I like the T-nos."

"—so it's not *his* audience."

"They still like him. 'Cause he's great."

"They loved the band in Ithaca two nights ago."

A pop fly off a Yankee bat snatches him away for five seconds. "Darn!" he curses; apparently the Sox catcher got it. Then I have him back. "Is Jack still singing great?"

"Well, he gets to the end of a set and can still talk."

"That Pedro," he hisses.

"Who?"

"Their pitcher. Martinez. I don't like him."

"Well, you wouldn't, would you? It's the Red Sox."

"They hate each other. The Yankees and them." Before I can ask what else is new he insists, "This year it's worse."

"How are you right now?"

"Down by three. It's the second inning." His voice becomes a vindictive whisper. "But we'll show 'em."

I take that as my cue to leave him with his other Number One.

The Flak Jackets' set is a rumble beyond the door. A minute after I pocket the cell phone the audience erupts with something between a gasp and a cheer. Not long after, the boys file in to infuse the room with their sweat.

A deflated beach ball hangs from the head of Caleb's bass. "That's Jack's kill." Caleb snorts. "We should mount it on the wall." And before putting away his instrument, he takes the Technicolor carcass and hooks it to the corner of a mirror at the far end of the room. The thing drops to the ground; he picks it up and starts scouting anew.

"The crowd was throwing it around the theater," Tim tells me.

Caleb squeezes past Tim, Jack, Wendy, and Joe. He pulls out the tack that holds the night's itinerary to the bulletin board on the back of the door. "Stupid idea—you do that in a stadium, where people are standing."

Tim reaches the couch but stays upright. "But no, it *made* them stand up. It helped us that way."

Caleb snorts again. He turns to face Tim, one hand on the ball, the other holding the tack, his bass swinging from his shoulders. "Who needs 'em standing for *that*?" He shakes his head. "That's like playing a show in the middle of a volleyball tournament!"

Jack and Wendy move to the couch. He heaves himself into the left side. She perches on the arm and leans his way. He rests his temple against her breast. "Not a great show," he says.

"Until they hit Joe!" Tim speaks in an almost-laugh.

Joe is closing his guitar case. He chuckles. "Yeah, I didn't see."

Tim continues. "The ball floated down in front, and someone spiked it at Joe." He breaks out in a childish grin. "Hit him in the head!"

Joe shrugs. "It's slow. It didn't hurt." He taps his black-mopped head. "But I wasn't looking."

"That got a roar from the crowd," Tim adds.

Caleb is still scouting the room for a suitable mount for their trophy. "So Jack sees this, and in, like, a second, he picks up his stand —" he zeroes in on a place above the center of the couch, "—over his head —" he leans between me and the kid and places the ball's remains on the wall, "—and *wham*!" He stabs the tack into the prize and backs away to view it. "Popped the thing."

"The crowd loved it!" Tim gushes. "Although I feel bad for whoever brought the ball. But they stayed standing after that."

"Not a great show," Jack repeats.

Caleb retrieves his bass case and opens it on the floor. "Why? Just 'cause you couldn't reach the high notes with a stepladder?" He tosses in his bass. "Who gives a rat's ass? We got cheered like headliners!"

The kid winces. "They shouldn't just be clapping for some stunt."

Caleb glares at the kid. "Well, shit, Jack, maybe *you* sucked, but I think *we* played pretty fantastic. I'll take some credit for those cheers!"

The kid lifts his head from his girl to glower back at Caleb, but the girl squeezes his elbow, and the affronted scowl melts from his face. "Fine," he says. "You got a point."

Before closing his case, Caleb digs into a small compartment and pulls something out. "Here." The ire is gone from his voice as well. He flashes the object at us: a long, slim joint. "We smoke peace pipe."

Wendy wriggles out from behind Jack. "I have to go to the bathroom," she says, and is out the door before the joint is lit.

⌘

September 7, 2003

Once again, after the roar of a theater, a Sunday-night club date in Rochester feels like a bad dream. The Flak Jackets shake it out of their heads on the road back to New York, where we settle into the same Midtown hotel Monday afternoon. Tim knocks on my door in the early evening and waves a newspaper in my face. "The *Village Voice*! The Beacon Theater show is in their 'Must-See' column!" He checks himself. "I mean, you know, the blurb is about the T-nos, but they mention Jack at the end."

I take the paper from him and leaf through it until I find that ubiquitous Torinos publicity photo. After two paragraphs of fluff about the headliners' unlikely reunion and a primer of what to expect, readers are encouraged to 'arrive early and see the antics of serial tantrum-thrower Jack Hackett.'

"It's a free paper," Tim tells me. "I just got five out of the box on the corner! You can keep that copy. I can't wait to show Jack!"

⌘

September 8, 2003

With the Beacon show mere hours away, the boys are back at their Thirtieth Street studio to rehearse. I remain behind in my dust-furred closet, typing up my backlog of musings, listening to the local television news anchors pep talk their way through the day's events. I take a few minutes to touch base with the West Coast.

Marty picks up on the first ring. "Uncle H, it's all coming together just like I pictured it!" His voice booms. "We're on the rise back here. The *L.A. Weekly* put them on a list of up-and-coming bands."

"What did they say about them?"

"Well, no, it was just a list." Purely by accident, I have deflated him. "We're goin' up, though. Give that paper four weeks and they'll be plugging the November show, harder than anybody!"

"How are you?"

He doesn't hesitate. "High on life. I've got breakfast right here in front of me, at my desk. You know what it is? An avocado! I've been on a real vegan kick lately. No meat, no dairy. If we get another hot spell, I may try and go raw."

"Good for you."

"But it's this band, Uncle H. It's Jack. All my life, I've dreamed of discovering a band and taking it to the top. And here it is! The Beacon tonight! The Beacon!" I let him keep his goose-bumps, refraining from reminding him that we're the openers. "This is the best part, too. Where it's all ahead of us. This is what we'll always come back to!"

⌘

The Beacon Theater is golden, gilded, ornate, magnificent. The Torinos' soundman breezes the Flak Jackets through their sound check; after four shows with them, he zooms in on their preferred levels with a few flicks of his wrist. Wendy sits beside me in the front row, in a plush velvet seat; when the one-two checking is done, her gravity pulls Jack from the stage to her side. From this the current is established, and soon all the Flak Jackets have migrated to us. Caleb is rubbing his neck.

"Still?" Jack shakes his head. "What'd she do to you? Fall asleep on your head?"

"Use your imagination."

"Geez, Caleb," Tim quips, "you oughta stay out of the beds of strange women!"

"You'd have done it if you could," Caleb shoots back. "Besides, her bed was a hell of a lot nicer than the milk crate with sheets I got back at the hotel." He rubs harder into his neck. "Why don't you bug Joe?"

Joe lifts his head.

"Joe left with a girl, not a fuckin'...Amazon." Jack gives Caleb his usual smirk. "Stick with Gabby, bud." He squeezes Wendy's hand on the armrest. "I mean, really. What does the good Lord think about his lost sheep?"

Caleb grins, an expression both amiable and menacing. "That's between the good Lord and me. Now, what say we track down a beer?"

"Count me out," says Jack, but the others agree, and our little huddle breaks up.

I spend the hour before showtime wandering the uptown streets. A warm breeze in the falling light gives a feeling of lingering summer to the city. Back on the sidewalk outside the theater, young people converge from all directions. A strict dress code distinguishes those coming to the show from passersby. A male Torinos fan can be picked out by his blue jeans torn at both knees, and by his white T-shirt with the band's name in a Western font branded across the front. Females, outnumbered two to one, wear tank tops and summer skirts. They wait outside in clusters. At the edge of the theater's foyer, a blue-jeaned, T-shirted fellow pulls a ukulele from a canvas bag, strikes up a few chords and begins singing. Within seconds the clusters have broken up and moved toward him, a growing number of people joining in singing.

I navigate between them, flash my laminate at the entrance and move through more clusters of young people in the lobby. Some I know I have seen at previous shows. I entertain the notion that the band has merely hired a busload of extras on a six-month contract to stock theater seats every tour date. *If only we had an extras budget....*

A rumble of applause vibrates through the open double doors ahead of me. Joe's guitar blasts through them as I flash my laminate to an usher. I walk slowly down the aisle, amazed at the vision on the stage.

Joe stands the same way, oblivious to the opulence that surrounds him, indifferent to the spotlit, phosphorescent glow that he gives off. They all glow; the spotlights sharpen the focus around them all, the gold frames them beautifully, they play snapping, tuneful, energetic rock 'n' roll, and I wish very much that this were the first time I were seeing them. For this, I know, is a good night. The band members are their usual selves, lean and tidy and loud and sloppy in just the right places. Jack is in tune, focused on his music, and seems to know better tonight than to try to find a way to bait the crowd. I would love to stumble upon this group, with virgin eyes and ears, and let them amaze me.

As it is, every beat of every song evokes a memory of another show, when the songs crackled with the thrill of discovery. Even when Jack ambles to the side of the stage, during Joe's solo near the end of the set, and climbs the curtains a good twelve feet, to a welter of applause, I cannot will the excitement into myself. When he slides back down to cheers, I shrug inwardly. It can never be new again—at least not all of it.

The applause intensifies suddenly, a collective gasp of delight. A fifth spotlight beams down to pick up the figure of Nick Torino swaggering onto the stage, his white guitar swinging from his shoulders. The Torino holds up his hand, more to quell the crowd than to greet it; the audience thunders at the mere sight of the great Enrique gracing the opening act's stage. As their cheer dies down, he sidles up beside Jack, running his hand along his pompadour. Standing a full six inches taller than the kid, he would cast a shadow over him were it not for Jack's own spotlight. Jack takes the Torino's proffered hand, allows it to shake his. Once released, his hand drops down to his side. He stands idle and lets the renewed, impatient bellows from the crowd go unanswered.

"Enrique!" a large, shaven-headed fan cries out down the front row. "I love you!" The audience's clamor creeps back up beneath his shout. Jack stands still. Nick Torino, the fabled Enrique, looks on, his gracious smile frozen on his face and congealing into an awkward baring of his yellowing teeth. The kid lets the tenor rise and still does nothing.

Nick gives up waiting and hijacks the kid's microphone. "New York!" he exclaims, and the crowd's volume spikes. "How about we do a little number together?" His legion roars again. Nick pats the kid on the back, turns and counts out the beat to Tim.

The opening chords get a unanimous vote of approval from the audience. Nick plays ear-pounding rhythm guitar and nods his endorsement at the band. Jack steps to the microphone and proceeds to wail the song's lyrics with such a slurred drawl that I cannot decipher a word. His pained expression and his anxious glances at his guest signal to one and all that this duet wasn't his idea.

At the second chorus, the Torino steps over to Jack and leans over to sing along into his mic. Facing away from him, the kid tilts the stand forward, walking it away from Nick and up to the lip of the stage. The whole motion seems awfully well-timed. By the third chorus, the Torino has skulked over to share a mic with Caleb, who is all too happy to press in close and sing along with a showman's verve.

To a man, the audience has fallen into singing for themselves, and when Jack's ordeal is through, before the song's coda is over, they cheer him heartily for his effort. Nick lifts his hands from his guitar and walks back to center stage to raise Jack's hand in the air. As the Flak Jackets bring the song to its conclusion, the kid and the Torino stand side by side to receive the fans' adulation. "Enrique!" they call. "Enrique!" And one stranger's voice, directly behind me but sounding like it's buried under a foot of earth, cries out, "All right Jack!"

⌘

September 9, 2003

Moving south through the Holland Tunnel and down the I-95 through New Jersey, the engine of this tour slides into a higher gear. Tonight and again tomorrow, we're in Baltimore. After that, it's Washington, DC. Then Richmond. The wheels are turning again.

Talk revolves in a wide arc around last night. "Can you believe it?" Tim repeats in variations at intervals down the Interstate. "We played, onstage, with Enrique Love!"

Caleb glances at Jack. "Well, treasure that memory, 'cause it ain't gonna happen again."

Jack squirms in his seat. "Let's just forget it, huh?"

"That's tough to forget." Spike assumes his professorial tone. "You were given an opportunity last night. And you damn near blew it." The kid squirms some more. "Now, from where I was, it was clear what you were doing, but the Torinos fans seemed too busy singing along to notice. Let's see if the reviews mention your attitude."

"You still haven't told us *why* you did it," Caleb says. "You seemed all right when Nick came to rehearsal."

"Let's just forget it," Jack says through gritted teeth, before tipping his head onto Wendy's shoulder.

Tim stares down at his splayed fingers. "To think that these hands played along with a Torino!"

I sit back and watch New Jersey slide past us. The post-industrial, concrete-wasteland terrain gives way quickly to rows of leafy trees on either side of the highway.

"Enrique Love! Nick!" Tim gushes. "This is something we'll tell our grandkids."

Caleb sits up. "Really, Jack. What was it? You thought you were being upstaged? Was it nerves? Or were things getting too good? Maybe you just needed to sabotage things."

A withering stare from the kid will not keep Caleb from hitting his stride. "Or was Nick too keen on us? Are you just not ready to be brought inside?" He leans forward and rests his elbows on his knees. The shift brings his face close to the kid's. Riding shotgun, two rows up, I have to strain to hear him. "Do you need them to hate you to be any good?"

Wendy lays a hand on the kid's arm; his jaw unclenches. Shaking his head he mutters, "Yeah, where's the fun in being liked, right?"

⌘

With Baltimore's brick-heavy skyline in the distance, we pull into our hotel. While we undergo the tedium of checking in, Tim spies a computer desk in the corner of the lobby. 'Internet use for guests only,' reads a laminated sheet on the wall beside it. "I *will* be a guest in a moment," he says, walking over. "Let's check if anyone's posted a review of the Beacon."

A few keystrokes and a couple of mouse-clicks bring him to the *Village Voice* website. I stand over his shoulder; a headline at the bottom of the main page snags my eye: 'Enrique & Co. Flare Out at the Beacon.' "Uh-oh," says Tim, and clicks on it.

The receptionist holds up the first room key for Jack to take. The fellow lets it dangle there for a full minute while Jack turns from him and lets Tim's reading voice pull him toward the computer.

"'Well,'" reads the drummer in a voice worthy of a news anchor, "'for those of you who have been eagerly awaiting a Torinos reunion ever since the band called it quits in 1998, you can stop biting your nails and rubbing your hands together, and start yawning again. That's right, you can yawn the way you did through the last two years of the band's original run.' That's low."

Tim is silent for a moment, reading some of the review for himself. The receptionist still holds the kid's room key over the desk. His expectant smile matches Nick Torino's onstage last night. As Tim resumes reading a few lines down, Jack takes another step toward the computer. Wendy relieves the poor clerk's arm, taking the key before stepping over beside her man.

"'It should have been apparent early on,'" Tim reads, "'when at the end of a blistering set by openers Jack Hackett and the Flak Jackets—'" he looks over his shoulder at us. "My God! We're getting a special mention from the *Voice*!"

"Just keep reading," says Spike, in a strangely soft growl, moving in close behind him to study the screen.

"Uh, here we are: '...a blistering set by openers Jack Hackett and the Flak Jackets, Enrique Love took the stage to back the support band up on a rollicking rehash of the T-nos' early B-side "Gunned Down". Singing wildly out-of-tune backup, adding guitar fills that sounded like he was in the next time zone, Love showed the Beacon crowd just how tired he is. His jittery excitement, during the duet and throughout the T-nos' own lackluster set, also leaves us wondering how serious his claims are that he's "clean as a whistle."' Gosh." Tim looks from the screen to his band. "Can they really say that in a review?"

"Gosh," answers Caleb. "They just did."

"'As if not being able to keep up with your own song isn't embarrassing enough, singer Jack Hackett (Love's own protégé) felt no need to be gracious about sharing the stage with his headliner. All but ignoring Love, Hackett tore through the song with a fire that proved he knew who the real star of the night was.'" Tim stops, reads on in silence. After a minute he exclaims, "Ouch!" He stands up from the chair, still gawking at the screen. "I hope Nick hasn't read this."

Spike pats him on the back. "Nick should be used to bad reviews by now." He puts a hand on Jack's shoulder. "And you," he says. "Man of the hour. You're fuckin' lucky that's the first time that reviewer saw you. I seen you do *so much* better." The kid wriggles out from under the roadie's hand. "I guess you're still pretty good after all." He chuckles at the kid's bewildered look. "But now you gotta be just as good, or better'n that. People expect somethin' from you now."

⌘

September 12, 2003

The band plays a tiny Baltimore club that smells of stale cigarettes, and as I sit among the dozen patrons, I feel as though we're slumming again. The kid tosses back two bottles of beer and hurtles around the stage, swinging his limbs and the mic stand around, shaking his head when his punches land on air.

The T-nos are absent from sound check the following evening. Their crew shove the Flak Jackets impatiently through each instrument's levels. "That'll do," the soundman grumbles after the band plays only a few bars all together.

Standing next to Spike, I mumble, "Do you think they read the review?"

Arms crossed, scowling at the sound booth across the stage from us, the roadie answers, "They wouldn't have to. They were there."

The show goes over well despite atrocious sound levels. Jack gives up trying to bore through a thick wall of bass, raises his glass to the crowd and begins to take his frustration out on his thigh. He saves some wrath for the mic stand as well but leaves stage and crowd intact. We leave the instant Spike has cleared the stage.

On to Washington, DC, where the band's 'Pick of the Week' status in a local indie paper garners them an extra dozen attendees. A few in the front row end up getting wet, but Jack escapes unharmed, and the remaining twenty in the audience give enough applause to overcome the jeers of the spattered few. Back in our Baltimore hotel that evening, when I tell the Fan on the phone that we just played DC, I feel almost ashamed to admit to him that, no, I didn't see the White House. Or Congress. Or the Washington Monument.

⌘

September 13, 2003

The other shoe has dropped; another door has closed. Johnny Cash is dead. Tim has just seen an obit segment on a morning news program. There are actual tears in his eyes as he tells me, standing in my hotel-room doorway. "That's another one down I'll never get to play with." With solemn face he loiters by my bed. When finally I clap a hand on his shoulder, he makes for the door. And when I see him next, in the lobby, he is dressed from head to toe in black.

Johnny Cash at Folsom Prison plays on the van stereo, and Jack keeps his arm draped over Wendy's shoulder from Washington to Richmond. Tim spends his time in his seat behind them, spouting the occasional word of wistful praise for the dearly departed and putting the first creases in the spine of Milan Kundera's *The Unbearable Lightness of Being*. "What a voice," he says after 'The Long Black Veil'. "He got such a big reaction from prisoners 'cause he felt a kinship with them," he expounds after 'Send a Picture of Mother'. And when Cash duets with June on 'Jackson', he sighs, "True love right there," and glances at Jack and Wendy.

Caleb shows the first sign that anyone is listening to Tim. "And they're together again." He leaves a beat before adding, "Praise God."

Wendy pulls away from Jack and turns to shoot Caleb a mocking look. "What," Caleb fires back, "you gonna go all Santa Claus on me again?"

Jack twists around. "What the hell are you talking about?"

"Your girl is on my ass 'cause I believe in God."

The kid lets a disinterested gape hang there for a second. "Uh-huh," he says. "Don't you have something more important to talk about? Like the G in the bridge of 'Hollerin' Blues'?"

"Right, go ahead," Caleb sneers back. "The one mistake I make in three weeks. I'll hold back about the whole first verse of 'Poor Boy' at Cornell."

Jack makes a face, sets his free hand on Wendy's thigh and returns his gaze to what scenery the Interstate has to offer. Her eyes follow his.

Johnny and June keep up their tuneful *tête-à-tête*. Caleb keeps talking. "You gotta have a pretty bleak outlook to think everything's just gonna go black in the end." The girl lets a mischievous grin rebut his argument. He continues, "I mean, what's the point of anything if it all goes up in smoke when you go? It's like it might as well have never happened."

"That's just what I'm reading about!" Tim waves his book around. "*The Unbearable Lightness of Being*! That's what he means!"

Caleb frowns. "Oh, dear Lord."

"No, really!" Tim is beaming. "He goes on about this in the beginning here. He's all about Nietzsche and Infinite Return. He doesn't touch God or Heaven. He just puts it like this: either we live this life once, and we die, and it's all over, or after we die, our lives are restarted from the beginning, and we relive the exact same moments as if it was the first time."

"Uh-huh." Jack and Caleb, apparently allies again, say it in deadpanned unison.

"So if it's just this one life, and then it's over, and we can't even remember it, then, like you said, what's the point? But on the other hand," Tim flips the book over, "if all history gets revisited forever, it has weight—you know, significance."

Success and failure. Great beginnings and terrible ends. A tragic birth here. A catastrophic death there. To be relived, re-grieved, revisited with the awful element of surprise ever intact. I, too, wish the subject would close.

"Yeah, well," Caleb retorts, "you'll never prove that one. Gotta have even more faith to believe that than to think God is real. At least I can point to miracles on Earth. All you got to go on is, what, *déjà vu*?"

"It's not just philosophy. I've read scientific stuff that sounds the same. Basically, you've got time starting with the Big Bang, going for however many zillions of years, and then ending with, whatever, the Big Crunch." He claps his book against his hand. "But the whole thing plays out on a loop, so once it stops, it starts right up again. And when we come in, we just live our lives the same way, and we don't know the difference. Heh heh. It's the gift that keeps on giving!"

Caleb opens the cooler behind his seat. "So, would Stephen Hawking here like a drink?"

"No, thanks." He wouldn't, but I sure as hell would.

Caleb takes a bottle out and swings it around the van. "Jack? Wendy? Nobody? Joe! You want one?"

Sitting silently beside Caleb, Joe smiles but holds up his hand to refuse.

"What do you believe, Joe?" Caleb leans into his friend. "You go for the Buddha? Or the Tay-o?"

At this Joe laughs. "I know the religions. I know Tao, I know Buddha, I give Christmas presents." Then his smile broadens, and his face becomes wise. "And I got music. Music is religion for me."

"Amen, brother!" Hitherto disinterested in such trivialities as the meaning of life, Spike lifts his hand from the steering wheel and holds it in the air, angled at his rear-view mirror. "You other fuckers take a cue from that boy, an' this outfit may actually get somewhere! Only repetition you should be thinkin' about, Tim, is bass-snare-bass-snare. And verse-chorus-verse-chorus; Caleb, that's your ticket to heaven."

⌘

Sound check in Richmond is spent hashing out a quickie tribute number. They rally around 'Hey Porter', for which the kid has no feel but which is redeemed by its sprightly rhythm and by Joe's surprising, blues-tinged guitar solo that closes with a six-string train whistle. With a thumbs-up from the soundman, we break for dinner, served in another wing of the venue. Jack earns a stern look from Wendy when he orders a second beer. We're left afterward with the customary two-hour wait back in the bar before the band goes on. Caleb fills that slot with a pitcher of beer, which he buys ostensibly for the whole group but which seems to flow only down his and Jack's throats.

I sit for some time at the empty bar, jotting in my notebook. As a new pitcher arrives at Caleb's table, Wendy tiptoes across to the stool beside me. "Henry?" Her voice is a worried murmur. "Do you think Jack's had too much?"

I look over at the kid, leaning back in his chair, a little dazed but serious, as he watches Caleb's hands tell some story or joke or nonsense. At length I mutter, "He's a kid. He can afford it."

My remark casts her eyes down at the floor. "All right," she mumbles. "I guess I'm being silly."

"You're being a doting girlfriend," I tell her. "You're good for him." Loneliness and guilt seep from those eyes even as they blink their thanks.

The night proceeds as usual. Early arrivals duck the cover charge. Others filter in from the restaurant. A lanky, crew-cut kid in a black T-shirt takes a post by the door as the lights dim to usher in the evening. The house music begins blasting, a soundtrack of songs which liberally apply country twang to a plodding, chunka-chunka, heavy-metal beat. I watch a steady stream of people fill up the room. It must be a weekend.

While the house PA blares, a group of four checks in at the door. Escorting a pair of full-figured blondes in dark dresses, two hefty men in Army fatigues pull out their wallets in tandem to pay the cover charge. The crew-cut fellow makes a cheerful salute, then waves off the servicemen's cash, to the delight of their dates.

The four take seats at a booth on the far side of the room. No more than twenty-five years old, they order a pitcher for their table and then assume serious expressions of digging the chunka-chunka music. When their beer arrives, they knock it back in manly swigs. Their hefty fingers tap regimental rhythms against their glasses, in time with the pounding beat.

Without a dressing room to retreat to, the Flak Jackets sit at their same table, watching the crowd grow around them. At a nod from the soundman, they stand and pick their way between tables to take the stage. Spike follows and takes his post at stage right, which, by an unfriendly quirk of building design, is situated next to the bathroom doors. Jack carries a new glass of beer and lists like a storm-tossed ship as he tries to hold it steady. They leave their table empty; Wendy, I suddenly realize, is absent. I look around the room and see her at the back, peering in from behind the porthole in the door that leads to the restaurant.

"Evenin', Richmond," mumbles the kid when the house music fades out. A few minutes of sporadic guitar noodling ensue while the soundman fixes a glitch in Joe's line. Jack says no more, just stands sipping his drink. A minute into the interlude he suddenly teeters off the side of the stage and staggers into the men's room. Two minutes later he's out again. Spike pulls him aside to tell him something. He gives the roadie a smirk and climbs back onstage. From there he raises his glass to the roadie. Bemused, Spike flips the bird at him while he takes another sip.

"Evenin', Richmond," the kid repeats. A patter of handclaps greets him. His bandmates kick in behind him, offering up a fairly tight rockabilly beat. "*Hey porter, hey porter,*" he sings with only a passing interest in the melody. With his eyes half shut, he sleepwalks through two verses. Joe steps up to deliver his solo with enough verve to keep the rest of us awake, but his spot can't last forever. The kid takes the song back, limps through another two verses, and covers the last line, "*I'm gonna set my feet on Southern soil and breathe that Southern air,*" like he's compiling a to-do list.

Nonetheless, their take gets a decent cheer. A guy up front in a red baseball cap yells out "Go Cash!" and the kid raises his glass to him.

The regular set ensues, and do I need to set down once more that the band is in fine form? A flawless, dynamic performance by Tim, Caleb, and Joe allows Jack to wobble through forty minutes and still come off as a decent act. Among those in this room, Spike alone doesn't clap, doesn't hoot. The roadie just stands there with arms crossed. And through the porthole across a room dimmed by cigarette smoke, each time I look I see Wendy, her face long with worry and hurt. Too late, I wish I could have shared her concern before Jack got more drinks in him.

Our hosts give hearty applause for the next-to-last number. Jack picks up his glass and scans the room. The alcohol only slightly glazes his eagle eye. At that moment, the larger of the military men passes in front of the stage on his way to the men's room. Jack's eyes narrow; my heart sinks. "Hey, officer," he calls out, and pauses. "'Officer', that's not right, is it?" The serviceman has stopped next to Spike. He looks up warily at the kid.

Something in the pause Jack leaves casts a shadow of suspicion over his audience. The goodwill is slowly sucked from the room. Joe plays a random lick. The kid speaks again: "Shouldn't you *all* be home by now?" This question does earn him a few scattered claps, but they die away quickly.

Eyes now turn to the soldier, who draws himself up to full height. His friend slides out of the booth over the frantic objections of their dates. This one strides up to join his bigger buddy at the kid's feet.

The kid's voice is sincere when he declares: "We want to thank you for what you all are doing..." The soldiers nod but maintain their posture.

"What's he doing?" The girl's voice is suddenly right at my ear, her hand on my elbow.

"...Goin' out to I-raq, riskin' your lives doin' all that killin' for our freedom."

Spike unglues himself from the wall, steps over to the men, and says something to them. The larger man raises his palm at the roadie. His friend gives a wan smile. A grumble rises from the audience. Wendy's fingers dig into my arm. "What's he doing?" she repeats, her voice trembling.

"No, really, boys," the kid soothes. "All kidding aside," and with his right hand he raises his glass toward the crowd. "All the best to you. Here's to ya." He jerks his left hand back at the band. Tim counts them off, the music starts, and the kid lights the fuse. Down comes his hand with the beer glass to stop at his side, at which point he thrusts it out with a look of triumph in a toasting motion. And of course he does so with just the right amount of force, jerks it to a stop at just the right time so that a dollop of beer from the half-full glass sloshes out.

The servicemen dodge a half-step backward; the beer slaps the floor. Wendy's fingers dig into me again. The kid smiles, pirouettes to face the band, swoops to set down his glass, and sweeps his mic stand off the stage floor. He sings 'Fifth Wheel/Third Rail' with a biting edge in his voice, standing with one foot in front of the other and hefting the stand like a poleax, the circular metal base cocked at the crowd.

The soldiers stand firm but don't advance. Every few seconds the larger fellow turns to shoot a glance back at their booth. His nostrils are flaring. His friend sucks in his lips and holds his narrowed eyes on the kid. I might have it wrong, but he looks on the verge of tears.

"*I'm a fifth wheel spinning backward...*"

Around the room arms cross, faces darken, and eyes beam curses at the kid. But the soldiers' stance appears to still them. No one stands or approaches the stage, except the servicemen's dates, handbags in hand.

"*Gonna light up like a comet's tail...*"

Tim and Caleb exchange wide-eyed glances. Wendy's eyes fill with water. Even Spike, near the epicenter, looks shiftily around the room. At least Joe is unconcerned, focused only on the next chord change.

"*When I run up against the third rail.*"

And then, of course, there's Jack, back in the song and giving it that edge, rising to the occasion for the first time all night.

"*Ooh, Fifth wheel.*"

He moves back from the mic, grinning down at the soldiers and at the girlfriends who now hang on their arms. While Caleb sings his backup vocals the four hold a steady gaze on Jack. The shorter soldier breaks his stare, looks down at his shoes.

"*Aah, Third rail.*"

The kid bows like Gene Kelly wrapping up a routine, bending deeply in the soldiers' direction. Then he whirls around and hops off the stage, passing the men's room, then the ladies' room and on out of sight. Nobody follows him, though.

The girl lets go of my elbow, though she can't shake the horror from her face. The band wraps up the song with an extra few bars from Joe's guitar. These feel tacked on, as a buffer between the departed singer and the rest of them. There is no applause to greet their finale; I am surprised to hear only a single, faint catcall.

Of course, the band doesn't enjoy the luxury that Jack gets of a quick exit. While they load their cases, a few members of the audience make their way to the stage. One by one they approach the soldiers and extend their hands or pat them on the back. Most move on to the edge of the stage and jeer at the band. I hear only one word distinctly from my vantage point at the bar: "Traitors!" The word comes from the man in the red baseball cap, he who had cheered for 'Hey Porter'. He hurls the word at Caleb, who winces but does not reply.

With a pained smile, Spike moves in to shake hands with the soldiers. They give him curt nods and then, arm-in-arm with their ladies, proceed to the exit. A wave of applause follows them out the door. At my last glimpse of him, the shorter soldier still watches the floor.

Wendy has watched all of this with me. Now she fixes me with a hard look. "Why'd he do that?" she asks, and I wonder, far too late, why I stayed her from pinning down his drinking arm.

Suddenly she's fanning the air from her face. "Let's get out of this smoke." We head out into the cool night air, across the parking lot to the van. Without the key, I stand stupidly by the passenger door like a dog waiting to be let inside. The girl spies Jack lurking in a corner by the wall of the bar. She storms over to him. Out of earshot, I watch her as by turns she harangues him and pleads with him. The kid is laconic even in body language. From this distance, his peeved expression betrays only faint lines of sympathy for his tormented girl.

"Don't let it get you down." Tim is kicking up pebbles across the pavement, toting his cymbal bags and imparting his wisdom to Joe, who holds two guitar cases and nods ruefully. "People are just jerks sometimes." He finds me by the van. "Somebody just insulted Joe." He repeats, "People can be jerks."

"I know," says Joe, eyes downcast at the asphalt.

"Guy called him a jap," Tim tells me. "In 2003."

Joe sets down his cases behind the van and sits down on them. "He thought I...was *with* Jack—you know. About the Army men."

Caleb shuffles up to our side. He sets down his bass case and with a forced grin claps Joe on the back. "Cheer up, kiddo," he says. "Some people are just assholes."

Tim's eyes widen. "That's just what I said!"

Caleb groans. Then he points at Jack, who seems to be letting Wendy sober him up. "There's one right there. Asshole, I mean." He shakes his head. "And we gotta answer for it." He lets out a long sigh. The sound of faraway cars follows for a few idle moments. Caleb sighs again, capping it with "Fucking war."

"I didn't say anything," says Joe. "I don't like war, you know, but..." He shrugs. "I just want to play."

⌘

Between the flare-ups, there is tedium. I run each morning. My puffing and sweating land me where I started, in a hotel room where I wait small eternities for the next moves in our itinerary. We climb into the van, sit idle as Spike brings us to our next stop. Spike shepherds us into the latest building: a hotel, a club, a café. The boys do what they are told: check in, sound check, performance. Wendy clings to Jack until the kid is set in motion at his next task. Then she steps back and watches, the growing gravity of worry gradually pulling down her smile.

I, too, observe. I am reduced to a machine of two functions: I observe, I report. And at this, as the same antics play themselves out with predictable regularity, I feel increasingly like a hamster on a wheel. Of course, a hamster will run its wheel. It will exert itself, expend energy. I, by contrast, am paralyzed. The wheel turns around me, and I can do nothing but watch it spin.

The process leaves me with a ball of static electricity buzzing in my chest. In the morning, I begin to sprint through the streets, shrugging off stitches and sending my heart into a pounding frenzy to push out the sparks. Back at the hotel, I rinse off the charged sweat, shovel in some solids to plug the recurring void, and climb, with just a shade more effort, back into the van.

The miles count down on the signposts: Pittsburgh 65, Pittsburgh 48, Pittsburgh 36. I count down to a date as well: October 25th. On that date, just forty-one, forty, thirty-nine days away, the wheels will stop. The band will fly back West. I will collect all of my observations, all of my notes and reports. I will fashion them into pieces and fit the pieces together. Two weeks later, I will observe one last time, take note as the Flak Jackets take the stage to record their breakout live album. I will pour the last of my energies into that show, fashion a pitch-perfect recap of the band's triumph, and turn it in. At that point, I will relinquish my duties and leave the wheels to turn around someone else.

⌘

October 16, 2003

"Not now, baby, please." Wendy's finger shoots back and forth across her collarbone. "For me?"

The bottle of Bud is at the kid's lips. Perhaps it's the way she bows her head in defeat and drops her hands to clasp in her lap. At any rate, the bottle drifts down to his own lap, then bobs this way and that around the van. "Anyone want it?"

"More for me!" Caleb swipes it from the kid's hand. He puckers up to it; in a minute it is empty.

Outside the van, a maze of avenues, on-ramps, off-ramps and side streets snakes around us under the artery of the freeway. Spike, at the wheel, shakes his head. He has just come off that freeway, two exits after the interchange from the I-95, and one exit after admitting with some amazement that he might have made a wrong turn. "I don't get it," he says. "I know Boston. I did the Cars."

Around us, the October sky darkens. Spike turns on his headlights at the next stoplight, turns left, and shouts "Fuck!" as the street he turns onto arcs to the right. A minute later, we are funneled back onto the street we just left, heading in the opposite direction.

"Spike," laughs Tim, "you're losing your touch!" Spike turns and shoots him down with a chilling glare.

The roadie takes his foot off the gas while he gets his bearings. An SUV shoots past us. From plastic poles attached to its rear doors, two small flags emblazoned with Red Sox logos flap in tandem. We pass a bar on our right. A huge banner in its front window screams, 'ALCS Live Here! BoSox Central!' From this side of the van's window, it's a faint reminder from the outside world—a reminder that there *is* an outside world. "Game Seven, isn't it?" Tim says.

Yes, it has come to this: I understand from news highlights, and from the Fan's incessant Yankee pep-talks, that an epic American League Championship Series has reached its climax. But among the Flak Jackets, Tim's question is the only reference to this monumental sporting event. No one answers.

Spike exhales a quick "Aha!" and jams the gas. The van lurches forward. We sail through two green lights before he curses again and pulls over to the curb. "Forget sound check," he says to the windshield. "I got a rough idea where we are now, but it's a ways if I gotta take surface streets."

"Like sound check ever does any good for a club date," Caleb sneers.

We wind uphill, downhill, crawl down busy thoroughfares, dart down empty side-streets. Cars zip by around us, duck under yellow lights, and zoom off into the dusk, their Red Sox flags flapping away at us with mocking glee. Ten minutes later, we come to a T-junction. Looking out across the street in front of us, Spike spies the banner at the same time I do: 'ALCS Live Here! BoSox Central!' His fist sends a shudder down the steering column and through the van. "Fuck!"

Lowering his voice to a grumble, he moves the van across and into the far lane, bringing it to a stop in front of the bar. Yanking the parking brake like he's trying to rip it out, he turns to his passengers with a solemn face. "I gotta go ask for directions." His door flies open; he all but flees into the bar.

"That's a first," says Tim. The thoughtful silence that follows is a fitting tribute to the fallen god. Even Joe's head bows in mourning.

Jack suddenly springs to life, bumping Wendy's head from his shoulder. "Wait here!" He pulls the sliding door open and hops out of the van, bounding across the sidewalk.

Caleb leans from the back seat and takes the door handle. "Hey, asshole!" he shouts to the kid's back. "It's cold out!" The kid disappears into a shop marked 'The Fan Zone' without looking back, leaving Caleb to haul the door shut.

"We're one short," I mention to Spike as he slides back into the driver's seat.

The roadie checks behind him through his rear-view mirror. "Where'd he go?" At that moment the kid reappears at the door, carrying a large, bulging plastic bag. "Get the fuck in here," the roadie barks. "We got another half hour 'fore we get to the club."

"What did you get?" asks Wendy, but the kid only smirks and kisses her cheek.

With directions in hand, we dodge through the traffic like a raft through rapids. From my front-seat vantage point, I can see ahead and brace for Spike's braking. This keeps the queasiness at bay. But when I look behind me, Wendy is looking pale and frazzled, one hand clutching Jack's in a white-knuckle vise grip, the other stroking her stomach.

The boys grab their guitar cases and gig bags upon our arrival. Jack hops out cradling his Fan Zone plastic bag like a swaddled infant. Spike hefts an amp across the sidewalk. But the girl shifts to the far side of the back seat and sits still, one hand on the window ledge as if to keep herself steady, and the other still holding her abdomen. Clutching a bag of cables, I stand at the open side door and ask if she needs time for her insides to settle.

"I'm fine," she says. Her nauseated expression fades. For a moment she closes her eyes. A smile spreads across her face. "He listened to me," she says.

"Yes, he did," is all I can say. Her smile is already fading; in an attempt to maintain it, I find myself adding, "Things have a habit of working out."

She furrows her brow. "You believe that?" She shuts her eyes, shakes her head. "That's not what my dad taught me." She opens her eyes and looks out onto the parking lot as though she's speaking in front of a class. "'There's no God up there to pull strings for you. You want things to work out? You have to pull your own strings!'" She looks at me again. Her eyes are pleading, as if to say 'Tell me I'm wrong.'

"Well, then," I muster, "that works out pretty well for you. That way you have all the power." I leave the sliding door open to allow her some fresh air.

There are so many reasons for dread as I walk inside. For one thing, I look across the bar over a sea of blue and red baseball caps. For another, though the opening band is onstage, thrashing through a lively hard-rock number, the baseball caps are motionless. Each capped head is trained on one of three screens showing the Big Game in progress.

Especially distracting is the giant screen installed obnoxiously at the very side of the stage. And the screen is large enough that a few paces into the club I can see the state of play: we're three innings in at Yankee Stadium, and the Yanks are down by three already. I can almost hear the Fan, a continent away, consoling himself as he rocks back and forth in his chair: "It's early. They can do it. Go Yankees!" But already I'm preparing a speech of condolence for him six innings hence.

The opening act finishes its song with a triumphant crash. The chatter in the room barely rises to applaud them. They launch into their next number. Two verses in, the crowd drowns them out with a delighted roar as, on the massive screen to the band's right, the Sox get a man on base and the Yankees' pitcher slinks off the field.

The Flak Jackets have piled their equipment behind the screen. Spike shoots out to collect more from the van. Joe tunes his guitar while his bandmates brood over glasses of beer. "This fucking band!" Caleb groans between two songs. "We've got the worst damn timing—it's like a fucking curse!"

"Hey," says Tim, clapping his hands together, "it's a challenge. We've got to win 'em over, right Jack?"

"Shut up, Tim."

We sit behind the screen and absorb the opening act's decibels. "And it's mostly guys, like, five-to-one!" Caleb hollers as the openers wind up another rocker. Spike hauls in the last of the amps. "The only chicks here are humoring their boyfriends!"

Spike sets the amp to the side. "Get your mind off all that!" he says. "You're here to play—a crowd of chicks is just gravy." He looks over the other three, his index finger coming up to underline the sermon. "These people paid money to get in here. You're a hot-shit outfit? Then you play for their money, whatever you get out of it. You give the best show you got, whether it's to twenty people or twenty thousand."

"It's not numbers!" Caleb gestures at the packed bar. "All these people here, you couldn't fit twenty people who *did* come for the bands!"

The stage remains silent; the players huddle at the drum riser. The crowd curses collectively as some play goes awry for the Sox. With that as their dubious cue, the players onstage return to the fore and count in a final number. Caleb snaps out of his sulk long enough to snicker, "That's rich— to take *that* as an encore!"

I head back out to the van, checking the score as I do: still three-nothing. The outside air has passed from cool to cold, and I have to zip up my jacket as I step to the curb.

Wendy hugs herself when I open the door. "You coming inside?" I ask. "It's warm."

"Is it smoky?"

"A bit. But it has a high ceiling."

"Is Jack drinking?"

A lie flies out before I can formulate a soft truth. "Not that I saw."

She gives a weary smile. "I'll be in soon."

Before going back inside I take out my phone and dial the Fan. He sounds harried and distracted when his roommate finally gets him to the phone. "Where are you?"

"In the belly of the beast."

"Where?"

"Boston."

"Are you joking?" he says after a long beat. And before I can answer, he's on a rant. "You tell those people. The Yankees are gonna do it. They're Number One. They'll do it."

"Jack's going on soon."

"You tell him from me he'll do great. He is great! Number One! You tell him!" And then he's back to "Yankees are gonna do it!"

Another lie escapes my lips. "I have no doubt. I'll call you when they do."

On the big screen inside, Yankee first baseman Jason Giambi has just smashed his team's goose egg with a solo home run. The noise level drops just a hair. Still, drinks are flowing, and the chatter bubbles on under the PA blare of generic guitar rock.

Jack is sipping the foam off a new glass when I rejoin the group. Spike has set the amps on the stage, and Tim is fitting his cymbals to the drum kit. Behind the big screen with me and the kid, a frowning Caleb takes his turn with the guitar tuner, while Joe experiments at slide guitar with the neck of an empty beer bottle. Jack purses his lips and rolls his plastic bag ever more tightly around itself, pulling it into his chest. Even Joe steals the occasional sweeping glance around the room.

Peeking around the screen, I see Wendy pass through the doorway just as a piercing burst of applause breaks out. Startled, she stops short at the door. It takes her a moment to comprehend that the Sox have just pounded out another home run, and her face remains timid as she tiptoes down the bar toward us.

Jack is two-thirds through his glass, in mid-sip when she steps around the TV screen and into view. *In flagrante delicto*, he lowers the glass to the floor of the stage. The girl only lowers her eyes.

Spike has been at the edge of the stage, talking with the sound man. Now he steps down into our midst. "The sound guy and I agreed, you guys'll have a better crowd if we hold off till the game's over. They're pushing you back, like, a half hour." He waves around the room. "This is a big deal for these kids. Long as the Red Sox nail this one, that crowd'll be so happy, you can *shit* onstage and you'll get an encore."

The minutes inch by, and there we stand. Wendy looks back and forth from Jack's beer glass to the floor. The kid sidles up to her, puts his arm around her waist. She lets him in close, but her face is unchanging. Joe and Caleb sit on the stage ledge with their guitars in their laps. Tim deposits his sticks on the bass drum and wanders past me on his way to the bar. "May as well watch the game."

The squeal of PA guitar grows in volume. Jack still has his arm around his girl as he brings her to sit on the edge of the stage. The bag stays clamped under his free arm.

The cranky guitar whine falls away; in its place, the chatter of the room has become eerily subdued. Taking advantage of the quiet, Wendy stands and says, "I'm going to get some fresh air." Bored myself, I leave the three Flak Jackets under Spike's care and escort the girl as far as the bar. As she walks off toward the entrance, I edge in next to Tim and turn to face the big screen.

The letup in the audience's celebration makes sense immediately. The Yankees are finally hitting. Derek Jeter has just crossed the plate, Bernie Williams is on second, and Japanese power-hitter Hidekei Matsui is at bat. My money would still be on Boston, but I can forgive our hosts for sweating a little. The Red Sox manager hobbles out for a talk with the pitcher; he hobbles back without calling for a reliever. Tim mimes looking at his watch. "I hope they get this done soon. I want to get some sleep tonight."

The easy laughter of the early evening is gone; now sporadic, frustrated groans punctuate the crowd's chatter. The place's manager, apparently more used to a music crowd than to a sports one, responds to the mood by turning up the PA music. The shuddering volume conspires with the fog of nervous cigarette smoking to bring the walls and ceiling in on us.

Onscreen, Matsui gets on, sending Williams to third. Two men on, one out, Boston's pitcher tired after seven-and-a-third innings, but with the Fan's favorite Jorge Posada stepping to the plate the Red Sox manager stays put in the dugout. The crowd starts murmuring at each other. Someone at a nearby table shouts, "Take him out!" Posada taps the plate. The Sox pitcher winds up.

Four pitches bring two strikes and two balls. There's a collective *whoosh*, the sound of the crowd exhaling, of hearts restarting, each time the ball hits the catcher's mitt. Posada digs in and for the fifth time the pitcher's leg goes up, his arm snaps forward and hearts stop again.

A brief gasp stretches into a horrified moan as a dozen images flash in dizzying rapid-fire at us: the ball firing off Posada's bat, shooting through the infield, out onto the grass; Williams over the plate; Posada rounding first; Matsui over the plate; frantic Red Sox scrambling; the ball flying back to second base. As the moan subsides, there is Jorge Posada, his foot on second, mouth ecstatically agape and fist pumping, quivering under the enormity of the moment. And here, all around me, there is the familiar sight: Boston heads falling into Boston hands. Tie game. Fucking Yankees.

Amid the hand-wringing, teeth-gnashing mass wades the club's soundman, his bald head shining with the light of the stage. Its lack of Red Sox headgear is an advertisement of his ignorance. He scoots behind the bar to confer with the bartender, then scurries off and ducks behind the big screen.

Spike emerges a minute later to retrieve Tim. He has to roar to overcome the music, which has reached a brain-rattling volume. A foot away, I have to read his lips to catch what he says: "They want you on!" He escorts Tim back to the stage, shaking his head.

Joe takes the stage first. To his right, it's the top of the ninth. He barely glances at the audience on his way to his amplifier. The audience returns the favor. Caleb is next, sneering openly at a crowd he despises. Tim's look of dutiful, sad resignation rounds out the range of emotions. The boys start their set, exchanging glances with faces like the entertainment on the *Titanic*.

Jack is wiping his mouth when he emerges from behind the big screen. He sets down his empty glass on the drum riser and places his bag in front of it, taking care to leave the bag closed at the top.

He howls into 'Fifth Wheel/Third Rail' with a force that blows Caleb back a foot. The lonely ire that first pricked up my ear to the song is back, though this time Jack is spitting it out at his surroundings rather than bringing it to a boil inside.

But Yankee closer Mariano Rivera is holding the Sox at bay, and I see not a foot tapping among the crowd. A few viewers have their hands over their ears. Their oblivious stares tell me these few are trying to block out more than the music.

The band members draw their groove from Jack's performance. The drums snap, the bass throbs, and Joe paints over that background with deft strokes of distorted guitar. Jack isn't perfect; his voice ties itself a little loosely around the melody. But competing with the ballgame for his audience's attention lends an edge to his vocal, and I find myself listening again.

The song ends; in the absence of PA music, we are treated to only the sound of the game from the little television that sits above the bar. The sustained rumble of the Yankee crowd wafts like smoke from the tiny speakers to mass in a black cloud above the Sox-capped heads. Jack surveys his audience with a bemused eye. He waits ten seconds, then raises his hands at his bandmates and claps slowly for them. A couple of girls near the stage take the hint, unhook their arms from their boyfriends' shoulders, and give a few soft sympathy claps.

The kid steps forward and nods a miniature bow. He leans out over the lip of the stage and turns sideways to see the big screen. Rivera has just retired another Boston bat; we're still tied. The kid shakes his head, rolling his eyes. Joe picks out the opening to 'Hollerin' Blues', and we go to commercial.

Only a few in the crowd give a half-hearted stab at enjoying the kid's impassioned take on the song. Some heads bob with the beat, but mostly these kids cup their mouths at their neighbors' ears and vent their anxiety.

Then, all too soon, the screen shows the aerial view of the Bronx, the grim score flashes across the bottom, and the hands and heads freeze once more. Game Seven. Tie game. Bottom of the ninth. Jack doesn't stand a chance.

The band starts to lose its pep. Tim's sticks don't bounce off his skins like they did. Caleb starts missing changes here and there, casting a jealous eye at the indifferent faces and the television sets before him. Jack carries on assaulting each number, but as three Yankee batters go down and the main attraction goes into extra innings, he starts losing steam.

"Oh, miss?" the kid calls as a waitress passes the stage. He digs into his shirt pocket and holds out a drink ticket. As the young lady takes it from him, he puts a hand up to block the stage lights and peers around the room. When he's finished scouting he says to her, "I'll have a beer, please." Though he's away from his microphone, I can hear him perfectly over the silent heads between us.

The waitress returns with his order in the middle of a verse. The kid receives it as he sings, mouthing "thank you" between lines. Thirty seconds later, when Joe steps in to solo, the kid starts guzzling. Half the glass's contents are gone when he brings it upright again. He shuffles to the drum riser, but he does not set the glass down. Instead, he sips delicately twice more, holding it out to see its level. When about a third remains, he picks up the empty glass he has already beside his mystery bag and puts it on the bass amp beside the riser. His new glass he places in the other's place by the bag. With that he returns to the chorus, the gleam restored in his eye.

His timing is pretty good; two minutes later, Wendy squeezes against the bar beside me. As the kid hefts the mic stand and growls through a bridge, she gives him a little wave. Her hand motion turns to fanning the smoke from her nostrils, while her other hand migrates once more to her stomach. But then her upper hand falls to the bar and begins tapping in time with the music. It is possibly the only motion offstage that *is* in time with the music. Because, offstage, we are all at Yankee Stadium, this city's collective neck in the guillotine going into the bottom of the eleventh.

We come back from commercial as the band start their last number. It's twelve-fifteen. Jack is leaning out to check the big screen. Caleb, Tim, and Joe lean into the song as best they can to finish off the set with dignity.

And then, first pitch—game's over! The crack of the Yankee bat (I don't even recognize the player) triggers the deafening whoosh, audible even over the band's fireball chorus. It's the rapid exhale of seventy bodies as that one swing sucks the air from the room. The ball rises up, up toward the stands. Its fall into the upper deck matches the fall of the blade into Boston's neck.

Jack can see this. He has the best view in the house for the despair that blankets the room. He looks out on pouring tears. Leaning out again to see the screen beside him, he sees the tormenting sight of pinstripes flooding the Yankee infield. He watches Mariano Rivera rush to the pitcher's mound and crumple into a heap in exhausted glee. He sees the crowd of Yankees massing to welcome their latest hero at the plate. He sees the despondent Red Sox players trudge off the field. He sees, no doubt, the blood running from seventy hearts in front of him. And seeing all of these things he gives his crooked smirk. He smirks at the heartbreak of his hosts, and I sense that he will live or die by his next act.

The kid runs back to the drum riser and reaches for his glass. He raises it at the crowd, glancing less than subtly at his girl as he brings it level, one-third full, by his face. He then takes a fortifying swig that leaves the glass empty, and returns to the drum riser. The only applause thus far has come from the television.

Joe and Caleb have thrown off their guitars. Tim is standing at the drum kit, twirling a wing-nut to remove his cymbal. "Hey!" Jack barks, and points at the drum stool. He speaks low, turning to direct the others as he does. I catch the words "just play." The guitars come back out of their cases. Tim sits and starts a lonely backbeat. Jack moves to rummage in his bag.

The bar manager does one thing right as the kid rummages: with a click of a remote he shuts off the televisions. All eyes turn in that instant to the movement onstage. The kid, likely sensing the new attention, turns his head so that for a second we see only his profile. He freezes, a skydiver in the plane doorway. The whimpering in the room dies down, leaving only the drummer's beat. I look to my side at the girl. A growing concern tightens her features. And then the kid leaps into the abyss.

With one swing of his arms, he yanks the great navy blue flag from his bag and unfurls it in the air above him. I leap forward at the same nanosecond that my brain registers the white interlocking letters, N and Y. The girl, a terrified yelp of "No!" leaving her lips, matches my step.

A cry of shock and anger rings out, almost drowning out the girl's exclamation, and in my first two paces already I see Sox-capped heads rise to ominous heights from the tables in front. He can't know what he's doing.

But he does. He makes three passes of the offending flag in wide arcs over his head. Wendy and I reach the stage as one and stop short, unsure what to do. The first few members of the mob stalk past the front tables at our flanks. Behind them, a phalanx of their supporters brandish their middle fingers like spears in the air. It is then, turning back to Jack, that I see a glint of metal and, a moment later, the spark off the flint.

The rushing bodies mass around us in front of the stage. There they stand for a heartbeat, a sudden confusion papering over the rage on their faces. Their confusion turns to astonishment as the flame catches.

The first tongue of bright orange flame licks across the bottom of the flag, curling up the side. Jack dangles it by the opposite corner and lets the flame build on the bottom until it begins to eat the bold white insignia. As blue and white fall under orange, the crowd begins to sound its approval. Scattered whoops and hollers play over the rumble of applause, as the flag becomes a ball of fire. The kid holds on with his left fingertips, the lighter held up triumphantly in his right hand. He clings to the burning rag as the crowd's rumble builds like thunder, holds it until his fingers disappear behind the leaping flame. The crowd roars, many rising to their feet as he lets it drop to the stage floor. And then, with both fists in the air, he jumps up, coming down with both feet stomping on the smoldering scrap.

The exultant, shuddering roar hits me in the solar plexus. I duck under its force, and feel Wendy's hand squeezing my arm as she, too, braces against its blast. Jack doesn't flinch. With his feet planted among the remaining shreds, he makes a motion to Joe at his left.

Joe takes the cue; as Tim's drumbeat resurfaces over the crowd's subsiding cheer, he strikes a mighty chord and lets it sustain. Caleb finds his bassline; two bars later, the guitar slips into the feverish riff to 'Poor Boy'. The kid steps from the ashes to his microphone amid a new wave of cheers. His voice, roughened from the set he's already sung, dry to the point of cracking from the smoke around his head, booms nonetheless. Rather than strain to reach the high notes, he bends the melody to his own ends. Howls of pleasure from behind me signal that the crowd is finally his. And so commanding is his performance, so energized is the band's playing behind it, that it isn't until they're bashing through the outro that I turn to see that the girl has walked out.

⌘

October 18, 2003

"Where is Wendy?" I ask after fifteen minutes at the breakfast table with no sign of the girl.

Tim answers for Jack. "She's visiting her family." The kid glowers at him. "They live just over in New Hampshire, somewhere between here and Danbury. Her brother picked her up this morning. He's bringing her to meet us at the gig tomorrow night."

"So we gotta enjoy our freedom while we can." Caleb gives Jack a playful elbow to the ribs.

It's easy to see what freedom means. Before the van pulls out of the hotel parking lot, Caleb is into the cooler, passing out bottles. He and the kid have polished off two Buds each before we stop for lunch. By dinner, I have lost count of their intake.

But their enjoyment seems to end there. Neither of them is a singing drunk, a laughing nor crying drunk. Caleb in the morning is as boisterous as ever, but by afternoon he grows quiet, content to watch New England roll by. And Jack remains Jack—only more so. When I ask him how he's enjoying his freedom, he cocks his head rather than shrugging. And when he takes the stage in Hartford and someone in the Torinos' crowd calls out for 'Fifth Wheel/Third Rail', the smirk that tugs at his cheek is that much more crooked.

But he's in bad form, and Caleb scatters bum notes across the set as well. The kid holds the mic stand for balance; when he ventures from it to pace the massive theater stage, his gait is an uneven zigzag. He manages only to mumble his lyrics, his voice swimming around the key.

"Boy, you laid an egg tonight, motherfucker," are Spike's words of wisdom as he rounds us into the van.

"I don't know, Spike," Tim ventures as he climbs in. "I think Jack exuded a certain aura."

The roadie rolls his eyes. "He exuded a certain *aroma*."

The kid's eyes would burn a hole in the roadie if they weren't doused in beer. "Who made you a critic?" he demands, sliding into the row behind the driver's seat. He is a bit late adding "Motherfucker?"

"Yeah, leave him alone." As he gropes his way in beside the kid, Caleb's taxed liver adds a surly edge to his voice. "He's allowed an off night."

Spike climbs into the driver's seat. "You just keep talkin' like that if you wanna be playin' the fuckin' Crooked Bar the rest of your life!" He turns the ignition. "Besides, you ain't one to talk, the way you played."

Jack and Caleb absorb his attack with silent scowls.

"You got a big opportunity on this tour." Spike negotiates a turn down the aisle of the parking lot one-handed, so that he can wag a finger at the rear-view mirror. "You can show twelve hundred people a night how great you are or just how hard you can suck." He shakes his head. "You just gave all those people an excuse to skip your next gig."

No one argues. But after some minutes of wordless brooding, Caleb reaches down and silently opens the cooler. Discreetly he passes a can of Coors to Jack and grabs one for himself. After a series of low hand signals between them, each holds his can at his knee. Caleb mouths "One, two, three," whereupon they hold out their cans and pull their tabs at the same time. The fizzy hiss sounds in stereo behind the roadie's ears.

⌘

October 19, 2003

Caleb and Jack match each other bottle for bottle on the drive to Danbury. Spike makes an early comment about a repeat offense, then limits his communication to reproachful glares through the rear-view mirror. By sound check, though, Caleb has switched from Bud to Starbucks.

Bass drum? Thump, thump, thump. Okay.

The kid is at the bar, his hands absently twisting a string of free-drinks tickets the promoter has handed to him. The bartender has only just moved behind the bar. Before the guy can set down his bag, Jack is waving one of the tickets in his face.

Snare? Bap, bap, bap.

"We're in for another dud." Spike is at my side in front of the stage. There is genuine worry in his sigh. "I hope the chick gets here soon." At my raised eyebrows, he raises his hands. "Hey, man. I know she's good for him. Keeps him grounded, all that. I get it."

Floor tom? Tom, tom, tom.

Spike snaps back into form. "She ain't bad, now that she puts out."

Full kit? Thump-bap, thump-thump-bap.

Jack's glass of beer is half gone. He shuffles from the bar to the stage. Staggering on and ambling back to the drums, he holds out a drink ticket to Tim, then pulls it back. "I can put it to better use," he slurs.

Bass? Dum-dum, dum-dum. That's enough.

Tim glances helplessly over the lip of the stage at Spike. "Uh, you know, I've had a hankering for a Coke all day," he says after a moment. "Maybe I can get you one, too?" He holds out his hand, waits, then smiles when the kid relents.

Now guitar? Ba-na-na-na-na.

Jack takes two swaying steps toward Caleb and tries the same prank with the bass player's ticket. But Caleb, sipping his coffee, his bass hanging free from his shoulders, snaps his ticket out of Jack's retreating hand.

Vocal?

"I think I'll have a Coke with Tim," Caleb says with a wry grin. The kid slinks away from him.

Vocal there?

He strides past his microphone and over to Joe. He hands Joe his drink ticket. "Lemme guess, a Coke for you too?" Joe gives a bewildered smile.

Vocal, come on.

"Reverb, high end, please," he says when at last he makes it to the microphone. "One, two, one, two, works for me." He stumbles back from the mic.

Backing vocals? One, two, one, two. Good. The kid paces dizzily from one end of the stage to the other.

Okay, full band?

They start a mechanical 'Hollerin' Blues'. Thump-bap, thump-bap, ba-na-na, dum-dum. Jack takes the mic stand, drags it back to the drum riser and unhooks the mic. Holding it limply in one hand, he parks himself in front of the bass drum, there to sing the entire song in drowsy tones until the sound man's 'okay' signal ends his ordeal.

As they disengage from their instruments, my cell phone rings. It's Wendy. "I'm leaving my parents' house now. My brother's driving me. Jack's got him on the guest list. He's gonna stay and watch the show." Jack sits down at the edge of the stage and prepares to roll himself off. "Is he there?"

"Jack? Of course, let me, uh, go look for him." I am a terrible liar.

I turn to the kid, mouth 'Wendy' at him and extend the phone toward him. His eyelids, heavy with drink, struggle to widen with his surprise. He shakes his head. I take the phone back. "Uh, no, Wendy, he's tied up right now. Sound check, you know."

"Oh."

"Hey, you'll see him at the show tonight, and then he's all yours again." This seems to satisfy her.

"I suppose you don't want her to hear the state you're in," I say to Jack after hanging up. He offers me his usual blank stare, slightly glazed over. I find myself fighting down a snarl. "Maybe you want her to get the full effect tonight."

He musters the best smirk his drink-palsied features will allow.

⌘

The place is half-full, buzzing with chattering bodies and pulsing with PA music when I spy the girl at the entrance. Standing next to her is a tall, strapping man of about thirty. And she's making hurt, confused faces at the bouncer, who looks up from his clipboard and reciprocates with a look of apology. I push off from the bar. I'm halfway to her when she reaches into her jacket pocket and hands the hulking creature a ten-dollar bill.

"We weren't on the list!" she exclaims when we meet a few paces past the door. "*I* wasn't on the list!" And then, as an afterthought, "This is Terry." Terry, just as tall, strapping, and thirtyish up close, nods gravely and shakes my hand.

We find three barstools, side by side. The girl's timing is perfect; the Flak Jackets emerge onstage almost as soon as we're seated.

The girl's face betrays her horror when the kid comes on, disheveled and glowering. She looks to her brother, then, with the embarrassment she has just shown him still apparent, at me. That reddish glow of humiliation turns to a pale pink of betrayal. Though it's her boy on the stage who has already and is about to further let her down, her eyes still shriek at *me*: *How could you?*

"*Oh, you say such things, I hear much more...*"

He's spitting as he sings, literally, shooting out little specks of alcoholic saliva from his lips and into the row of tables in front of the stage. I see the silhouette of one fellow right in front of him, lifting a hand to wipe the dew from his brow and shield against any more. A group of three young men crowd around a table touching the corner of the stage. Seeing Jack's rather disgusting display, they chortle together, pointing mocking fingers at him.

"*Here I stand in the hurricane, hollerin' asking why...*"

Like last night, he leans against his mic stand like a drunkard against a lamppost. The band, even Caleb, holds down the rhythm, and the song flows smoothly. Jack's uneven melody floats over it, unhinged from it in pitch and cadence, like a piece of trash on a pristine stream.

"But I'm standing on my blistered feet, and here you thought I'd die..."

Terry speaks into the girl's ear. He draws back, his stern face gauging her reaction. She shakes her head at him, answers back. Her hands wring in horror.

The three at the stage right table are still laughing it up as they flag down a waitress for another round. One crosses his eyes and mimes Jack's clinging to the mic stand. His tongue sticks out of the corner of his mouth. The waitress picks up an empty pitcher from their table, leaving only their also empty glasses behind.

"I'm hollerin', I'm screamin' bloody murder bloody blues..."

The kid slurs so badly that I can only decipher the lyrics because I have heard them a hundred times before. Caleb winces down at his bass; Tim's eyebrows are raised halfway to the ceiling, as if the sheer force of his buoyant expression can pull the kid's voice up into the right key. Joe glides into a solo, which he finishes walking over to turn up his amplifier. When Jack approaches the mic again, guitar chords overpower his caterwauling. Off-balance as it is now, the mix is easier on the ears.

"You think you can just say that we're through..."

The waitress drops off the refilled pitcher with the merry trio. Each fellow fills his glass to the brim. They toss back giant gulps in rapid succession. One of them, a skinny guy with short, spiky hair, makes some comment to the fellow beside him, and they collapse into one another in laughter. This catches the kid's eye.

"You think you can just—" He starts repeating the last line, realizes his mistake, and mumbles the correct last words, *"...someone new,"* a beat behind.

"What's wrong with him?" Wendy's voice is shrill and accusing in my ear. Her eyes are lit by fire even as they fill with water. And what can I say to answer her that will not make me, in my inaction, the kid's accomplice?

Joe relieves us with another guitar break. The kid is inching over to stage right, dragging the microphone with him. The three at the table lose their laugh lines. A staring contest, three against one, begins.

Thump-bap, dum-dum, ba-na-na.

The kid pulls himself up, stands as tall as his hampered equilibrium will permit. The three respond by sitting up in their chairs.

Wendy shifts in her seat. "He's gonna do something..." she starts in my ear.

Thump-bap, dum-dum, dum-dum.

Joe takes a bar after his solo to figure out that Jack isn't yet ready to sing. The hole in the mix is gaping. Wendy shifts again and addresses her brother.

Her arms flail in worry.

Ba-na-na-na. Ba-na-na-na.

Joe carries another verse. Caleb, still playing a reasonably steady line, steps up behind the kid and says something. His smile is stiff. The kid shakes his head, still intent on his adversaries.

Ba-na-na, ba-na-na, thump-thump, tom-tom, bap.

He brings the mic to his lips. Caleb eases back to his station. Wendy doesn't buy the apparent climb-down, though. "We've got to..." Her words turn into motion as the kid starts spitting the next verse, sheer hostility in his growl.

"Caught between two barbed-wire fences, my loneliness, my pride..."

She's off the stool and picking her way past tables on her way to the stage. Her brother bolts after her. I feel my own legs carry me up and forward in their wake. Up front, the fellow nearest to the stage is holding up his hand to shelter himself from Jack's shower.

"Love ain't nothin' on—"

Jack shuts his mouth and sucks in his lips. The song rolls on without him. We're halfway to the stage, Wendy still leading, squeezing between tables, chairs, and patrons rapt with the standoff in progress.

Thump-bap, dum-dum, ba-na-na.

Joe starts yet another guitar solo, thinks better, and retreats back into playing chords. Once again the kid makes no move, but his three foes are laughing now. One of them tops off the three glasses, emptying the pitcher. And then the three raise their glasses to Jack, each beaming madly.

Thump-bap, dum-dum, tom-tom-tom-tom.

The kid's foot comes down the instant their glasses return to the table. The spike-haired guy pulls his hand back just in time as his glass shatters under the kid's shoe. A frothy wave of beer sweeps over the table. Wendy shrieks and stops short a few feet from the blast. The three friends push back from the table and shoot to their feet. Each gapes first at his drenched outfit and then at the lunatic who straddles, like the Colossus, one foot on the stage, the other still planted amid the wreckage on their table.

"What the fuck!" the spike-haired guy shouts. His cry is clearly audible to the entire room; the band has, for once, stopped playing. There is a moment of complete silence, broken only by the sound of Spike leaping onto the side of the stage. The three young men stand in place, chests heaving, hands trembling.

And then they lunge. Jack staggers back, escaping the table before the three can get hold of his leg. With Wendy's cry of "No!" following behind them, they clear the lip of the stage in one bound. Jack darts back behind the approaching Spike, past Caleb, and into the wings. He stops, though, clearly within view, and turns to look back.

Spike is quick, and deftly grapples with two of the three, his hands against one's elbow and the other's forearm. "Easy! He's not worth it!" These two are foolish enough to engage in shouted dialogue with the roadie, buying Jack valuable seconds. But Spike is just one man, and the third adversary, the spike-haired one, has dashed past his friends without slowing. Caleb steps up as the next line of defense. He strides forward with the neck of his bass extended to his left like a toll bar. The guy charges through it, knocking the instrument backward and spinning Caleb sideways. Caleb makes a half-hearted grab for the fellow. When his hand closes on nothing, he yells out to Jack, "Go!"

For the kid is still in the wings, watching the melee with a look of dazed wonder. And only now, when the two held at bay pull away from Spike, does he make a break for the backstage area. Their more nimble friend is almost upon him.

We fly onto the stage, Wendy with a scream. Spike bolts back toward the scene forming in the wings. But the first to get to the kid's side is Tim, who has leaped from his drum riser to land within feet of his friend. The kid stumbles down the corridor that leads backstage. We arrive at the opening to witness Tim's brave stand. He wedges himself between Jack and his foe, turning on the stranger so that the kid can make his getaway.

But Tim makes two fatal errors: first, he assumes that he can stop a charging bull with calming words. Yelps of "Easy now!" and "Hold on!" slow the attacker, but only long enough for his friends to catch up with him, and for him to wind up. When the fellow swings, it would seem from Tim's expression that he is sent sprawling as much by his surprise as by the force of the guy's fist against his jaw. He lands half on the floor, half against the wall, and stays slumped there, stunned, a human roadblock that in their drunken state the three have to tread over with care.

Their balance is uneasy, and Spike has just snagged one of them by his shirt. These boys have no need to hurry, though, for Tim's second mistake is to think that the kid will use his gallant intervention to gain some distance on his opponents. Instead, Jack stands at the end of the hall, between the backstage lounge and the men's room, strangely immobilized and staring stupidly at Tim's great fall. And when the three marauders surround him, Spike pulling in vain at one of them, the kid succeeds in sending just one punch into empty air before they start landing blows.

Bodies cram in front of me, obscuring my view of the attack. Joe and Caleb rush into the corridor. Wendy screams, claws her way past her brother and over poor, prone Tim. She comes up against Spike's back as the roadie wrenches his adversary from over Jack's ducked head. The roadie swings the guy around to get between him and Jack, inadvertently slamming the guy into the hysterical girl. She lets out another shout as the guy's torso knocks her into the wall. Spike turns back to the fray without looking at her. And as the girl shouts helplessly at the tangle of people, as Tim pulls himself slowly to his feet beside her, beyond them I can see only the spike-haired guy's elbow flashing in and out of view as he pummels the kid.

Suddenly I am heaved into the wall as the bouncer plows through the hallway. He passes Spike, who has managed to pull a second body away from the kid. The brute then swoops down to take hold of the spike-haired fellow in a half-nelson. "Get out!" he bellows, and at the rest of us, "Move!" He rounds the guy's two henchmen up with his massive free arm, and herds them all back to the bar area. My last view, as I am swept out of the corridor, is of the girl, diving past the group and farther down the hall to tend to her man.

Her brother Terry accosts me. "What the hell is going on here?" he demands, voice shaking. My own voice trembling to match his, I confess that I don't know.

The bouncer gives a final shove to the trio at the entrance, then returns down the corridor to deal with Jack. Terry follows the man back down the hall to find his sister. I wait where I am, leaning against the pillar that forms the corner of the stage. After a minute, Caleb, Joe, and an ashen Tim stumble back into view. The bouncer follows, arguing over his shoulder with Spike, who, along with Wendy, props the slumping kid up by his arms. Terry walks just behind his sister, mumbling to her in tones which could be soothing or scolding.

Spike and Wendy lead the kid to the nearest table and pour him into a chair. Behind the blood, his face has kept its shape. His nose, though bleeding, is on straight. The only mark on him is a cut over his right cheekbone. But he leaves it to Wendy to wipe the blood from his face with a napkin; instead, he holds his sides with both hands and groans as he tries gingerly to twist from left to right.

Frantic chatter rises around us as the crowd discusses the spectacle. I peer past the wide-eyed faces and survey the trail of destruction. At the table by the stage, a man with an apron dumps a dustpan full of glass shards into a garbage pail. Jack's mic stand lies across center stage, while Caleb's bass and Joe's guitar lean at odd angles against the drum riser. A glass lies on its side in front of Joe's amp.

"I'm going." Terry has moved from his sister's side. "She wants me to leave," he says to me. "I can't believe this!"

"I'm sorry you had to see it," I feel foolish to say. "It's never turned out like this." I leave out just how close it's come in the past.

He shakes his head. "I told her to come back with me, but she's insisting on staying with this asshole." Then he holds out his hand. As I shake it he looks me in the eye. "It's a shame. I've read your book. Wendy told me all about you. I was looking forward to meeting you."

A new, irrational sense of authority compels me to say, "Jack is a good kid." My authority melts against his sudden look of contempt. With another shake of his head, he turns to leave.

Spike gets up from the kid's side and makes his way to the stage. There he starts pulling together the band's gear. Needing some activity to work the adrenaline from my veins, and to clear the swirl of ill thoughts from my brain, I hop up with him and wordlessly lend him a hand.

⌘

She's gone. Through. Off the tour. I can't write any more.

⌘

October 21, 2003

"I didn't mean to hurt him!" My brain has stopped superimposing glasses onto Tim's face. Without them this morning, the drummer's eyes are red-rimmed, bloodshot and pleading. He sits alone with me at the breakfast table. His small, white plate has on it only a bun and an unopened packet of butter. He has just confessed to whisking the girl away from Jack last night, to leaving the kid half hanging over the side of his hotel bed with one last bruise to add to his collection.

I ask him what exactly happened. His face contorts. "Oh, God," he starts, and tears his bread in half. "I was just...he was gonna..." He raises his eyes to the ceiling.

"Just start where we left off." I put my hand on the table, palm up, between us. I don't know how the gesture might comfort him, but it comforts me. "What happened after I turned in?" That would be right after our party fell out of the van and escorted the kid *en masse* to his and Wendy's room.

He picks up one of the two halves of bread and rips it in two. "Well, I went to my room—I was right next door to them—and I just lay on the bed. My jaw was still hurting a bit—" he puts down the bread morsels and massages the side of his face, "—and I just wanted to cool out before going to sleep." He takes a deep breath. "So then, five minutes later I hear a bunch of crashing and thumping through the wall. And I listened for a minute. I thought it would die down—I *hoped* it would die down. But it didn't." His voice rises. "So I went in the hall, and I listened some more at their door. And I could hear Wendy screaming. So I started banging on the door, and I'm thinking, *He's beating her up, she won't be able to get to the door*. But she did come, she just about tore the door off its hinges." He rips another hunk of bread off the half he's left intact. "And she was crying like rain, all red-faced, and the way she covered her mouth I thought he'd socked her."

"But he hadn't."

"No, as it turned out." He starts shaking his head. "But the room was a mess. The bedside lamp was on the floor, the curtain rod was off one of its hooks, and the blinds were all crooked. There were clothes sorta strewn everywhere, on the bed, over the TV." He breathes in deep once more. "And Jack was still just flipping out. He had his suitcase and he was swinging it around, smashing everything he could see. He sent the lamp flying off the TV table. And he smashed the suitcase into the TV, and it's a miracle the screen didn't shatter. And he was coming toward the door, and he hit the mirror, and that *did* shatter, and Wendy screamed. And I was getting pretty spooked, and he was close enough to us that he could have swung and hit us, so I grabbed Wendy and sorta pushed her out the door..."

He pauses for breath. "And the light in there was crazy, 'cause the lamps were upside down on the floor, but at least one of them was working, and with the light sort of cast up on his face, he looked like a madman, just terrifying. And he yelled something at me, like, 'What are you doing with my baby?' And he was coming toward me, and like I said, the light was crazy, and *he* was looking crazy—you know, fire-in-his-eyes sort of thing—and he lifted the suitcase up over his head..." Here he takes in a long breath. His admission comes out in a quiet, trembling sigh: "And then I hit him."

I close my eyes as I picture the blow, the suitcase crashing to the floor, the kid's stunned face as he follows it. "I didn't mean to hurt him," he repeats in earnest. "I was scared, the adrenaline was flowing..." He steals a glance at Jack, who sits across the room, cradling his head in his hands. "I didn't even know you could knock a guy out cold with one punch." He puts his hands to his own, shaking head. "Spike says it was probably more the beer that made him stay down." He looks over to the other corner of the room, at another table where the roadie sits picking at his bacon and eggs and exchanging murmurs with Joe and Caleb.

"That's what he told you last night?"

Tim nods. "Wendy was crying her eyes out, and I took her to Spike's room. And Spike came back with me and we kind of lifted Jack up on the bed, and Spike told him in his ear just to stay asleep. So Spike stayed with him, and I went back to Wendy, and I told her I thought she ought to go home—I mean, it's lucky we happened to be so close to her folks." He takes a shred of soft bread and presses it between his thumb and forefinger. "We came to you then, 'cause she didn't know her brother's cell number. She wanted to call him so she wouldn't freak her mother out in the middle of the night. She'd called you from his cell and all." He closes his eyes and swallows hard. "Oh, God."

From this point I have the story: the girl calling on her brother to turn right around and retrieve her, no questions asked; the roadie's quick tidying of the room, gathering together the girl's things and spiriting them out to us while the kid slept off the blow; and his mannered diplomacy at the kid's door when the hotel's night manager came belatedly to investigate the disturbance. And of course there is the subsequent scene of haggling outside Jack's room, during which a wad of cash flew out of my wallet, to cover the damage that Spike could not conceal, and to buy us the last few hours of our stay. After all, we had the girl to attend to.

"How was she when the two of you went back to your room?" This is one gap in the chain of events: the two hours of waiting for Terry to turn up, which the girl spent locked safely away from the berserker next door.

His face softens. "She was pretty shook up." Again he looks over at Jack. The kid remains in the same position as at last glance. When Tim speaks again, it's at half volume. "I turned on the TV and flipped channels for awhile, you know, to get her mind off things. And she just talked over it."

"About what?"

"Well, she was mighty distraught to be leaving. I tried to tell her it was best. She kept saying that she loves him, and that he's a good guy, and all that. And then she told me..." and his eye roves over to my tape recorder, winding away between us. He picks up again, speaking closer to full volume. "She said, uh, how she was going to be in trouble, uh, with her mom and dad." His voice lowers anew. "She cried a whole lot. I gave her a hug every so often—just to comfort her. Near the end she kinda rallied, and she told me, 'It's time to start pulling my own strings.' And then you knocked with Terry."

Yes, I knocked with Terry. I had waited for him in the hotel lobby, my pajama top tucked into my slacks. When he stormed in, I brought him to Tim's room, from which Wendy emerged in tears, hugged her brother, hugged me, and vanished down the hall. Solemn-faced, Terry took her suitcase and disappeared behind her. The lump she left in my throat remains even now.

Tim sighs. "What are we gonna do? I can't see Jack ever talking to me again. I tried to say I was sorry when he came out of his room this morning, but he just looked at me and kept walking. What can I do? I don't want Jack to hate me. He's my friend. I love the guy, you know?" He pauses, then whispers, "Oh, God."

We stand soon after, leaving Tim's untouched packet of butter amid a dozen shreds of bread. My pristine roll rests in my own plate beside it.

⌘

October 23, 2003

We're at the finish line: Freeport. We are to play one final show, sleep at the Holiday Inn by JFK, and fly home tomorrow morning. We should be exultant. The mood backstage tonight should not be that of a wake.

But it is. Catatonic, the kid sits on a metal folding chair in the vacant kitchen that serves as the backstage area of the night's venue. In a triangle around him, the Flak Jackets pick and slap, Caleb and Joe on unplugged guitars, Tim at the vertex with sticks against his thighs. Their focus is deep: they stare at one another, watching for changes; at Jack, looking for approval. Caleb looks for reaction. Joe, for once visibly concerned, waits for a nod. With each glance at his friend and leader, Tim pleads for a sign of life. The three are deaf to the music blasting from the bar PA, and to the buzz of a near-capacity crowd behind the grease-covered tile of the kitchen wall. They seem not to sense it, just as Jack seems not to sense *them*.

I maintain my distance, leaning against the frame of the screen door that opens out to the back alley. The cool outside air wafts under my open jacket. It's a chilly comfort: something tender rests inside me, behind a barrier of stoic strength that has congealed over the course of years. That tender spot has flared up behind that dam on this day, applying new pressure which the dam is dismayingly ill-prepared to take. If I step into the band's circle, if I get too close to Jack's burning grief, the dam might burst, I might feel that dreaded flood of tenderness. And if that happens, the fragile peace of mind that for years I have delicately crafted will dissolve like a sand castle in its midst.

They rehearse, an apparently untried number, for twenty minutes. Members of the opening act cart guitar cases and amplifiers through the room, past my post, and out the screen door to a waiting minivan. The tight quarters make for difficult maneuvering to avoid crashing into any of the seated Flak Jackets, but none of my boys makes any effort to make way. The band members follow Jack's mumbled directions, inaudible to me, as though they've been shouted.

At length I make my way through the cluttered kitchen to the front room. On a high stage Spike fusses with the club's soundman, flapping a hand at the microphone and at the giant black speakers that hang by chains on either side. He puts his mouth to the mic, says a terse "Check," and a shriek of feedback consumes the room. All forty-odd people in the room duck against the barrage—all but Spike, who merely shakes his head at the soundman and raises his palm at the offending mic.

I take a seat at the bar and look out over the audience, three or four dozen Long Islanders, some of whom I reckon I rubbed shoulders with at the Beacon a few weeks ago. Watching the stage, they shout into each other's ears to overcome 'Sweet Home Alabama' playing over the scene. As the song fades out, a stringy-haired, leather-jacketed little fellow appears in the entranceway, holding a beer glass in one hand, and a cigarette in the other. The man lifts his glass in the direction of the stage and yells, "Yeah!" He takes a hefty drag from his cigarette and stubs the thing out on the threshold before stepping in. Then he cranes his neck and exhales straight up in the air, obviously eager to demonstrate his feelings for the state's new anti-smoking law. The smoke billows swiftly up into the high arched ceiling.

Two PA tracks later, the soundman retreats from Spike and the stage, the roadie ducks out to the kitchen, and the stringy-haired fellow lets out another whoop. This time three or four sympathizers take up his call.

A heavy-metal number ensues, long and loud. A satisfied patter rises from the floor to greet Tim as he climbs to the stage over the fade-out. The clamor increases, augmented by a couple of shouts as Caleb and Joe follow, guitars in hand. And when the kid shuffles into view behind them and wanders over to center stage, there's even a hint of a roar: the crowd is expecting a good time. Of course, I know better.

Caleb plugs in and comes to his microphone. A ring emits from the speaker as he opens his mouth. "Check!" It turns piercing at the utterance. The agonized wince Jack makes as the sound subsides is the first burst of feeling I have seen from him all night. It brings pain to his face, to be sure, but moreover it invokes in his puppy-dog eyes a sorrow, like the feedback is some shrill aural distillation of his misfortune. He shudders and staggers back. When he regains his composure he opts to hang back by the drum kit. He looks mournfully out over the audience, past them, like a lost toddler looking for his mother in a crowd of strangers.

The chatter of the audience rises to an awkward level. Joe tries to make eye contact with the kid before beginning the set. When he fails to get a response, he looks to Tim, who sits bewildered at the sight of his bandleader. Finally, the tension of their inaction goads Tim, and after another few uncomfortable seconds, he points a drumstick at Joe to start.

A slow arpeggio introduces the first song. This is no furious rocker, no song to start a party, and it catches the audience off guard. Heads turn, people make puzzled faces. But the sweet soulful tones relax the kid, and as the chords change and begin to ring familiar to me, he gathers himself and rediscovers center stage.

A short stab of feedback accompanies Jack's first words: *"To know..."* A threatening ring persists from that point. But the initial screech fails to stop me from recognizing Jack's song. And the hum that follows fails to smother the sound of his soul weeping.

"To know you were there,
Waiting,
Behind me."

And none of it can keep my heart from turning to molasses.

"If I got lost,
To know,
That you'd find me."

Jack Hackett, whose own flame can burn brightly when he sets his mind to stoking it, turns all his efforts to remaining upright and simply lets the song pour from him. Gone are the grimaces at missed notes. Absent are the lines of intense concentration in his brow. The mind that would work so hard at perfecting the kid's delivery has been melted down, reduced to a single synapse which can do naught but blink at his loss. And so rather than take careful aim and shoot fireballs at us, he merely stands and glows.

Caleb comes to the microphone. The speaker hum grows as he sings harmony:

"Nothin' to do now but cry,
But my tears, they run over a smile."

Caleb. Caleb who sat by and snickered each time people or events conspired to drive Jack's love away. He watches his friend, and in perfect sync he moans, as though Jack's pain were his own.

"I smile, as I bleed my eyes dry."

When again Jack sings alone, *"To know you were there,"* he finds me in the crowd. The music swells behind him for a bar as I endure his pitiable stare. *"For awhile."* The line passes; the kid looks away.

Joe steps forward to take the solo, moving into the kid's space as he plays. He shifts his gaze from the kid, to his fingers, back to the kid. He tilts his guitar up and swings the neck toward him, offering up his licks. He plays heroically; the kid shuts his eyes.

Joe retreats, returning to arpeggios. Jack returns to the fore, eyes still closed, stopping in front of the mic when the whine of feedback rises again. His lyric quells the ringing:

"No, there's nothin' to do now but cry,
But those tears still run over my smile,
Can't forget, no I ain't gonna try,
Sweet pain,
You were there,

For awhile."

And though he makes no visible movements in body or face, an aura of serenity radiates from him. In this tender moment I envy him. Pity him, yes, that too, but I envy him somehow for his sublime pain, and that he can use it to break *my* heart.

"Oh I had you, for awhile."

The lights on him wash out the finer details of his face. I can't see if he's crying. No, he's not—or at least he's not shedding tears.

But in the final pleading climax, he bellows, *"Oh, I still want you!"* and it's the holler of the field hand among the cotton rows.

He wails, *"I still need you!"* and he's the solitary, redneck truck driver on a desolate nighttime highway.

"And to think—oh, baby..."

And he's Patrick Barclay, getting over his lover Stacy, or the death of Mister Rogers, or better, looking over his mother's open casket and trying with all his poor power to work out a reason for a tragic turn of events that positively defies reasoning.

"To think you were there..."

And he's Patrick's sadly inadequate father, trying, in the face of the most staggering catastrophe he can imagine, to stay on his feet, to be strong, to be *there* for his son in a way he's never been before. He's Henry Barclay after Cherie, and he's Johnny Cash missing June, Elvis losing his mama or kissing his Lisa Marie goodbye. He's every two-bit nobody in the cold, cruel world who has ever been left suddenly *without*. And each of them, every one who sobs over loss, is Jack Hackett without Wendy.

"For awhile."

In that moment I feel my inner dam begin to crack. I close my welling eyes and brace myself for the flood. I am saved, though, by what happens next.

The kid is spent with his last bawling line. He begins to tilt back like a tree falling over. As his voice trails off, the hum of feedback springs up to overpower it in a piercing banshee scream. As ear-shattering as it is, I am thankful for its merciful timing. My eyes squeeze shut in a pained grimace for a split second. I look out again; in that instant, Jack's reflexes kick in.

While forty heads duck into their hands against the speakers' assault, the kid grabs the mic stand and yanks the cable from the base of the mic. With Caleb's mic still screeching, Jack uproots his stand and, holding it by the top, pirouettes in his place. The round metal base sweeps up from the stage floor, swings briefly like a pendulum, then rises in a widening spiral around him. First Joe must jump out of its way, then Caleb. As it passes over the lip of the stage, with a furious final heave the kid lets it go.

Screams erupt from the crowd, loud enough to rise over the persistent feedback. Those directly under the stand's path dive to either side, knocking over chairs, jostling tables, and spilling drinks. The stand arcs through the smoke just beneath the high ceiling, a front-loaded missile that surrenders to gravity and comes down, base first, with an almighty crash against the mixing board. The sound man, more agile in his movements than he is with his equipment, darts out of the way just in time to avoid the rebounding base, which lodges itself with a final thud in the seat he has just vacated.

Silence descends upon the room. The feedback is gone, which I at first take to mean that the kid has killed the mixing board. I look back at the stage; Caleb stands at his microphone, holding in his hand its disconnected cable. He looks stunned, eyes and mouth gaping in perfect awe of the spectacle the kid has just created, Jack's *pièce de résistance* of high violent art. Joe and Tim remain pinned in their places, robbed of speech and motion by their sheer surprise, their disbelief.

For a moment, the crowd remains motionless as well, some members still in various duck-and-cover positions, some just looking on, bug-eyed and openmouthed. At the two ends of the disaster stand its perpetrator and its near victim. The sound man has just dodged a bullet, and carries in his face a mixture of rage and relief. The kid, still in the stance of his follow-through, looks in body like a golfer assessing his drive. His slack face tells a different story, one of befuddlement at the spectacle he himself has created. Befuddlement, bewilderment, tempered with something else. His eyes begin to narrow, and his jaw sets into the sad scowl of one who has just driven the final nail into his own coffin, and is ready to lie down in it.

The place is locked in this shocked stasis until the stringy-haired gnome in the back breaks our collective trance. Leaping from his seat, he pumps his fist above his head with a triumphant "Yeah!" With this outburst, the crowd exhales as one. Hands drop from ears, heads rise like turtles' from their shells. An excited murmur spreads throughout the room.

The sound man, too, finds his breath. With trembling hand he removes his black baseball cap, and with his forearm wipes his forehead. Flipping his cap hastily back on, he storms toward the stage.

From his station by the wall to our right comes Spike to intercept the charging bull. He snakes his way around tables and chairs, and ends up wedging himself into a gap in the front row, where the somewhat shorter sound man suddenly finds his face against the roadie's blockading chest. Hurling abuse at each other, the two fall into a new round of finger-pointing, the soundman poking savagely at the stage and at his precious board, Spike stabbing at the speakers and then at his ears. Perhaps frightened that the chaotic scene will lose him his crowd, the bartender hurries from behind the bar over to the board and turns on the house music. The distorted guitar riff that springs up over their cussing gives the two parties pause. They break off their fight and look around, first at the speakers, then at the board.

After a second of contemplation, the sound man is the first to return to the matter at hand. He turns back to the stage to find an empty space where until now the melancholy shell of Jack Hackett has stood. Immediately he bolts backstage, followed by a suddenly calm Spike. When the little man emerges a long minute later, looking frustrated and angry, I am relieved. The kid still has some presence of mind after all.

Spike and the Flak Jackets begin tearing down their equipment and carting it out the door. It has occurred to them, before our slower-witted engineer friend, that their gear could become collateral for the damaged board. While the fellow busies himself berating them all, I take stock of the crowd.

Jack is clearly not coming back. These people paid an eight dollar cover to get in the door tonight. They have just now seen only five minutes of what should have been a forty-minute headlining set. A dozen of them sit before tipped, empty glasses of drinks the kid put on the floor before they could put them down their throats. But where there should be anger, I see only astonishment. These folks seem content to order another round and gawk some more, at the argument unfolding onstage, at the mic stand that still rests cockeyed on the seat behind the mixing board. They've seen the spectacle they were promised. Jack's four-minute catharsis of grief, his grand spasm of aggression, have rendered superfluous any further half hour set in which the kid might have to contrive the angst which in truth has been drained from his shattered heart.

Final *Chorus*

November 5, 2003

"We want Jack! We want Jack!"

Patrick Barclay, heretofore the Fan, looks on speechless at the husk of Jack Hackett. His jaw hangs open, his eyes squint through his glasses. At the fadeout of 'Memphis, Tennessee' (to which Jack has treated himself three times already), the clamor of the nightclub crowd seeps into our control-room cocoon. The kid presses a button on the console; for a fourth time Berry's falsetto guitar and plaintive plea, "*Get in touch with my Marie*," push back the outside noise.

"Are you gonna sing this song tonight, Jack?" the Fan asks. The kid's deep-sunk eyes rise from the floor to gaze through Patrick's face. Patrick fidgets under the kid's stare. "I bet you'd do it great!" he finally blurts.

The kid's eyes find their focus. "You think so." His voice is a flat, hollow breath, devoid of tone, half bereft of life. Before the Fan can answer him, he's back at the stereo system, turning up the volume against the crowd's renewed chant.

"We want Jack! We want Jack!"

The door swings open. The chant crushes Berry's soft moans until Marty shuts the door behind him. He holds a glass of red wine up to me. "My first." Then he strides up to the heap of sorrows that is Jack Hackett and claps him on the back. "Jack! Listen to that crowd! You're the man tonight!" He raises his glass to the kid. "I just walked through that crowd. Lots of gorgeous girls out there." His eyebrows leap up and down as though they're on a trampoline. "They're yelling your name just as loud as the guys." He slaps the kid between his shoulder blades again. "Put on a great show tonight—the kind I *know* you can do—you'll be glad you're single."

Marty's free hand shoots up to catch the kid's fist before it can reach his jaw. Jack leaves his teeth bared, but he seems to have spent his last ounce of energy on the punch; he leaves his fist up, wrapped in Marty's fingers.

"Hey." Marty deposits the kid's fist on the edge of the mixing board. "What's that for?" He places his wine glass on top of the stereo rack, freeing himself to take the kid lightly, fraternally, by the shoulders. "Jack. We all liked Wendy. We're sad she's gone. But it's been *two weeks*." He lets a second go by, then repeats, "Two weeks, Jack." Jack's eyes, anchored now to Marty's face, brim with water. "At a certain point, Jack, you have to push off again."

"We want Jack! We want Jack!"

Marty lets go of the kid's shoulders, steps back, and lets the chant swamp all other noise, lets it vibrate its way under all of our hides. When the shouting ebbs again, he picks up his argument. "And dammit, Jack, you lucky bastard, *this* is what you get to push off into!"

"We want Jack! We want Jack!" The call crescendos, incredibly, yet again.

The kid cranks the volume knob on the stereo. Even at its loudest, the chant can't overcome Chuck's lament. Everyone in the control room, Flak Jackets, Spike, engineers, all give up trying to ignore the drama surrounding the kid. Just then Marty lunges at the power button. Chuck is silenced in mid-plea.

This time the kid does connect, sending Marty sprawling with a yelp onto the carpet by the door. Nearest to him, I grab his arm and pull him to his knees. Red rivers run from both nostrils over his upper lip. I reach over to the coffee table in front of the couch, grab a wad of napkins, and press them against his face. The kid is busy pushing buttons on the stereo; he displays no emotion, only a single-minded intensity that does not ease until Chuck's guitar jangles the intro we've heard four times before.

Marty sways almost to the tipping point when he reaches his feet. One hand takes over holding the napkins to his nose, while the other moves to steady itself on the back of the couch. "I'm okay," he murmurs at my look of concern. Then, to the kid, "I'll let that slide, Jack." He staggers over to stand by the Fan, steadying himself on my son's shoulder. His words are clear and loud, despite the mass of paper over his face. "You're hurting. I'm rubbing salt. I understand. But why not use tonight to show you're bigger than the hurt inside you? Look at me." He straightens up and lowers the napkins from his nose. He has to jam it against his face again when a trickle of blood escapes his left nostril. "Just look at me," he repeats. "I got over some nasty demons this year. I did it, I'm a better person now, and I managed to do it because of *this band*." He drops the napkins once more and lets the blood drip. "You can do it too."

The kid lets the second verse of 'Memphis' begin. When he opens his mouth, his words cut through the music and outside noise like daggers aimed at Marty's head. "What do *you* know about hurting?"

"We want Jack! We want Jack!" The chant bursts in again as the door opens.

A man with a white apron around his waist leans in and looks around the control room. Spike springs forward and crosses to the door to confer with him. The standoff breaks as Marty turns from Jack to watch the roadie in conference.

"We want Jack! We want Jack!"

Roadie and waiter exchange hand-waving words for a minute before the waiter leaves, bottling the crowd back up behind the door. The roadie addresses the room: "The crowd's gettin' restless. They want you on now." He points at the Flak Jackets, who rise from their couch. He swings his finger around to Jack. "Kid, you've got the goods. You showed up tonight, so some part of you wants this. I don't think you're gonna fuck it all up now." He lets a stern glare be his summation.

The kid matches him for thirty long seconds. The record switches to a more upbeat number. Berry's trademark guitar intro tries to lift the pall from the room. Jack reaches for the 'Stop' button and kills the guitar dead.

"We want Jack! We want Jack!" The welter of cheers boils over the chant once again.

Spike breaks away from the confrontation. "All right boys." He points at the three Flak Jackets, then heaves the door open and points toward the stage.

The engineer pushes back his bangs and gives the roadie a thumbs-up. "We're ready to record!" He softens his voice to tell Jack, "We get a great live sound here. We'll listen back later tonight—that'll make you feel better." The kid lets the cheers coming through the open doorway swallow up the words.

The Flak Jackets shuffle to the door. All three eye the kid, Caleb with a look of mild reproach, Joe with tight-lipped pity, Tim with the same mix of horror and guilt he has worn since that awful night in Danbury.

Caleb is the first to stop before the door. He takes one giant step toward the stereo, leans over so his face is inches from the kid's. "Jack," he says as if through a megaphone. "You know I love ya. I'll love you even more when you've finished kicking ass tonight!" He withdraws toward the door.

Joe takes his turn before disappearing into the club. "It'll feel good to play." He lets his words float to the kid, shrugs when he gets no response, and adds, "I like playing with you."

Before Joe has the sentence out, Tim bursts forth. "Jack! I got it! Call her when the show's over! Tell her you love her, you're a changed man, all that stuff!" His face begs for the kid to take his advice.

The kid spits his response over the rumble of the crowd: "You got her number now?"

Tim flinches. "No," he admits. Caleb, waiting in the doorway for the exchange to finish, takes this as the sad conclusion and breaks for the stage.

Joe follows, head down and with a weight in his step that the crowd's sudden eruption fails to lift.

"But Jack!" Tim suddenly takes a step to my side and grabs my shoulder. "We called her brother from Henry's phone! That night! The number'll still be in his phone! You can call *him* when we're done! Or maybe you'll call him tomorrow morning?"

The clamor of the crowd demands that the drummer end his talk here, that he take the stage and calm the beast with his soothing beat. Still, he stands clutching my shoulder. The cheers outside dissolve into confused chatter. Finally Tim throws the kid his last line: "I just want everybody to be all right."

The kid gains his focus once more to fire back: "Well shit, not taking her away might've helped!" The fire retreats from his eyes, doused by welling tears. "Ah, damn," he breathes, and it sounds like an apology. A tear makes it past his eyelids.

Tim slinks out the door. A wave of applause rises from the crowd a few seconds later.

Whoops and whistles serve as the prelude to the Flak Jackets' instrumental intro. The engineer plays with a fader on the mixing board. "We're rolling."

The roadie still holds the door open. "Jack." He leans toward the kid. Just then the guitar-bass-drum attack on 'Fifth Wheel/Third Rail' peals from the stage, from the club PA, and from the speakers above the mixing board. Spike has to yell to get his message over the mix of cheers and guitars. He points past the doorway. "I'm goin' out there. Take a minute. Let them warm up. After this, do what you want. But right now, you do what you have to do, and you be fuckin' great!" He leaves the door open behind him, letting the maelstrom of the chugging music and the edgy crowd flood the control room.

Marty dabs at his nose and looks for fresh blood on the napkins. Seeing none, he pockets the wad and walks to the doorway. "Jack! You're on!" he shouts, broadly grinning, before plunging into the noise. "I know you'll make me proud!" The kid gives no reaction.

"We want Jack! We want Jack!" The chant reaches an apex again, bellowing past the guitar and drums. The engineer springs to his feet and darts past the kid to shut the door. The Flak Jackets' riffing sharpens, coming now mainly through the two speakers mounted over the board.

"We want Jack! We want Jack!" The cry will not be quelled. It bleeds its way into the soundtrack, through the walls, through the onstage mix in the speakers.

The kid opens his mouth. His jaw hangs slack for a moment while his eyes rise to meet mine. He speaks, so softly that I only fully catch his words by reading his lips: "Gimme your phone."

The Fan doesn't hear him. "Jack," he begins, "I know you're sad. You lost your girlfriend."

"The phone." The kid looks from my face to my pants pocket.

"We want Jack! We want Jack!"

"I lost *my* girlfriend, too." The Fan sounds deeply earnest. "Last February," he goes on. "I was real sad. But my dad took me to see you play, and guess what, Jack!"

"Give it to me." The kid rears up to his full height, eyes red, nostrils flaring.

"Guess what, Jack!" my son repeats. "I was sad, but I saw you play. It made me feel better!"

"Shut up." The kid holds a hand out like a stop sign at my boy. He steps toward me, in slow motion, with his arms out and ready to grapple with me if he needs to.

"We want Jack! We want Jack!"

Patrick will not shut up. "You made me feel better! If you go and play now, *you'll* feel better!"

Months with the kid have trained my eye, and I can see the tension that grips his whole body. One more word from Patrick will snap the kid. I do the only thing I can to avert this explosion: in a split-second motion I pluck the phone from my pocket.

"We want Jack! We want Jack!" The chant crescendos as if the closed door were flung open. They are becoming ferocious in their impatience.

The kid's aggression, a swell of it about to burst its banks, is suddenly channeled toward me. His hand swoops down on mine, tearing the phone from my grip before I can make another move.

"You're great, Jack!" Patrick gushes over the kid's shoulder while the kid stabs frantically at the buttons on the phone. "You'll show 'em all!"

"We want Jack! We want Jack!" The chant now follows the rhythm of the Flak Jackets' intro. The engineer rocks in his seat at the board. "We want Jack!" His fist goes up with each shouted word.

The kid's hands tremble as he scans back through the dialed numbers. Suddenly his grip tightens around the phone, and I know he's hit the date of her call to her brother. A second more, and he mashes the keypad one last time.

"We want Jack! We want Jack!"

He brings the phone to his left ear and sticks a finger into his right. "We want Jack!" I can't imagine that he can hear anything over this clamor.

Patrick speaks while the kid listens for a voice on the other end of the line. "You tell her you're great, Jack!"

"We want Jack! We want Jack!"

Once again the chant dissolves. For a few moments at least, we can hear over the music. Into the lull my son injects his last drive at reaching the kid. "You're great, Jack! You'll show her! Number One!"

"Hello?" The kid's voice breaks. He hangs onto the phone without speaking further.

In that moment my son's voice is soft, but still it manages to reach the kid. "You're great, Jack!" he says. "Number One!" And a moment later, softer still: "Whatever you do." The kid's eyes meet my son's for a heartbeat. Then a force three thousand miles distant pulls the kid away.

"Hello? Terry!" The kid jams his palm against his open ear. "I need Wendy." Outside, the sound of Joe playing for his life can't quell the crowd's temper. "I know it's late! I'm sorry! But wake her up! Please!"

"We want Jack! We want Jack!" The words pelt the control room walls like volleys of arrows.

"Please, Terry! I don't have time for this!"

"We want Jack!"

"I'm *not* drunk! I'm not high, I'm not anything! I'm backstage, and there's a million people wanting me to do the same shit again, and I can't do it unless I talk to my girl first!"

"We want Jack! We want Jack!"

The kid's face darkens to a deep pink. I catch a whiff of his sweat as he shouts, droplets of spittle flying from his mouth. "Yes, I was! You want to hear it? Yes, I was a jackass, yes I fucked up, and *you* can hate me for it, but guess what! I'm better now! *She* made me better, and all I want is to prove it to her!"

"We want Jack! We want Jack!"

The door swings open, slamming hard into the kid's elbow. Though I can hear the thud over the din, the kid doesn't flinch. Marty and Spike stand in the doorway. The roadie's face borders on anger; Marty's skin shines with sweat, and his eyes bulge with fear.

"We want Jack! We want Jack!" Each syllable makes Marty shudder.

The kid turns his back on them, wrenching his arm away when Marty tries to pull him back. "Listen to me!" he begs down the phone. "She's my girl, you hear? She saved me, and she's mine, and I'm hers!"

"We want Jack!"

"And the baby. The baby's *ours.*"

"Baby?" The Fan squints at the kid. "Did you say 'baby,' Jack?"

"We want Jack!"

Marty makes another move to wrest Jack from the control room. I reach out to hold Marty back; Spike already has him by the shoulder. The anger has left the roadie's face.

"Listen! Terry! Just shut up and listen! I'm sorry! I'm sorry I woke you, I'm sorry I put everybody through all this. But that kid is ours, Wendy saved me, and I'm gonna be there for her! You can't keep me from—"

"We want Jack! We want Jack!"

The kid presses his palm harder against his ear. He bends over, away from the doorway. Spike pulls Marty inside the control room and shuts the door.

"We want Jack!" The chant barely loses a decibel, but the closed-off feeling seems to draw us closer. The engineer stops grooving to the beat coming from his speakers and turns from his board to look at the kid.

Patrick steps closer, his jaw slack. "Jack?" he ventures.

The kid doesn't hear. Of course he wouldn't. Not at this exact second. "What's an amnio?" he says into the phone. And at the utterance of the word, gears start to turn in my head.

"We want Jack! We want Jack!"

"Wait! Terry! Please! I don't know what that is!"

"We want Jack! We want Jack!" The control room quakes with the synchronized stomping of a hundred and eighty feet.

The kid stabs his finger back into his open eardrum. His face contorts into the act of hearing what the girl's brother is telling him over my phone. The explanation reaches the kid at the same time that the meaning and significance of that technical term meet up in the forefront of my mind.

"We want Jack! We want Jack!"

Patrick stands staring at him, jaw still slack, straining unabashedly to eavesdrop. The kid's gaze falls on him for a second. From there, his eyes flit to meet mine.

"We want Jack!"

In the space between the beats of the chant outside, the kid's right cheek twitches just below his eye.

"We want Jack!"

And this is the moment I will always come back to: Jack Hackett, world wailing and stomping at his door, phone at his ear, flinching at the boom that resounds over all other noises, the deafening thud of a door behind him slamming irrevocably shut.

"We want Jack! We want Jack!"

His face pales. His eyes loosen their focus, his jaw drops, and he lets out a slow, hissing sigh. If the voice that speaks to him from across the country is saying anything now, the words are wasted; the kid's phone hand slides down from his ear and hovers in the air somewhere past his shoulder. His pupils cross as his lids drape over them; the roadie moves toward him with his arms out when he begins to swoon.

"We want Jack! We want Jack!"

But he steadies himself. He clamps his eyes shut until crow's feet spread back to his temples. He sets his jaw and brings the phone back to his ear. When he opens his eyes, they fix on the confused, bewildered face of my son, Patrick Barclay, the Fan. "I don't care!" he shouts. "The kid's not perfect? Hah! That's fine! You hear me? Fine! Lemme talk to Wendy! Jesus Christ, let me talk to Wendy! We can do this! That's my girl! That's our kid! Dear God, don't get rid of that kid! You listen to—Hello?!"

"We want Jack! We want Jack!"

The phone slides from his ear again. His face, frozen in its frantic, wide-eyed pleading, swings to meet mine. His eyes drop to look at my shoes.

"We want Jack! We want Jack!"

He lifts his gaze up my legs, past my waist, over my chest. His lips move silently as he meets my stare.

"We want Jack!"

Those lips curl back into a smile, a full, winning grin, betrayed only by his flooding eyes.

"We want Jack! We want Jack!"

I catch his words only by watching his mouth move. "He said 'she'."

"We want Jack!"

He emits the tiniest chuckle.

"We want Jack!"

"It's a girl," he tells me. His forlorn glance at Patrick, the renewed, heroic attempt at a smile he points at my son, both of these serve to confirm the rest.

"We want Jack! We want Jack!"

John Preston Hackett turns and floats toward the door, past a dumbfounded Marty, past the roadie, whose face finally sheds its permanent mask of cool. He opens the door.

"We want Jack! We want Jack!" The thunder of stomping feet taps against my solar plexus. I, the Fan, Marty, and Spike find our bodies as one, rushing after him as he disappears.

"We want Jack! We want Jack!" A tsunami of cheers smothers the chant. An excited battery on Tim's snare, all but swallowed up by the crowd's roar, greets Jack as he steps onto stage left. Suddenly aglow in the blazing stage lights, Jack pays no attention to the flourish. He gives no sign to the crowd. The band cuts to the build-up to the verse while he picks up speed. From the side of the stage I see only his back, but he stays facing dead ahead, and I think I can tell what he's looking at.

"We want Jack! We want Jack!"

The faint green light ahead of him must occupy his entire field of vision.

"We want Jack! We want Jack!"

The mass of humans crammed into this club is a dimwitted beast, impossibly slow on the uptake. Their riotous applause rages on after Jack has sailed past his microphone, after his flying leap off the stage and onto the only vacant patch of floor in the packed house. Long after his disappearance through the curtained doorway above which the 'Exit' sign glows a pale green, their cheer refuses to die.

It evolves slowly. The Flak Jackets turn the verse into an impromptu guitar solo while exchanging confused glances. For a minute, the roar from half the crowd breaks up into laughter. But slowly, well into the lyricless chorus, while Caleb leans over Tim's cymbals and mouths "What the fuck?" with laughing lips and terror-stricken eyes, while Joe pours visceral notes out of his amplifier, while all three musicians struggle to hold up 'Fifth Wheel/Third Rail' against the crush of the beast until Jack returns to his senses and the stage, the beast rediscovers its roar.

"We want Jack! We want Jack!"

Ten or twenty voices have taken it up before I start to hear the renewed chant over the general deluge of shouts.

"We want Jack!"

A dozen more join in, and in the next instant the entire crowd belts it as one.

"We want Jack! We want Jack!" The floor begins to shake anew with each word. *"We want Jack!"* Fists beat out the rhythm in the air. *"We want Jack!"* No longer buoyant with anticipation, each word is now a punch at the stage.

"We want Jack! We want Jack!" The smell of the beast changes. Its sweat begins to overpower, and its alcohol breath turns sour, then suddenly bitter. These are fumes awaiting a spark.

"We want Jack!"

Spike and I catch the scent in the same breath. We work in tandem; while I throw my weight into Patrick and Marty, pushing them toward the control room door, the roadie hurls himself onstage and lunges for Joe. Out of the corner of my eye before I turn my head away, I see him collar Joe with his right arm and reach for Caleb with his left. 'Fifth Wheel/Third Rail' chokes to death in half a bar, to a collective groan from the crowd.

"We want Jack! We want Jack!"

Patrick holds his ground at first, leaning into me as he gapes at the unfolding disaster. With a yell I heave into him; he relents, but his stubbornness costs me my grip on Marty's jacket.

"We want Jack!"

"Don't stop!" Marty shrugs himself free and leaps onstage before I can swat him back down. Without pausing I shove Patrick back to the control room door. *"We want Jack!"* The shout blasts at our backs like dragon's breath.

We come up against the engineer at the door. "What's happened?" he shouts, craning his neck to see beyond us.

"Let us in!" I stab a finger at the control room behind him, but he doesn't budge. I step to the side to give him a view of the unraveling of events. Spike is shepherding the Flak Jackets off the stage amid a blizzard of napkins, straws, and coasters flung at their backs.

"Shit," the engineer says, but shakes his head when I once again point to the door. "Here!" He grabs the collar of Patrick's jacket and swings him around. My boy, who has been staring at the mayhem with his mouth hanging open, jolts as if awoken from a dream, as the engineer pushes him through a doorway tucked into a corner opposite the control room door. I follow them through, into a passageway running behind the stage, cluttered to shoulder height with cases, crates, instruments, and sound equipment.

"We want Jack!"

Behind me scurries Tim, with Caleb and Joe at his heels, and Spike as rear guard. No one pursues us, though I can feel the crowd's pulse against the length of the stage-side wall.

"We want Jack! We want Jack!"

Once through the doorway at the far end, the engineer pats me and my son on the shoulder and dashes back, presumably to guard his precious mixing board. I gather my bearings; through curtains to our right I can see the many-headed beast still chucking light debris at the stage. "We want Jack! We want Jack!" some still cry, though the beast's voice becomes more and more an incoherent howl.

"Everybody just calm down!" Marty. My poor, stupid godson, sounding at once authoritative like a schoolmarm and helpless like the mouse before the lion's jaws. I part the curtains and yell his name, but he stays at Jack's microphone. "Cool out! The band'll be right back—"

In the middle of this desperate lie, the first of the bottles flies out from somewhere near the bar. The blaring stage lights obscure Marty's vision, or else his panic hampers his reflexes. The bottle strikes him in the right temple, sending him reeling.

"We want Jack!"

Another bottle, some copycat from the other side of the room, flies over his head to smash into pieces on Caleb's amp. Sensing more to come, I surge forward through the curtains, holding my jacket lapel up in front of my face, and yank the staggering Marty off the side of the stage.

"We want Jack!"

It must be about now that the beast turns on itself. More debris pelts the equipment onstage. At a certain point—perhaps as Marty and I pass through the curtains underneath the green 'Exit' beacon, or as we six members of the disgraced Flak Jackets party grope through a dark passage to the fire doors that Jack in his stupor has left ajar—the spark is touched off. A bottle or glass or ice cube falls short of the stage, hitting a clubgoer in the back of the head. Or maybe in the tight quarters one of the throwers elbows one of the chanters. Whatever the catalyst, it is inevitable: some member of this crowd will hit some other, the other will retaliate, and as arms, legs, shoes and fists fly, the blows will land further afield.

And as these flare-ups spread through the club, the innocent will bolt as one for the doors. Those dozens who make their way as far as the rear alley where I and the Flak Jackets' party stand in collective shell-shock will count themselves lucky; several more who fall under the stampede will have to wait for the first responders with their stretchers to carry them out.

We will stand among a throng that will grow more numerous, more dazed, more shell-shocked, listening in disbelief to the riot inside as the beast slaughters itself. And incredibly, shortly before the lights flash in the street, before the authorities come to pronounce the beast dead and take statements on its passing, we will hear its cry again.

"We want Jack! We want Jack!"

As before, it will start with just one voice, some battered holdout, stumbling among the broken chairs, the shattered glass and the half-dead bodies, proclaiming his survival with the only words his drunken, beaten brain can muster.

"We want Jack!"

Inane even when the hungry mob first adopted it this evening, in the aftermath of Jack's apocalypse the chant will sound positively psychotic.

"We want Jack!"

But other survivors among the ruins, still bursting with the same psychosis, will be eager to shout their defiance, or will be too drunk to have good taste.

"We want Jack! We want Jack!"

They will shout it inside, at least a dozen voices, with such vigor that a few out here in the alley with us will pick it up, if only for a few repetitions. "We want Jack!" They will go on for minutes, until they exhaust themselves, or until the first man in blue appears at the front door—or until at long last it dawns on them that they won't get what they want.

"We want Jack! We want Jack!"

The crowd will chant for minutes that feel like hours, and the object of their call will elude them. I will picture him floating on, through the network of alleys that shadow the streets of West L.A. In my mind he will drift until he reaches his apartment, if it's near enough, or until the crushing weight of this evening pushes him to the pavement.

"We want Jack!"

And there, ensconced indoors or lost in the alley maze, he will avoid capture. The record company, his management, his band, all those who invested time and money in his cause will no doubt want to get at him, to wave contracts in his face and bombard him with scoldings and threats. The police might well like to speak with him, to dangle a possible charge of incitement to riot in his face, though it would be hard to make such a charge stick on one who merely walked across a stage.

"We want Jack!"

They will shout it like a mantra, as though by some miracle their chant might alter the laws of time and space, and bring them Jack Hackett and the Flak Jackets, back from the dead and ready to deliver the awe-inspiring spectacle they in their ignorance had expected to see.

"We want Jack! We want Jack!"

They will shout it, scream it, thunder it to rattle foundations, but they won't get what they wanted.

"We want Jack! We want Jack!"

And poor, poor Jack Hackett. Neither will he.

Coda

Pity Jack Hackett. Pity Wendy, his girl. Pity the Flak Jackets, and their entourage, and anyone caught under the crush of people as tonight turns from debacle to catastrophe. But don't pity them past Thanksgiving. And certainly don't pity me.

The billiard balls and marbles keep colliding. They are indeed powerful things. It takes only one of them, a well-placed atom happening into another near enough to us, to envelop us into their chemical reaction.

By brainless luck, a single sperm among thousands makes it to an egg. At the instant the two cells pass their chromosomes to one another, the egg lets go of one too many. It's miniscule, that chromosome, so tiny that a powerful microscope will give only a blurry picture of it. Yet for its size that one mote wields power on the level of an atom bomb. Its blast covers one entire human body, and can shake to their very cores the bodies of all those around it.

Jack has disappeared. We won't find out where he's gone by the time the cops leave and we all stumble home. News will reach me in the next month, via Patrick: "Tim emailed me. Jack's apartment's empty!" My boy will send many a note to Jack's email address. All will go unanswered.

The Flak Jackets' rise was set to be meteoric; like any meteor, they make quite a flash when they fall to Earth. Their name will appear in the local papers from the *Times* on down. Only the *L.A. Weekly* will devote a paragraph to the trio's heroic performance (a shame, since their ten-minute intro will play back on the Mint's player as the most searing piece of gutbucket rock 'n' roll they have ever served up). Tim will use a quote from the *Weekly* as the lead-off to a mass mailing announcing the band's debut as a three-piece. Patrick and I will be among the twelve at two of their shows a few months later. We will compliment Caleb on his voice when they convene at our table after their allotted forty minutes. Patrick will shower them all with praise, though he will withhold the superlative 'Number One'.

At the second of these shows we will share a booth with Marty. Between sips of orange juice, Marty will complain about his loss of status at Farley Management. A few jibes from Patrick will be enough to break through his melancholy shell; by evening's end we'll see a few flashes of that old grin that used to make me so nervous.

Little eddies in the current of Time will drift us apart. The Kevlars (as the three remaining Flak Jackets will bill themselves) will send regular emails to Patrick advertising upcoming shows. But my boy will admit to me that "It makes me sad—no Jack." I will hear less frequently about the band's plans as the months graduate into years, until one day my boy announces that Caleb will be getting married. "You remember his girlfriend Gabby?" he'll ask me. My cackling reply will puzzle him.

I will return to work. By chance I will cross paths with the owner of an antiquarian bookstore, one of those hideously elitist establishments that open their doors to clients 'by appointment only.' This man will know my authorial vintage (which, when I consider his line of work, will disturb me more than a little), and will declare me the ideal candidate for the role of his assistant. Who knows if I will do properly all of the things an assistant manager is supposed to do, but this man will keep me on for years with nary a complaint.

I will have cause for sorrow in the years to come. Dear Leader's reelection, hot on the heels of a crushing postseason defeat of the Yankees at the hands of the Red Sox, will hurt me to the point of weeping. In fact, my threshold for tears will fall steeply in the coming years.

Increasingly, though, I will seek out those tears. Two Gram Parsons LPs and half a dozen Françoise Hardy albums will join my record collection, alongside new CD copies of my favorite Chuck Berry and Little Richard sides. With just a few bars of that country-boy wail or that soft French moan, a hundred conflicting emotions, tangled together in a great and growing knot in my head, will melt and flow free. The release will often leave me wet faced but feeling the calm of one who has just made love.

The tears I shed for Patrick I will not seek. My boy will begin to forget, little things at first, but steadily more important items, and with greater frequency. I will know that his deterioration is real the day he goes missing for a couple of hours after his work; I will find him wandering the street a block away from his building, unable to find his way home. That same month I will see a doctor about a swollen patch under my arm. Tests will reveal lymphoma.

Moments will pile on moments, arranging themselves into passages, paragraphs, and chapters. Stories, great collections of these moments, will begin and end, lining themselves up haphazardly in my memory like the overflowing bookshelves I look upon each workday. With the constant influx they will become harder to arrange, to access.

But they will all be there. Once a moment happens, it enters into eternity. I cannot travel back to it once it's passed, just as I can't reach the moon no matter how much force I put into jumping at it. But like the moon that moment is there. Its imprint is made in space, in time, and we can see that imprint from beyond the physical reach of the moment itself.

Elvis Presley has long since bloated and died, but with the DVD copy of the '68 Comeback Special that I'll place between Gram and Françoise, I can watch him stalk a tiny stage in black leather, I can listen to him cut through the hot pulsing heart of a song with a voice like a chainsaw. Over and over on my TV screen, I can watch him perform his own resurrection. With the right appliance, at the push of a button, Elvis reigns on. And in the same way, with the telescope of memory I can return to any of an innumerable collection of moments, choosing from a catalog as long and varied as my life itself.

But this is the moment I will always come back to: John Preston Hackett, phone at his ear, broken already, flinching as a new sledgehammer comes down on the ruin that still stands.

I will visit that moment at different times. I will bring it to mind whenever sorry, senseless news comes my way. The light it sheds will cut down the shadows any horrible event might cast. The marking of Patrick's birthday each year will begin with visions of 1968. That year will serve as 'In the beginning'; 2003 will be my 'Amen'. Sometimes, so powerful is the imprint of Jack's moment, it will flare up unbidden in my consciousness. In these times, whatever I'm doing, I will stop to bask a moment in its glow.

Look at him, poor, young Jack Hackett, wincing at the blow delivered from three thousand miles away. Watch his cheek twitch, see the explosion of comprehension radiate from that point across his face. Pity Jack Hackett. Pity him as he stumbles from the room, across a lit stage, out the exit and into the night. Don't pity him for long, though, for I know what will happen next.

For years, without news from him, I will know his fate through faith alone. But a gift will come to me, nearly a decade on, and its timing will vindicate me as much as its contents.

I will come home one morning in early December, unable to enjoy the warmth of the California sun that so easily banishes the briskness of a winter L.A. night. A heavy frost will have blanketed my heart with the doctor's news, an hour prior, that my cancer has spread. I will be thinking of thawing it out over a whiskey flame when I pull the envelope from my mailbox.

The envelope itself will bear no return address. The New Hampshire postmark which should ring a happy bell will not, thankfully: I will therefore feel the rush of recognition in one blast. There they will stand in the over-glossy Christmas card photo, beaming their tidings of comfort and joy. Look at them: huddled together, standing on gymnasium floorboards, gunmetal folding chairs flanking them, a low stage adorned with a blurry backdrop of bright greens and reds over their shoulders. Look at the girl, my Wendy, dolled up in a cartoonish Victorian dress, mountain of tresses concealed beneath a Mother Goose bonnet. See how her smile strains to touch the giant red dot painted on each of her cheeks. Look at Jack, John Preston Hackett, dressed in a jacket and tie but still managing, with his overlong arms outdistancing his sleeves by three or four inches and his priapic cowlick standing proud atop his head, to come off like a vagrant. Look at the half smile planted firmly back on his face. Then follow the length of his arm to see his hand on the little one's shoulder.

It's a girl. See her mugging for the camera, all crooked baby teeth and thick, deep pink gums. Smile at her chipmunk cheeks, bulging against the flaps of gray cloth that frame her face. That hood—what is it? It tops an equally gray costume of fur; two pink circles of felt protrude from its peak. The mouse-eared hood covers her real, human ears. I will be left to imagine them, though I'll have a pretty good idea: tiny, soft, sticking outward and perhaps folded slightly over. Hooked to them underneath the gray fur, her black-rimmed, thick lenses serve as two magnifying glasses for her eyes. Look closely at them, past the spot of glare from the camera's flash. They are beautiful. The smooth, broad lids that squeeze them into almond shapes squint away all her whites and most of her pupils as she smiles. But peer in, get your face up almost against the glossy surface, and you'll be able to pick out a trace, a few pixels, of blue ringing the black irises. She is gorgeous, from the twinkling eyes, across her cherubic face and every square inch of her squat frame, down to the stubby fingers that barely poke out of her mouse-gray sleeves.

Feel the pops of recognition, of vindication, at each sight: at my Wendy's sweet smile, at Jack's arm around her, at the little girl in the mouse costume between them. Feel another rush on reading the message printed in red and green italics across the white bottom of the card: '*Merry Christmas from the Hacketts!*'

The signatures on the back of the card will send another thrill to further warm my heart. Up at the top, in a neat but flowing script: 'Wendy'. Next to Jack's four-letter scribble, in a small, tidy print, a cryptic message in six words: 'And here you thought I'd die.' Cute, Jack, but false. I know, from the minute you disappear under the exit sign at the Mint, that you've jumped two steps away from Death.

A certain regret will tug on me when Jack's story plays in my mind. I am missing a critical piece. As a writer, a teller of stories, I appreciate the irony: Fate hands me a story, fully-formed, when my powers of imagination have long since petered out, then robs me of the great pay-off scene that will tie the tale together. But I am no longer idle. Let's see if I can jump-start the old creative engine and come up with a scene of my own to fit the open space.

Might Jack reach Wendy by phone? By email? Perhaps. But I lean toward on a more old-fashioned plot development: Jack blows the last of his advance, maxes out his credit card, and buys himself a ticket back East. He has her father's address; a college professor's home is probably easy enough to find online. On arrival at a New England airport, station, or depot, he disembarks and marches without stopping to a car-rental counter or taxi stand. Or else he simply steps out into the street and keeps on marching.

He reaches her father's door. I picture the sun dipping in an azure sky strung with pink cirrus clouds. His breath shows, as does the smoke from a nearby chimney that gives the neighborhood the scent of burning pine. Though the doorbell is a bright yellow button clearly visible on a black frame, his momentum drives his weight into his knuckles, and he makes the door shudder with his knocking.

A wiry, bespectacled man opens the door halfway. His eyebrows crowd in behind his lenses. He straightens up to give himself extra height, and lets his silence turn thumbscrews on the disheveled stranger. "Yes?" he says finally. *Who are you?* the word asks, and *What do you want?* and *Why are you staring behind me?*

Jack doesn't have to explain. Wendy peers out from the hall, a few feet behind her father. The realization of who this is and what it means hits her at the same time that Jack's eyes adjust to the inside light and catch her face.

Here my romantic's heart gets carried away, giving Wendy a seven- rather than four-month baby belly, and a face streaked with weeks' worth of tears. I have the girl, her father, and her mother in the hall behind her, preparing that very minute to leave for the dreaded appointment.

Jack sees Wendy gasp, and feels an urge to lunge toward her, kiss her, relearn the feel of her body. But a barrier blocks his path, in the form of her angry father. Jack fumbles for words to pry the man from between them, but the father refuses to let words dislodge his image of the young punk who knocked up his little girl. His scowl turns poor Jack's tongue to stone.

But then Jack shuts his eyes. He takes in a sharp breath through his nose to suck back his tears. When his lids part again, he is looking past the professor once more. He has remembered his gift for vibrations.

With care he gathers all his emotions: his love for this girl and the child inside of her; the torment that has consumed him this past month; the strength he has found to heave the great weight of his ambitions and expectations from his shoulders and hurl himself across the country. These he bundles together and holds at the back of his throat. As he speaks anew, they seep out like air from a balloon; their undercurrent boosts the resonance in his voice. Invisibly it radiates out, pulses through the professor, makes him step reflexively back into his doorway.

What might our hero say? Jack has endured weeks of torment, crossed mountains, valleys, rivers and plains, all the while with a song repeating in his heart to sustain him. And so I have that record spin again in his head as he levels his gaze at lovely Wendy and speaks: "I have a name for her."

More words will follow, none of them important. The professor protests, but in backing away from the doorway he has shown his wavering hand. Wedging himself inside, Jack can cast his vibrations out to Wendy's mother and build himself some sympathy.

He won't need to build a thing further with his girl, though, since from the instant she has seen him at her doorstep, she is his girl again. And from the moment he touches her arm, the vibration his touch sends through her seals her decision. Jack Hackett will have his way. If he wants this baby, with all its imperfections, she will gladly give it to him. And the child will bear the name he has chosen.

Strike that—the father in the doorway, the standoff—cross it all out. Let Jack come up Wendy's driveway as the girl happens to emerge at her door. Have their eyes meet, let her leap from the doorstep and into his arms, and from that tearful, glorious moment let their fate be sealed. That, after all, is all it ought to take.

Jack will get to name their little girl. That much I know for certain. She will write it, in sloppy black letters, likely with hand-over-hand assistance from her mother or father: 'Marie'. And the moment my brain ties together those five letters, I will feel a twitch in my cheek: a tiny flinch at the inner sound of a door being thrown open. These doors, which shut so often behind us, they can sometimes open up again. And the one just unlocked by the writing of a child will open the way back to this moment: John Preston Hackett, on the phone backstage with the strains of 'Memphis, Tennessee' still reverberating in his head, trying the patience of a volatile crowd, flinching at the blow dealt to him from a continent away. The two moments will tie together, fused in my mind by the exalting heat of a thousand emotions. The first is the beginning; the second will be the end. But then again, each is both a start and a finish. In each, one cycle of my life draws to a close while another starts up.

And with each of these two moments, with each of these doors, a window is opened, albeit briefly. Outside is a mountaintop view, beneath a clear, boundless nighttime sky. There, before my eyes, the stars line themselves up in a perfect geometric pattern, and in these fleeting instants I believe I catch the universe making sense.

Maybe it happens that night at the Mint; I will feel it happen as I stare down at a Christmas card photo on a cool L.A. December afternoon: I will feel the corner of my mouth pull back on one side, so that when I flip the card over again, my half smile will mirror the smirk Jack Hackett's image beams back at me. My own half grin will linger for hours after I clear the piles of red-streaked pages on my writing desk and place the card at an angle beside my laptop keyboard. For a few moments, the grin will broaden to cover both sides of my mouth when I notice Cherie, circa 1968, inches away in a silver frame, holding a tiny pink creature swaddled in white. It will crest when I see how closely her eyes match Wendy's, and how closely my son's almond eyes match those of Wendy's daughter. I wonder, in fact, if that half smile will ever fully fade from my face.

And then, almost as soon as I've set the card down, I will pluck it back up. I will make a beeline for my closet, moving a little faster with each step, and dig out my tracksuit. I will lace up my sneakers and zoom out the door. Even hobbling as I will, a man pushing seventy trying to work long-hardened joints and pump blood through a system riddled with tumors, I will ring Patrick's bell only a few minutes later.

With my breath almost gone, I will puff out the exclamation "Here!" and shove the card into his hand before he has fully opened the door to his room. With that drowsy blank stare that his face will have taken on in recent months, my boy will peer down through his thick bifocals at the photograph. The scalp will show through the graying wisps on top as he tilts his head down for a closer look.

Suddenly his eyes will bulge. "That's their baby!" he will shout. He will hold the photo up at me, his cheeks glowing a brilliant pink, squinting at me as though staring into the sun. "She looks like me," he will say like a proud parent. "I could be her Dad!" I will lose my breath again in the burst of laughter that follows.

I will arrange to pick Patrick up for dinner, then hop from his doorstep and break once more into a jog. My joints will creak, and I will have to work to get both feet off the ground. In my heart, though, I will be flying. I will stagger through my door and land in a sweaty heap at my writing desk. Setting the precious card back beside my computer, I will type these words. Though such a feeling cannot possibly last, I will feel, while I tap at my keyboard, that somewhere between these lines is the password into Heaven.

From then the picture blurs. Ruth will be planning to visit me for Christmas. Should she follow through, the family she has found to rent her Winsted house will see to it that she can stay here at least six months. Maybe in the springtime I will stage a remarkable comeback. Patrick's decline will likely be slow, unless a fall or illness hastens it; I hope we will share more moments, that Ruth will find the same joys in him that she always has, and that together we can bring some remnant of my boy's buoyant personality bubbling back up to his surface before it slips away forever. And if I do go, I wish them both love and strength to stay standing on their own.

There will be Death; each day that passes shows that this is certain. But I will start to run again, resolving to make it once more a daily ritual until my condition precludes it. And here is another certainty while I run: my gaze will not be over my shoulder but straight on to the horizon, and I will rejoice at every step.

And when I am finally beaten, what then? Shall I find myself at the gates of Paradise, pleading my case to some heavenly bouncer? If so, while I sweat over my eternal destiny, I will relish the notion that perhaps Caleb will have put my name on the guest list.

There is, of course, an outside chance that Tim and his Nietzsche have figured out the way things work. In that case, even in those waning days of November, it will all stretch out ahead of me. Death will be just one more door slamming shut, depositing me naked and soaking back at the starting marker of a circular path, with all its doors re-opened.

In this reality, I will revisit every moment, each hit and every miss, with a fresh perspective. The spillway's splash will be once more the parting of an ocean. My father will stoop again to touch my shoulders. I will meet my darling, and enjoy the thrill of learning love from her anew. I will walk the road of fatherhood, stumbling badly at first, but gaining my stride in time to enjoy its fruits. I will fall again, fall hard, for Wendy and Jack Hackett; I'll feel that full flutter that only tickles the heart so strongly in its first flush.

It all awaits me, for all time. My life, then, becomes a song of eternity, a never-ending cadence of joys and sorrows, and aren't I lucky that I might forever dance to its rhythm? "It's the gift that keeps on giving!" echoes Tim's voice in my head. And indeed, such a future might be the sweetest of all.

Gratitude

Without the help of the following friends, this book would have been far less than what it is. Each of them has my heartfelt thanks.

Zoe Hannon
Robi Banerji
Paul Feilzer
Gene Hayworth
Benjy King
Sarah Heacox-Jackson
Hiro Kawashima
Brittney Inman
Jeb Lipson
Rebecca Molloy
Orlando Ortega-Medina
Glen Palmer
Suzanne Reisman
Mark Reynolds
Tony Russell
Jan Swanson
Sirius Trixon
My co-workers at Manny's Music between 1998 and 2001
The Durangos: Dennis, Adam, Shawn, and Buddy J
The Scramblers: Dennis (again), and Vince
The various lineups of the Mat Treiber Group
The Treiber Family: Mum, Dad, Katie, Holly

Special thanks, and extra love, go to my wife, Roxanne Fontana, who took my hand and led me into all of the real-life adventures that found their way into these pages. Every good thing I have today I owe in some way to her.